Countdown To Oblivion

Allies and Aliens
Book 1

Shaka Bry

Copyright

This is a work of fiction. Names, characters, places, and incidents either are the product of the author's imagination or are used fictitiously. Any resemblance to actual persons, living or dead, events, or locales is entirely coincidental.

Copyright © 2022 by Shaka Bry

All rights reserved. No part of this book may be reproduced or used in any manner without written permission of the copyright owner except for the use of quotations in a book review.

Cover art by May Dawney Designs

Fiction is stranger than truth.
shakabry.com

For Skye

Part One

February

There is nothing noble in being superior to your fellow man. True nobility is being superior to your former self.

— Ernest Hemingway

Chapter One

It won't be the end of the world if Craig breaks up with me.

I have to keep telling myself this. There's no justifiable reason I should be with him. It's obvious to anyone with a brain that I'm not his type. By extension, he's not mine either. When we kiss, it's like two fish bumping snouts (or whatever they have). Our mouths smack together like two slippery, slimy, grotesque slugs. When we're doing the sloppy sloshy lip dance, Craig's patchy facial hair tickles me in all the wrong ways. The first time I bumped up against his prickly whiskers, I choked back uncomfortable laughter. Or maybe that was vomit? I hate to admit it, but these days, it's almost impossible to suppress the awkward giggles when we're going at it. So no, it's not great.

I always thought Craig was a decent guy, and I'm convinced we'll eventually get in synch with each other. This stuff doesn't always start out perfect. But Alicia is relentless and never shy about her intense hatred of my froggy relationship.

"So, where's Prince Charming today?" she asks, scanning the cafeteria for my boyfriend's long, silky, bleach blond hair. I've already assessed the perimeter—he's not here, and likely not coming.

"Beats me," I say, failing at nonchalance. "I'm not his keeper."

The truth is, I haven't seen or heard from Craig since yesterday afternoon. Is he ghosting me? I didn't think he had it in him. He sent his last meaningless, mundane text nearly ten hours ago. But who's counting?

"Honestly, Rain, you need to dump his ass! He hasn't even sent you so much as a lubby dubby heart emoji on V-Day! C'mon! He's got some nerve! Of all the days to disappear!"

"I'm sure he's just, eh, busy?"

"No, forget that. He's trash. You don't need him, Rain. Mark my words. You are too good for that poser. Who does he think he is? Lemme get ahold of him. Let him show his face in here right now. I'll —" She wrings her hands around a defenseless pear, attempting to squeeze the juicy life out of it. I can't help but smirk at her cruel intent.

"Thanks Leash," I tell her, because she's right, of course. "But—"

"But nothing. Stop making excuses for the jerk! He's leading you on!" She mutters this next bit under her breath, "He's leading himself on, too."

A stack of trays drops in the kitchen, making a noisy blur of the otherwise commonplace, chaotic lunchtime activity. It's a rare event when someone causes such a clatter; but when an obnoxious tray drop occurs, a quick pickup usually follows the sound. This mishap, however, is accompanied by the sound of tinkling silverware and crashing plastic cups. The ensuing noise continues for far too long, as if someone had slowly backed into and knocked over many great big stacks.

Next comes a bloodcurdling scream. I qualify it as *bloodcurdling*, because having never heard the likes of such a thing before (not in real life, anyway), I can describe it as nothing else.

"Jee-sus!" Alicia declares, laughing, perhaps inappropriately. "Someone should be fired over that."

Everyone in the caf is in a state of premature pandemonium over the uproarious distraction. Through the echoing din, I spy the culprit through the kitchen's side door—one of the cafeteria ladies stands amidst a gigantic mess of her own making. She drops a hard gasp, then makes a run for the exit, but not before nearly spilling herself over the disarray of dishware she's toppled. She finds her balance and steadies herself, then backs her way out, away from dozens of judging teenage eyes.

"It's—It's impossible." The heretofore shrieking daffodil dashes off. I watch her ungraceful exit, noticing a sole, solid tear breaking across her sad crow's feet.

And she goes.

So unaware is she of herself and her belongings, that when her phone drops from her hand, she does not stop to retrieve it. She's good and gone by the time Tina Hatfield picks it up and chases after her.

"Ms. Gretchen," Tina chimes. "You dropped your phone."

"I didn't know she had a name," says Leash. We sit back at our table.

"What do you suppose that's all about?" Peggy asks, taking a seat opposite us. "You can't act like a psycho in a menial school job and expect not to suffer some consequences. I'm not saying she'll be fired. Who knows? But she should be put on notice."

The rest of the cafeteria staff hustle out, unexpectedly, tripping over themselves to follow in Ms. Gretchen's hurried footsteps, all the while staring at their phones in horror.

"Something's up," Ronni says, entirely uninterested in her unopened, bagged lunch.

I don't know what to say. So I shut up.

Halfway across the cafeteria, making an effort I never would have guessed her capable, Connie Blackburn stumble-jumps out from her royal table by the long front window. Unabashedly free of its hiding place (her bra), Connie's not-so-secret, secret phone glows ominously in her cupped hands.

"It's the end," Connie announces blandly. And everyone watches her face as it turns to an unlikely shade of fear and/or horror. "They say it's the end of the world!"

Those nearest Connie, her minions, huddle around the most popular girl in school as she doom scrolls through her social feeds. Their growing disbelief and desolate wonder are enough to chill anyone's bones. Even mine.

A herd of six—no, eight teachers and counselors burst in. Every one of them looks as if they've just seen the sun explode. Their faces —drained of all color and wiped of all expression—unintentionally add to our growing distress.

"Children, come!"

"They're not children, Barb. They're young adults." Mrs. Clysdale chides Ms. Langson. She's always spoken plainly to us, and treated us as human beings. Also, rumor has it, Mrs. Clysdale and Ms. Langson are lovers. I can totally see it.

"Everyone, please," Ms. Langson continues. "An emergency assembly will be held in the theater."

"What for?" Peter Gannigan wants to know. I figure Pete hasn't grasped the sincere level of potentially national tragedy-sized proportions we might be dealing with. How long can teachers stall before divulging that there's been another 9/11, or that the president's been assassinated, or that California was destroyed by a nuclear bomb or… I don't know, something much worse or unimaginable. My nervous wreck of a brain can fathom a host of unlikely scenarios, but I shouldn't jump to conclusions just because the cafeteria staff and stupid Connie Blackburn had a bit of a freak out.

"What's going on?" someone asks. I don't catch who it is, but others raise their voices in support of uncovering the unknown.

"There have been news reports—" Mrs. Clysdale pauses, as if she's afraid that speaking the words aloud might make them true. "There are reports of an alarming nature. Now, I don't want anyone to panic because—Hold it! Mr. Stiner, where are you going?"

"To the theater," Jaime Stiner, a senior, says. "To get answers. And my phone."

He marches off, followed shortly by others, then everyone else, and me. It's times like these (has there ever been a time like this?) where our uptight private school's policy of confiscating phones at first bell really rings fascist.

"Do you think we're at war with China or something?" Carmen Lux asks no one in particular as she forces her way through the cluster of pushy students in the hall. Separated from her clan, Carmen needs to hear herself talk, I guess. "I mean... It's gotta be super bad, right?"

"Yeah," I say, because I agree. Not with the China bit—well, maybe—but more so with Carmen's assessment of the severity of the day. Remarkably, I find myself suddenly famished and wishing this news could have waited to drop at least another twenty minutes, so I could have finished my egg salad sandwich. I left it sitting on the cafeteria table with everyone else's forgotten food.

Thad Reynolds bumps my shoulder hard as he joins the other idiots plowing through the still-obedient crowd. They have to do most things with half strength, because any overt signs of aggression might land them in detention.

"Watch it, Thad!" Carmen stands up for me, but maybe it's only because she received a minor, tertiary bump as he passed. Thad couldn't care less. He's set his sights on the John J. Wilkins High Theater, where a hastily put together informational meeting is about to commence.

"Give us our phones!" someone shouts. It's really too crowded to be safe here in the hall. Finally, the theater doors open and the entire student body pours in. And not a moment too soon, either. Another minute or so, and I just know there would have been severe shoving. Then who knows what?

"Everyone sit, sit. Please. Take a seat." Principal Detroit does his best to keep us all calm, like we're a match strike away from inevitable ignition.

But the way he holds his jacket—

"Why is Detroit clutching his threads?" Leash asks. I'm thankful she's still with me, right on my wavelength—my one and only, truly. What I appreciate more than anything about Leash is her sameness. She is my home.

We sit. Others stand.

Mr. Jeffries, the school janitor, walks onto the stage, dragging a microphone stand. Before he reaches center, Principal Detroit meets him and snatches the microphone. He speaks a few words, but of course the thing's not plugged in.

"Jackass," Leash spouts. Plenty others in the auditorium call him worse. Annoyed but not waiting for Mr. Jeffries to plug him in, Detroit speaks loudly to get everyone's attention.

"If you do not sit, we will never get started!" he shouts. And surprisingly, everyone listens. The microphone screeches to on, and Mr. Jeffries gives Principal Detroit the thumbs up.

"We are going to have an early dismissal today. You can all go home to your families." His pronouncement is met with muttering, denial, astonished, confused faces. He holds us all with his unspoken news. "All right. I'm just going to come out and tell you this. You're old enough to hear the truth, and you're going to get it as soon as you leave here anyway. There are various, prestigious news outlets reporting there is an asteroid heading for Earth."

We self-proclaimed young adults bellow like children—like baboon children.

"Not today, kids! Please! Settle down!" Principal Detroit waves his arms in the air to get some point across. What, I don't know. It's the end of the freaking world. What else is there left to say?

"They're saying it will hit in October," he utters.

"What?!" Jaime Stiner refuses. "Of this year?!"

"This is nuts," Leash says. I can't even fathom a reply. Her gaze fixes on some vacant spot in the distance. The news broke her brain. And probably mine.

"The buses will line up shortly. We have notified your parents. Those who drove to school today will also take the bus."

"Screw that!" Jaime Stiner is aghast. He stands and runs out of the theater. Nobody stops him; nor does anyone attempt to hold back the others who follow his lead.

With Leash tugging my sleeve, I watch as Principal Detroit comes down the front steps of the stage to console some girl in the front row. He's mouthing, "It's okay. It's okay." Or at least, I think that's what he's telling her.

"It's not okay," I say to Leash, and we stand to leave as calmly as everyone else, which is to say, with no self-restraint at all.

"If it's true," Leash says, almost distantly, as we push our way forward through the auditorium. "Then at least your dirtbag boyfriend will get what's coming to him!"

"Are you kidding me with this right now, Leash?" I can't even with her. If it's true, we're all gonna get it. Big time. The last thing on my mind right now is stupid Craig and his big, dumb, rude, and hurtful V-Day disappearing act.

As challenging as it was to edge our way out of the auditorium, exiting the building is proving to be even worse. The phone re-distribution is turning sour, and a few seniors are getting grabby. I'm actually shocked this whole thing hasn't escalated more. And maybe that's why it hasn't—the state of mutual shock we're all in has numbed us. Does knowing you're in shock make you any more or less susceptible to shock's effects?

Sarah Lesinger, one of the student aids, is passing out phones as fast as she can from behind a table full of crates. I'm handed mine pretty quickly. Sarah's on her game, considering the day's events. I push past those still waiting impatiently, and look for Leash once I'm outside. Somewhere along the way, she'd snatched her phone from the bin and escaped the boiling madness before I could.

It is immensely cold out here, and too bright—a typical February day in our gentle coastal Maine town. A day that would otherwise be full of possibilities.

"We've lost our possibilities," I tell no one.

Leash's Saab pulls up to the curb. I grab the handle and step in, shivering. I don't even get my door shut before she pulls away.

"We didn't get our jackets," I mention. It's such a superfluous thing, but it *is* freaken freezing.

As Alicia drives calmly with purpose through the school parking lot, I realize, "Are we really the first ones out of here? How is that possible?"

She signals left out of the lot, as if it's any other ordinary day. "Everyone is staring at their phones," Leash comments as we pass a group of girls who seem to be upset, not by the horrific news, but at their phones themselves. One girl, Maya Kinsey, chucks her precious cellphone at a nearby tree. It smashes on impact, and even with the windows closed, I can hear Maya cursing her foul temper.

"It's bad, Rain. I know it. We gotta get home and lock our doors before things get any worse. Hey, can you look? Get the news!" She points furiously at the useless rock in my hand. It might as well be one. I hold the screen up to her. *NO SERVICE* is all it says. It's upsetting, sure, but I'm not about to destroy my phone over it. Sheesh.

As Leash drives, I wonder briefly what she meant when she said, "before things get any worse," but then I go back to worrying about the giant asteroid, and the lack of cell service. Absolutely in that order.

Route One isn't nearly as heavy with traffic as you'd expect—I mean, if the (literally) Earth shattering news is accurate.

I snap the radio on, fuddle with it. Nothing goes.

"It broke, remember?" Leash points out, raising her speed just over the limit. I doubt any cop will care.

"What the hell, Leash?" I say, pointlessly snapping the knob to off. Everything is futile. I should just cram into this uncomfortable car seat and accept our fate. Because it's coming. With each passing second, it seems more of a pressing inevitability.

You know nothing for sure.

"I don't understand." Leash is unraveling. Her fists grip the wheel, and she's misting. She's in that fragile moment she sometimes gets to, just before breaking into a cold sweat or a hot cry.

"Just get us home," I tell her. And she nods, focusing on the quick trip.

Leash drops me at the top of my driveway, and I don't put up a fuss about it. She's mad itching to get herself home.

"Text me," she says, then looks at her phone again. Still no service, I suspect, by her reaction. "Text me when you can, I mean. It's going to be all right." The only reason I pretend to believe her is to help her believe it herself.

"Sure," I say. She blows three rapid kisses my way, as if this will be the last time we ever meet. *Should I catch your wayward love out of thin air, Leash?*

"Weirdo," I say. And she's gone.

I pretend I'm not losing my mind for as long as I can and saunter toward my front door. This is undoubtedly the first time I've done such a thing, but if I can keep a cool head and a relaxed stride, maybe the reality won't be as bad as I think.

I'm still in some half-state of shock (if that's a thing), where reason suggests it could all be one global-sized mistake. Or maybe everyone misheard, and they're overreacting. I can still hold these contrary thoughts until I see proof otherwise. I still have plausible deniability, or something. Maybe I should stay out here on the lawn for the rest of the day? Maybe forever.

"You're home early. I guess you heard?" It's Ang. He's done some stealthy sauntering himself prior to quietly announcing his presence. We've talked about that, Ang and I—about how I don't appreciate his skulks.

"It can't be," I say, turning to face him. He's holding a rake that's too small for him, and wearing work gloves like it's just an ordinary Saturday in June, not an apocalypse nightmare in February.

You're living in pre-apocalypsia, Rain. The apocalypse hasn't happened yet.

"What are you raking? *Why* are you raking?"

"Just cleaning up some dirt in the backyard," he says, and it's totally normal. Ang is the kind of neighbor you never see coming—in more ways than I care to count.

"The world's ending, and you're playing in dirt. How perfect."

But it is.

Part of me is pulling me toward my house, but a bigger part wants to appreciate and absorb every detail of modern life while we still have it. Sitting in wild wonder and joining the world in shock and sorrow can wait, because Ang is holding a rake.

"I don't know," he says, glinting into the sun. Is he searching the sky for the asteroid? "I just don't see it."

Neither do I, even when I squint.

I hear Mom's beat up engine before her car turns the corner onto our street.

"Rain! Oh my God, Rain!" Her big-haired head hangs out her open window. She's acting even more like a crazy lady than ever.

"That's my cue," Ang says, winking. "Don't freak too much. That's all. I'm sure everything will work itself out." He walks off into his garage with his too-small rake slung over his right shoulder, framed against the sun like some Norman Rockwell painting that never was.

"Sweetie baby Rain child, come here!"

Mom parks askew in the driveway, barrels out of the car, sweeps me across the lawn and into the presumed safety of our home. But not before I get one last look at the early afternoon sky.

All is deceptively clear.

Chapter Two

When the crying and hugging finally come to a halt, Mom suggests we order a pizza. But even if the phones were working, I doubt any restaurant would be open for deliveries. The entire world is going to be glued to the news, for however long the networks continue to broadcast. I have a funny, pessimistic feeling people are going to lose their desire to work soon, if it hasn't happened already.

I turn on the T.V. just in time to catch the tail end of a minor story amidst an otherwise insurmountably newsworthy day. The reporter standing in the middle of Scarborough Square is wrapping up her piece on a sputtering lack of cell service in the area. "Though there is no official word on the cause," she says, "local authorities have hinted that the flood of network overuse has caused the lag."

"You think?" I rarely make a habit of talking back to the television. But I'm sure a lot worse is going to change in pre-apocalypsia.

"Based on people I've spoken to on the street today, and my personal experience—" The reporter holds up her phone and the camera quickly zooms in to show the now familiar "no service" symbol. "—I'd say it's more than just a lag. If anyone in the area has received cell service in the past couple hours, I haven't spoken to them. Reporting live from Scarborough Square, I'm Stephanie Haddish."

Mom's humming (actually humming!) as she moves through the kitchen. The unsettling sound of drawers opening and closing, utensils being shuffled around and dropped, and her frazzled tune indicates she's attempting to mask her emotions with whatever it is she's decided to cook.

I click immediately away from the commercial break where Channel 30 is, for some reason, trying to sell me on visiting the Bahamas. On the National News Network (NNN), an astronomer named Stuart Pilsley is breaking down the science, pinpointing exactly when the asteroid will strike Earth.

Mom pops her head in. She's not heard the astronomer's detailed explanation. All she sees is the headline below his name that reads: 99.4 percent certainty the moment of impact will be:

October 18, 12:02 p.m. E.S.T.

"Oh no! Rain, your birthday!"

"I'm well aware, Mom."

"Well, we'll just have to celebrate a day early then. How can they know the exact impact time, down to the minute?"

"It's sensationalism," I tell her, doubting my own words. "They can't possibly know."

Mom shakes her head and walks out of the room. She's still in denial. Maybe I am too, but at least I'm aware of it.

Over the course of the evening, I listen to countless reports on numerous stations rehashing the same information over and over again.

A top secret contingent of the world's leading astrophysicists, astronomers, scientists, and brainiacs has been studying the asteroid for almost ten weeks! They've come to the horrifying conclusion that yes, believe it or not, October 18, the day I turn 18 (my golden birthday!), is the day we all die.

The countdown to our inevitable destruction ticks away. Every channel has its own unique doomsday clock; and it is impossible to look away.

Countdown To Oblivion: 8 months, 3 days, 11 hours, 59 minutes, 56 seconds... 55... 54...

"Oh. What time is it?" Mom asks in a dreary haze. Our forgotten plates of half-eaten, half-cooked angel hair pasta sit on the coffee table, begging to be cleaned.

"12:02, Mom. It's going to hit at 12:02 p.m. They've said it a million times."

"No, not the asteroid strike. I mean, what time is it right now?" She stares blindly at the cardinal-decorated clock on the wall. She straightens in her chair, narrows her eyes. Her eyesight's just plain awful without her glasses.

"It's 12:02, Mom," I tell her, stunned. What are the chances?

I don't breathe for almost a full minute.

"12:03," Mom says, registering my fear.

Our remaining midnights are numbered. Time will march on in the hollow shell of our non-existence, sure. But when we're gone, the minutes that pass will be meaningless—just as they were for billions of years before we sentient, time-telling beings came to be.

"We should go to bed," Mom says, and gets up. I sink back into her warm spot on the sofa as she goes. "I can't do this anymore. Not tonight. The end of the world will still be here tomorrow."

"Mom," I begin, appalled by her apathy. "We're all going to die. Every living thing on Earth is going to be obliterated. How can you even *think* of sleeping at a time like this?"

"Because I am tired, Rain. And obsessing over The End will not change anything." She recognizes she's overstepped her motherly bounds, but is too zonked to care. What she doesn't know is that scared seventeen-year-olds still need unbreakable Doris Roches in their life to be the voice of blind optimism. Or maybe right now I need my Doris Roche to just be my mom.

"Come in and sleep in my bed tonight," she says. "Not for you. You're strong, Rain. But for me." She kisses my forehead as a weak declaration of being alive, maybe, then limps off to her bedroom, declaring she loves me as she goes.

You have each other, the dad I vaguely once knew agrees, then hedges his bet. *Until the bitter end.*

My pretend image of him has never been this wishy washy. Usually when he appears (which is not often), he imparts me with some fatherly wisdom, the likes of which I probably picked up from old family sitcom reruns. I've always attributed the slick way Imaginary Dad wears his dapper suit and mustachioed grin as a testament to Lon Savvy, the debonair family man/investment banker from the 1960s drama, *Daddy's Rules*. I never admitted it to anyone (not even to Leash), but I used to watch all those cheesy shows on the late night *T.V. World* channel. They gave me a bloated sense of what I was lacking. What they also did was give me an unappreciated disdain for my own life, such as it was—which wasn't fair. Mom's always tried her best to give me everything I ever need, want, and to some extent, don't deserve.

"Everyone's making way too much out of this, right?" I ask him. But Imaginary Dad's gone quiet, standing in the corner by Mom's full, glass case of not-so fine China, drinking a crisp scotch out of a glass tumbler we don't own.

Wherever my real dad is, he probably doesn't drink scotch. But I like to pretend that he does, because the caustic, smoky smell of it on his ghost breath is tangible and profound.

"Surely our government and the world at large will figure a way to stop it. We gotta have hope, right?"

I dunno, Chicken.

I love that he calls me Chicken. Imaginary Dad (or ID, I guess, for short—though that's a bit on the nose), has been calling me Chicken since he first showed up, when I was six.

I picture myself standing by the couch as he walks over to me. I embrace him long and hard, then reluctantly let him go, and he fades.

Don't stay up all night, Rainbow.

Somehow, I hold back the tears as he goes. There will be plenty of time for crying in the months to come, no doubt.

Back to the present horror, I flip from news channel to news channel, but it's all the same droning terribleness. When an image of the clear, star-filled sky appears on screen, the reporter makes a piss poor attempt at narrating what he sees. There is no visible sign of the asteroid. Not yet.

The world's leading eggheads predict our naked eyes should be able to see our coming death in about three months. Every sorry future milestone has a sorrier countdown these days.

I've heard enough for one night. I turn off the television, then shut the lights as I go. The soothing hum of the heating vent near the floorboards by my bare feet gives off the opposite effect: a chill ruptures my nerves.

How long before the power grid shuts down? How long until humans devolve into cannibalistic cretins? I give it a month. You could say I have little to no faith in our species.

Scrunched beneath my tight covers, I lie awake for hours. I check my phone a billion times, but even in the dead of night, it's useless. You'd think our Wi-Fi could access the Internet. We're the only ones using it, that I know of. It's password protected, and not even I could hack the thing without going into the dining room junk drawer and retrieving that shred of paper with the obnoxiously long password.

Something more significant is at work here. The lie the news propagated about an overage on the nation's 5G network is just ridiculous enough for some people to believe. I'm not a conspiracy theorist by any means; logically speaking, though, it makes little sense. Not that I know anything about the inner workings of the web. For all I know, the asteroid could have destroyed the Internet's outer galactic satellite.

All nonsense. I'm clinging to absurdity in the wee hours of the night.

How am I going to sleep? I might never again. Are there people on the other side of the world waking up to the news? How long has it been since it broke? I'm sure everyone everywhere knows by now... except maybe invalids who don't understand, those unfortunate souls (or maybe in this case, they're the fortunate ones?) confined to their comfortable comas, and perhaps some of the mentally insane. Maybe they've taken to big city streets to collect righteousness points for years of tireless Armageddon prophesying. The time is nigh. Repent!

We should have heeded their warnings. The wild-faced maniacs with rotted teeth in their head, frazzled, mud-caked hair and eight layers of baggy, torn, smelly clothes were right. I've always felt bad for society's discarded prophets. How did they get to that devolved stage of life? What could snap a person's brain to have such an everlasting effect? Could someone as relatively average and (I think) sane as me wind up spouting nonsense in the gutters, too? If that's going to happen, then I'd better get cracking on the crazy. There's only 8 months, 3 days, and 9 hours (give or take) to get there.

I toss. I turn. I toss again and kick my comforter off the side of the bed. I roll, angry at my body's uncertain discomfort, and pull the blanket back up and over my head.

With eyes fastened wide, I can't help but think that maybe I *have* gone bonkers and this is all really my psychotic break. But that's pretty selfish of me—to think I could destroy the world on a whim, in my mind.

This *is* real. This *is* happening.

Despite my train wreck of logical apprehensions, I close my eyes and try to remember what it's like to fall asleep. Instead, I am met with incomprehensible flashes of the unexplainable—brief images of alien-humanoid creatures waltz through my darkened peripheral. I blot them out by using an old trick Imaginary Dad taught me as a kid.

"They aren't real. They aren't real. They aren't real," I whisper, fully aware of the irony—the mantra originated from a manifested, false father figure.

In days long gone, when they would come creeping in to my room, I might turn my head from the alien-like silhouettes, only to discover an insignificant shadow or unassuming leaf riding on the wind. These unfounded daydreams never added up to anything more than paranoia. Like vague déjà vu, they dissolved into the past. I dismissed each as an effect of my overactive imagination... until the next alien-humanoid visitors came shambling in. Once or twice, I processed these flitting delusions into coherent dreams. In them, it was as if some entity were trying to contact me.

Remembering unreal alien ghosts from my past lightens my head, which is what I want. In the morning, there will be better ways to cope, process, or at the very least, understand. Or maybe the coming asteroid will have just been a bad dream. Wouldn't that be fine?

I close my eyes once more and am immediately assaulted by blinding streams of light. Instead of screaming, I ride them outward or inward, wherever they may lead. This is how it happens sometimes, though it's never seemed so real. Tonight, I'll allow the alien presence to have no physical body—not in my headspace.

Regardless of my dreamy mind's wants, it's here, somewhere. Logically, I know I'm mentally exhausted from the day's events, subconsciously clutching to some make-believe part of my psyche for warmth. But then someone (some *thing*) squeezes my hand. Beyond a shadow of a doubt, my hand is, in actuality, clutching tight to my flowery bedsheet. I know this. But the soft linens feel like... leathery skin.

"Rain," a voice whispers. I bolt upright in bed. The sun shines bright and oppressive through my window. I raise my right hand to my face, and for a moment, I can still feel that alien presence. When Mom knocks and enters my room, the dream (or whatever it was) vanishes.

"Rise and shine, honey," she says, seemingly unaffected that I slept in my bed, and not with her. "Breakfast is on the table. We must carry on, right?"

Mom makes a point of smiling wide and stupid. She waits patiently in the doorway for me to return her emotion. Though I can't mimic her feigned enthusiasm, I throw her a quick, toothy grin.

"Good girl," she says, then bops on her pseudo-merry way. Oh, to be old and full of denial.

Before I join her for our Saturday morning breakfast ritual, unrested as the dead, I check my phone for signs of life. There is nothing.

In the living room, I plant myself back on the couch and switch on the T.V. The headline on NNN reads: *Earth Doomed.*

Fantastic.

"Well, that's subtle," Mom says. She brings me a plate loaded with pancakes on a breakfast tray.

I eat, because I guess I have to, and watch as a steady barrage of scientists, talking heads, and everyday folks line up to give their input, emotions, research, and two cents on the only news that matters. On the right side of the screen (beneath the ticking doomsday clock), is a programming note of authoritative guests scheduled until noon.

The science being spouted across different channels is sound and widely unchallenged. Those who know about this sort of thing agree. The Torino Scale, a method for categorizing the impact hazard of potential near-Earth objects (NEOs), rates the coming asteroid as a ten out of ten.

It's undeniable. The math is irrefutable. We're headed for the end of the world as we know it. Please, pass the orange juice.

The news anchor on NNN cuts off his current correspondent's expert interview when he gets word through his earpiece that a representative from a Think Tank calling themselves "The Sky Watchers," has released a statement to the media. The anchor waits in momentary, awkward silence as someone passes him a printout.

"They're using paper," I mutter.

"So?" Mom says, sitting next to me.

"So that means the Internet is down where they are too."

"Too many cooks," Mom replies. She's clinging to out-of-place idioms now?

She's still in denial. Give your Mom a break.

"Okay," the anchor begins again, scanning the sheet in front of him. He speaks to someone off camera quietly, but with no attempt to mute his mic. "This has been verified, then? Okay." He turns back to the camera. "Ladies and gentleman, I'm just going to read this to you, word for word. These are the facts as 'The Sky Watchers' have presented them." He clears his throat and reads. "The asteroid speeding on a collision course with Earth is approximately 135,475,910 miles away, languishing in the solar apex. We've long known about Vesta and can spot it with high-powered telescopes in the night sky."

"Vesta," I speak our destroyer's name.

"On Christmas Eve of last year, Don Roberts, a forty-five-year-old Lansing, Pennsylvania farmer, self-proclaimed amateur astronomer, and frequent contributor to 'The Sky Watchers' blog, noticed Vesta's unnatural brightness through his telescope. After eight days of studying the asteroid, it astonished Roberts to learn he'd plucked an apocalyptic event out of the stars.

"When Roberts alerted 'The Sky Watchers' about the asteroid, we immediately forwarded his findings to renowned astronomers and astrophysicists around the globe. In our fifteen years of service to the planet, we have seen nothing like what Mr. Roberts has uncovered. After just a few days of deliberation, those same astronomers and astrophysicists gathered all findings and delivered them to the highest levels of the United States government."

"The government's known about this for over a month and a half?" I say.

Mom lets out another huff of distaste as a response. "I'm shocked they kept the lid on it that long."

"Asteroid C-4390 a.k.a 'Vesta' is all threats rolled into one," the news anchor continues to read the prepared statement. "As much as we are certain Vesta is humanity's inevitable end, there is no resolute agreement on how, or why, the 330-mile in diameter rock dislodged from the asteroid belt whence it came. Nor can we understand how, in its theorized multi-billion year lifespan, Vesta hasn't broken up into thousands or millions of smaller pieces."

I've got a theory for them. Perhaps Vesta *has* broken up in its long history. How could anyone say for sure? It's not like there's someone out there who has a super-powered telescope that can see into the past.

My dead phone on the coffee table suddenly comes to life, vibrating like crazy. I grab it, leaving the unsatisfactory news report to linger in the background. Immediately, I stumble and stutter around the web with mad intensity. I scroll my *SelfLife* page but find only complaining and terror. People I know—people in my own Life Circle—are outright blaming the government for this. Opinions are wild, rampant, and there's definitely no shortage of them on social media (not that there ever was); still, in retrospect, I was naively hoping the world would just chill out for a minute to take a breath.

Nope.

Rather than poison my already destroyed morning vibe with more vehemence, I skirt away from *SelfLife* to watch a live feed broadcast on a Lansing news site. A reporter is shouting to Farmer Roberts, who peers out his window, "What do you think about the name? Does it bother you not to get credit for the discovery?" I can't imagine anyone would want their name attached to Vesta. What a stupid question. Vesta was named long before Roberts caught it hurtling through space.

The old man in zoom camera focus closes his curtain in a huff, and the reporter switches gears.

Through various reports detailing a well-documented online history of 'The Sky Watchers' chat rooms, I learn that Roberts' high-powered telescope was housed atop his grain silo for twenty years. During that time, the farmer got hitched, had a daughter, lost his wife, and raised his now-eight-year-old "Suzy Bee" as a single dad. He and Suzy Bee have long taken midnight climbs up the lengthy silo ladder to gaze at the stars. On Christmas Eve, they jokingly spotted Santa. But when Don returned to his telescope the next night, and the next, and the next, he formed a clearer understanding of the strange light that was originally "Santa's sleigh."

Mom is saying something unimportant from the other side of the room. I lost track of whatever the NNN anchor had been saying long ago.

I revert my attention back to my phone. It's useless once again. I've been absorbing content for the past twenty minutes, and didn't think to text or call Leash. I'm such a jerk.

"Mom?" She's standing by the window, staring out at the overcast February morning. "Mom?" I say again, a little louder, and this time she turns.

She smiles, takes a deep breath, and says, "I was just thinking about your Grandma."

I don't even know how to respond. She hasn't spoken of grandma... well, ever.

"What about her? She's in Virginia," I manage, dully. It's practically the only thing I know about the woman. That, plus her favorite candy is Milk Duds. Mom let that gem of a nugget slip when we went to see *Hip-Hop Puppet Massacre* in the theater a couple years ago. We'd gone in thinking it would be hilariously bad, but were served a lesson in cinema for our ignorance.

I follow Mom to the kitchen, and she pours herself another cup of coffee. If my caffeine measurements are accurate, from the looks of the simmering pot, she's had three already. That is, if ID hasn't slurped some of it down. Not that he would. Imaginary Dad's not real. And as far as I know, he only drinks scotch.

"She called just before dawn. Maybe around 6:30? I'm not sure. I was so out of it. It surprised me awake. You know that thing never rings unless you're calling. And what with the cell service being so spotty. I didn't even know she still had my number."

"God, Mom. What did she say?" Whatever it was, it couldn't have been good. I get the feeling none of what Grandma has ever said or done in the presence of Mom has been what one might consider *good*.

They argued, I'm sure, because Grandma's extreme stubbornness has kept her sheltered in her home, seven hundred miles away. Whatever falling out she and Mom had, that was decades ago. And Mom's never broached the subject, let alone be open about it when I ask.

"She wanted me to know that she was okay. She said she's been waiting for a time like this for a while now."

"O...K?"

"She apologized, said the past didn't matter. And that I should make my peace with God, and with you."

"With me? What about me? She doesn't even know me!" I guess it makes sense that estranged family members would call in the middle of the night (or first thing in the morning) after the whole wide world learns we're going extinct. But why would grandma mention me at all? I honestly didn't even realize she knew I existed.

I still do, for now.

Mom turns her back on me, pulls a clean dish from the rack, and scrubs it with her soapy sponge. "It's nothing, Rain. She's just a mean old woman looking to make amends."

I sit in the silence, then think better on it. "And did you?"

"Did I what?"

"Did you forgive her? For whatever she did?"

Mom puts the doubly clean dish back on the rack and turns her attention to a sparkling glass. "Eat your breakfast, Rain," she says, then puts down the glass to go get dressed or cry. More often than not, I think Mom was the actual cause of their rift. But today, I'll give her the benefit of the doubt.

I feel bad for her. I do. But Mom and Grandma have problems that go back so far and involve so much that I could never understand. The few times I've asked about our only living relative, she's put me off, pushed me aside, or yelled at me for "sticking my nose in other people's business." After so many disappointing one-sided conversations, a girl just has to throw in the towel, you know?

Despite my queasy stomach, I help myself to a few more bites of Mom's delicious pancakes and drink the tall glass of orange juice she's poured for me. Mid-swallow, there's a knock at our door. A quick glance out the front window reveals none other than Craig, my long-lost boyfriend. In the grand scheme of things, he hasn't been that long, or that lost—not at all. In reality, I haven't heard from him in roughly 38 hours, but who's counting?

Half-surprised my off-her-meds mother hasn't emerged from her room to pry, I go to the door and open it to the sight of Craig's pain stricken face. The light, tan foundation he secretly applies every morning is stained with his true feelings. It breaks my heart to see him suffer.

"Craig," I say, and leap out to embrace the bastard.

I'm just happy we're both alive. For now.

Chapter Three

"Rain," Craig whispers in my ear after my embarrassing display of hitching and sobbing comes to an indulgent end. I would have held onto him for longer, except for two simple facts: 1) Despite her initial indifference to my early morning gentleman caller, Mom's now peeking out the window at us; and 2) This son of a bitch ghosted me on V-Day! The all-consuming blow now swirls back into my consciousness, pushing aside other recent, Earth shattering events.

"Don't *Rain* me, Craig! I know you're sad. For Chrissakes, the entire world is crying an ocean today. But I'm still here." I push him off of me, careful not to lose my balance beneath the weightlessness of my weight. "Where have you been hiding?"

There's a universe of B.S. between us that remains unsaid, but I need him to start. He needs to lay the first stones of our path.

"Rain—"

Without knowing it's coming, I punch my so-called boyfriend in the face and he goes down, reeling.

"It was Valentine's Day, Craig," I state my case. "And don't give me any whiny crybaby story about the end of the world because you were ghosting me all day and the night before!"

"You punched me," he states the obvious, licking his chops.

"Only because you deserved it. Now talk." I stand on the front stoop with my arms crossed while Mom no doubt sticks her nose out from behind her bedroom curtains again.

That Craig clearly knows his behavior was atrocious but came to my doorstep empty-handed anyway—that he didn't care enough to apologize with flowers or chocolates or whatever other romantic crap girls are supposed to go gaga over—solidifies my long-held theory about him. The only shocker will be if he has the guts to divulge his truth.

"I'm sorry, Rain. I could have handled everything much better. I know that now. I just didn't want to ruin all your future Valentines with the memory of what I have to do." He hangs his head. "Now my timing couldn't be worse. What with the end of the world coming, it just seems like it doesn't matter anymore. You know? No more Valentines. Ever."

"You're stalling," I say.

"I'm getting to it! Please, this isn't easy for me."

"I'll bet it's easy for Nate Clark, though," I blurt, and immediately regret it. A person's sexuality is theirs alone to divulge, when (or if) they so choose. But I haven't been deaf to the rumor mill. A person would have to be ignorant to not interpret the snickers that fall along my back as I walk through the judgmental halls of John J. Wilkins High.

"You know?" He doesn't deny it.

"Of course I know, Craig. Everyone knows. It wouldn't surprise me if I was the laughingstock of the entire school."

"Nobody's thinking about that anymore, Rain."

"I should have had the nerve and the dignity to pull out of this so-called relationship. But I didn't. Even though I knew who you really were... probably from the start. And maybe that was before you knew yourself. Maybe not. I don't want to know."

"Why did you stay with me, then?" His upturned face shows lines of remorse. Craig appears torn up over this—over his actions and the way he's treated me (or not treated me). Suddenly, unbelievably, *I* feel sorry for *him*. I want to comfort him and tell him it's okay that he's dumping me. Because maybe it is.

"You're right." I bend willingly. "Nothing matters anymore. You should be happy. You should be who you are for the short time we have left. We all should."

I'm not sure what I meant about that last bit. If I had my head held to fire, I couldn't tell you who I'm really supposed to be. Maybe it's this girl I'm seeing now—the one letting go of her anger and holding on to some fleeting sense of serenity. Because if I can't have peace staring into the void, then what's the point?

Craig's car idles in the street. The smoke coming from his exhaust pipe tells me all I need to know about the boy I pretended to love; that he intended for a quick getaway. He's angling for it now with his phony apologetic body leaning in that direction.

"I'm sorry, Rain. I really am. If I could turn back time, I would have told you. Right after I told myself."

He's lingering longer. Is he waiting for something else? Do I owe him money, for God's sake?

"There's been looting already," he says, as if we're not standing here floundering in the wake of our false loves' post-mortem. "There's too much news. How can anyone follow it all?" He checks his phone for updates and finds one immediately. It barely registers that cell service has been restored. I'm too mad to think straight. "In most major cities overnight—Detroit, Chicago, Philly, New York. People are already losing their grasp on civility. Maybe we never had it. Maybe we're all primal beasts just waiting for an excuse to revert to our ancestral cave dweller forms."

Though he might be right, I honestly do not want to get into any kind of discussion about morality or humanity with him. From now on, *I* get to decide who I share my mental acumen nuggets with.

Ang appears from behind our garage. He must have come out

through his back porch and crossed our shared backyard while Craig and I were verbally sparring... or whatever that was. It's no surprise my next-door neighbor's outside on a Saturday morning. I wonder how much of our conversation he's overheard.

"Hey," he says, walking over. "Everything all right over here?"

Is he extremely perceptive, overly nosy, uncannily lucky, or all of the above?

"Yeah," Craig answers for us both. "I was just leaving. Take care, Rain. Things are going to get..." He struggles to fetch the right word. "Difficult." I don't think he nailed it. Things are going to get unprecedented, that's for sure. They already are. But even that does not fully encompass the hellfire likely brewing in every nation on Earth.

"Goodbye, Craig," I tell him awkwardly. Part of me feels like we should hug in this moment, but a much bigger part is screaming, *Screw that!* So when he comes in for one, I flinch from his embrace, sending an unmuddied message.

"Bye, Rain," he says, turns, and leaves. As he drives down my street and out of my life, I force myself not to cry. It hurts, because of course it does. It hurts beyond anything I've ever known, and it's so incredibly stupid I should feel this way. My long-standing lack of intimacy, both physical and emotional, piles on.

I've never allowed myself to fully realize what I was doing, being with Craig. But I feel it all now. And he'll never know how much he hurt me. He'll live the rest of his brief life, entirely ignorant of the suffering he inflicted. And I guess that's fine. We've all got too much to worry about to have any extra crap in our heads.

"You wanna go for a walk later?" Ang asks. I run my arm across my eyes just to dab the faux drops swelling there.

"Yeah," I say, because the world isn't over yet. "I'll come by." If Ang can be nebulous about when *later* actually is, so can I. Another sad example of how time no longer has meaning.

On the other side of the door, Mom is waiting. She says nothing at first. She waits for me to open up to her. I can't remember a time I've been more vulnerable to her charms.

I watch Ang through the window, cuz he's slow strolling away. He scans both his right and left for a long time. Is he... looking for potential threats?

"We're going for a walk later." I give her nothing else, and I know it's killing her. But Mom doesn't pry. For that alone, I've forever cherished her, and only occasionally resented her indifference.

"Okay hon," she says. "You left your phone in your room. It sounds like it's blowing up. Guess we're back online!"

Annoyed at the jinx, I sprint up the stairs to my room, where a flurry of notifications pours in. Most are texts from Alicia, but there's a bunch of other messages on *SelfLife* from people I barely know. I read one of them in full and glaze over the rest.

— Omigosh, Rain! Are you okay? I'm so sorry he did this to you. Please let me know if there's anything I can do to help.

Does everyone know already? That's impossible.

And now I see it.

Craig has changed his status from *In a Relationship* to *Single*. Not only that, but he's written a lengthy status about his feelings. My eyes boil as they blaze through it. Phrases like "ended things amicably," and "Rain's one of the good ones," and "we'll always be friends," and "she's a piece of my heart" jab tiny daggers into my soul. For one, why couldn't he say these things to my face? And for two, he was *just here!* How did he write such an elaborate post in the two minutes since he drove away? The answer is obvious. He had that status in the bank and probably just hit the Post button as he was walking back to his car. Slime ball!

I notice that nothing in his long, weepy analysis of our "mutual" breakup remotely mentions him being gay... or Nate Clark.

"Oh, Craig," I say, feeling truly sorry for him and his new boyfriend, or whatever. I hope he can get it together someday soon. The time for being a closeted homosexual is over. Then again, I suppose that's easy for me to say. I don't know what Craig's family is like, for starters. He never let me in.

I shoot Alicia a quick response—*I'm fine. Really. But thanks. Talk later*. I silence my phone and chuck it on the bed. The hitching in my chest barely begins when I end it.

* * *

"Don't be gone long, please," Mom says later (which, incidentally, I have discerned to mean 11:04). "Give Angus my love."

It's killing her to let me out of her sight, what with the better side of humanity likely wavering on the head of a pin.

Or maybe that's just you projecting your fears onto her.

What it comes down to, though, is this: If I had to walk through Hell with someone, Mom would want that person to be Ang Finnegan. In her eyes, he's a golden angel in human skin.

Her love of our friendly, coy neighbor stems from two events (that I know of). One: We were four years old the first time Ang saved my life. As legend has it, we were playing in the shallow waters at Brigmere Cove. Ang's dad was watching us, but also *not* watching us. He was fishing over to the side.

We were close enough so Mr. Finnegan could run and pick one of us out of the three inches of water if he had to; but by age four, I guess Ang's dad mostly assumed we were fine. As it turned out, I wasn't—not when a giant wave (well, it was giant for a pipsqueak like me) knocked me head over heels into deeper water. I'm sure I could have stood on my own two feet if I'd had the wherewithal to do so, but I was up to my eyeballs in terror. Plus, you know, I was four. So there was that.

Just as I was sucking saltwater and watching my tender life flash before my eyes (a flash, incidentally, I have but a fleeting memory of), Ang's dad proclaimed he was "reeling something big!"

The ocean penetrated my lungs. But not exactly. I know if that were true, I'd be dead. I looked it up. Water plus lungs equals sayonara.

Ang's small but strong hands were suddenly on me, grasping to hold on. I knew his forceful touch, even then, though I couldn't see his face through the ocean spray.

He lifted me, set me in sea muck, pushing me back to where we were most comfortable.

At that point, I let loose a massive wailing screech that drew his dad's attention. The poor guy's legendary fish spun off his hook, and he came running.

Mr. Finnegan probably would have liked it if I'd kept the incident hush hush, but being the mommy's girl that I was, it took me all of two seconds to unleash what had happened when I got home.

I'd by lying if I said I didn't have shards of guilt for ratting out Ang's dad. Things were never the same between him and my Mom after that.

Because perfect memories are slippery creatures, I wouldn't have these were it not for Mom's undying devotion to Ang. Despite her disapproval of his father, she's always held the ridiculous notion that me and Ang were made for each other. That's like saying a rose could fall in love with a moose. And that he's saved my life no less than twice, well, that's just what brothers do. They look out for you. That's what he's doing now.

Okay. Calm down, Rain. You're only going for a walk.

Even in February, the coldest month on the coast, there's never a shortage of beach walkers. This afternoon, however, is the exception that proves the rule. Not a soul can be seen for miles. Not on the road, nor the path through the woods to the beach. Nor the beach itself.

"Well, this is just eerie, isn't it?" Ang says, as we wind our way down to compact sand. "You'd think people would want to enjoy the splendor Mother Nature has to offer before it's all gone."

"People are scared. They're glued to the news. Not everyone can be as elevated as you, you know. Plus, it's freaken freezing out here." My body responds to my words with a shiver, and Ang, true to form, removes his coat. "Please, I'm fine." It's a half-lie, but the chivalrous goof believes it just the same.

"Sure you are," he mentions noncommittally and puts his jacket back on. We walk a little faster, and the exercise warms me until my embarrassing breakup and six-month sham relationship rears its brutal head in mine, making me cold again.

"Six months," I say, and Ang politely ignores my muttering, probably because he can sense a tirade coming. "I can't believe I wasted six months on him. What was I thinking? I'll tell you what—if I'd known the world was going to end, I wouldn't have wasted a minute on Craig."

"He's a decent guy," Ang defends my ex, a dangerous route to take, given the circumstance. "Maybe just confused, is all."

"Well, he's not confused anymore! I all but solidified his position for him. That's me! Rain, the ogre. Rain, the hideous. Rain, the gay maker."

"Ooh, I like that last one. It has a nice ring to it. You should pay for a tasteful embroidery. You know, really flaunt it as your style. Or no! Start a band. *Rain and the Gay Makers*. Of course, you'll have to learn how to play an instrument. And your bandmates will also have to repulse the opposite sex."

He's right. In his own losery way, he's showing me how ridiculous I sound. The whole Craigscapade was just a dumb thing that happened to me in my tragically short life. I should move on, and fast, because there's not much living left to do.

"There's two hundred and forty-four days. That's all we have left."

"Wait, so you do watch T.V."

"Huh?"

"You know the countdown. But everywhere I've seen it, they show a breakdown of months and days. They have it down to the minute."

"That's dark." A dying foam wave comes close to brushing our feet, but we're seasoned enough to sashay around it.

"So how'd you figure the days?"

Ang takes a beat. "It's just what Dad told me. He's the T.V. zombie."

"Oh," I utter. Because what else is there?

We watch the waves in silence for a while. I wonder, how will the asteroid change the tides? Will there still be tides? Or will Vesta explode the planet into infinite celestial particles? Why haven't the science nerds reported on *that*?

"I guess we'd better make the most of our days, then. Right?" Ang picks up a perfectly flat stone, and skims it across the water. Perhaps sensing the opportunity for moments of truth all around us, he shifts the focus to his own, progressively saddening situation. "I don't know what I'm going to do when things get bad. And you know they're going to. Probably sooner rather than later."

"How's he doing?" I ask, regretting it's been so long since I'd been over to see Mr. Finnegan. In my defense, my head's been lodged way up in my butt.

"I used to tell people he has his good days and his bad ones. But the truth is, the times he's lucid are far outnumbered by the times he's… gone."

We come to a natural stop about a half mile from home. Ang sits on the sand, and I join him. We stare longingly west at some dancing dolphins.

"I don't know what to say," I say. "I should have come by. I've been so self-involved this year, I don't even know who I am anymore." As I'm trying to apologize, I hear the narcissism monopolize my words, and it sickens me. "I'll make him an apple crumb." That makes Ang smile. It means everything that I'm able to give the vaguest ray of solace. "It must be so hard for you, I'm sure. Just cherish the times when he's… present." I grasp to keep his optimism alive. "Your dad's a fighter. He's in it for the long haul."

"I hope so. I'll consider myself lucky if we can make it to the grand finale together."

"Yeah, we've got months," I say. In meaning to sound optimistic, my feeble words do just the opposite, jolting us back to reality. How strange that this ever-looming asteroid can weave its way in and out of our consciousness. How long will that phase last?

"When he's at his worst, Dad rants and raves about—" Ang stops, as if wondering whether he should trust me with some terrible family secret. Have I lost his trust in my absence?

"It's okay, Ang." I speak into a crisp breeze. And whether by my words or my tone, I've given him the acceptance to press on.

"He's obsessed with aliens," Ang reveals with a despondent chuckle. "From everything we've been told about dementia, people slowly deteriorate. Their minds self-destruct, and they forget who they once were. It gets worse and worse, and the worst-case scenario is when they become a shell of the person they used to be. Then they die."

"It's awful," I say, not just to be supportive.

"But with Dad—it's like… it's like these very specific ideas of his… I feel like they've always been there, hiding under the surface. He's never felt comfortable sharing them before. Now, his disease is letting them fly because he's flown the coop."

"Have you tried talking to him about his delusions when he's lucid?"

"I have. But he looks at me as if *I'm* the crazy one. And I don't want to spend the dwindling amount of time we have together discussing his lunatic ravings." Ang physically recoils from his own statement. "I shouldn't say that. He's not a lunatic."

"He's unwell," I say, and leave it at that.

Ang stands and helps me to my feet. We walk back the half mile along the beach, and this time, I accept the gift of his jacket when he offers it. I can't shake what he's told me, though. Ang's dad was always so solid. His degradation started a couple years ago, and by the sounds of it, it's progressed exponentially in my absence.

"Come fly with me tonight?" Ang asks once we've reached the path to our street. Although I nearly got sick from the altitude the last time I went up with him and his dad, Ang's proposition is intriguing.

"Does he still fly with you?" I ask.

"Technically, I know, he's supposed to. I'm only five chaperoned flights away from being eligible to test for my license. But if there was ever a time to carpe the living crap outta some diem, it's now." He flashes his pearly whites my way, and that old, cheesy, boyish charm of his works its magic.

"Sure, Ang," I give in, because he's right. Why not go buck nutty and live a little before we die? "But if we crash, I'm gonna kill you."

Chapter Four

Over the next three hours, I bake. After being subjected to a bit of incessant bickering, I've turned off my phone to make Mom happy. We're leaving all doom and gloom outside our door for now.

Mom tidies up around the house, pretending it's just another normal day, and I let her indulge in the fantasy. She folds laundry with aplomb and cleans the mantle over the fireplace as if she was born to dust.

Mom was, in her day (which wasn't too long ago), a baker supreme. Starting with an initial investment from Berkshire Bank, she opened her first bakery when I was still toddling alongside her. By the time I was kicking ass in the first grade, she'd rapidly expanded into a statewide enterprise with 23 store fronts across southern Maine and into New Hampshire! As it became clear she needn't oversee the day-to-day activities at any of the branches, Mom relaxed into her most comfortable self, and she's been content being Doris Homemaker ever since.

And yes, Mom's name is actually Doris. The *Homemaker* surname is false (obv.). We're the Roches, which is French. Mom's great grandmother came to America from the land of bread and wine and cheese. I don't know much else about our lineage, if you're asking. And don't get me started on how many times I've been teased about being a roach. The number is far from zero.

When the clock strikes four, I take out my fresh-baked apple crumb pie and lay it on the counter. Were this any other time of the year when the temperature wasn't below freezing, I'd set it on the windowsill over the sink. The February air would eat away every delicious element I'm trying to retain.

While the pie cools, Mom frets. She's been back and forth from the front window to every other space in the house so many times I can actually see where she's laid tracks in the carpet. "While you were out with Angus," she told me, "I received another call from Grandma."

I never imagined a scenario when we'd see the old woman again. Although, I hadn't guessed an asteroid would wipe us out, either. Apparently, that's all it takes for a miraculous family reunion.

"I think it's a good thing she's coming," I say. I'm not sure if I'm angling to press Mom's buttons or if I truly believe it. "Why wouldn't we want the whole family together to the bitter end?"

She doesn't speak, ignoring my obvious allusion to the prominent, missing father figure in our home. She's hiding something—some big info we've skirted for years—the true nature of her relationship with Grandma. Not that I care.

With the pie cooling, I have some time to breathe and to think. A steady, uncomfortable itch to check the news creeps along my skin. I'm halfway to my phone when an obnoxious tire squeal stops me. If only I hadn't waited for the flaming pie to cool and brought it next door steaming, I wouldn't be here for the inevitable powder keg match that's about to blow. Or maybe *because* I am here, the long, built-up sparks will simmer.

Plus, yay Granny.

Are we being sarcastic, Rain?

Mom hurries to the kitchen and gets to work washing the pile of pans and utensils I've left in the sink. Normally, I'd clean my mess, but desperate times call for selfish measures. Mom's best defense, upon Grandma's arrival, is a distracted one, albeit phony.

The side door off the garage opens suddenly, and there she is, lugging a suitcase and about a lifetime's worth of grief. She's made her way in, without waiting for an invitation, as if this was second nature—as if she visits all the time.

"Hey Pumpkin," my long-lost Grandma says with no audible tone of affection. She looks toward the kitchen where Mom stubbornly still has her back turned.

"Make yourself at home then." No emotion. Eyes on suds.

Grandma continues past me, bringing her one, sad suitcase to the guest room. I brace myself, wondering what will come next as the old lady's slow footsteps make their way up the stairs.

"Don't mind me. I'm only seventy years old, I can manage, carry my own things, and whatnot."

"Omigosh," I say, remembering my manners too late. When I reach out to help her with her luggage, I'm shockingly unprepared for how much she's aged.

"Grandma," I say, trying my best to hide my surprise.

"You've gotten big, Rain," she says, also recognizing a change in me. Time happens, I guess.

"We made the guest room up. I assume it will be satisfactory," Mom regards her with a recalled coldness I'd all but suppressed. Grandma doesn't acknowledge that Mom's spoken; instead, she continues her way up, remembering the simple layout of our home from what must be eons ago.

"So this is where we're all gonna die then," she murmurs, then enters her hastily made room at the top of the stairs. I drop her suitcase by the bed and ask if there's anything else I can get her from the car. "That won't be necessary, Child, but thank you all the same. Everything I need in this world is there in that case. I left the rest behind for the wolves, I imagine."

I'm not sure wolves would be interested in Grandma's cozy

knickknacks, trinkets, and bedsheets, though they'd probably go for whatever deviled eggs and deli roast beef that's souring in her fridge. Unless the wolves she referred to aren't of the foraging, canine variety? Is she expecting human predators and just too polite to scare me?

There's not much polite in her. Don't give her that much credit.

"Well, I'll let you get settled," I tell her. Before she can offer another awkward word, I slink out of the room, go downstairs, collect my jacket and still-cooling pie, then peace out without a *Good luck, Mom*, or anything. The two of them made their bed, they can sweat in it together. I'm like ninety-five percent sure they won't kill each other. Not my problem.

The drastic contrast between our yard and Ang's says so much about what he's been busying himself with lately. His well-kept lawn is a shining testament to his ability to make things as pleasant as possible for his ailing father. Even in the dead of winter, Ang's walkway is attractive. Sure, the flowers he's decorated with are all plastic, but that doesn't matter. It's the way each one compliments the next that catches your eye. The color scheme blends so well, you can't tell where one fake stem ends and its neighbor's petals begin.

I've seen Ang building his elaborate, welcoming awning for months; but I've yet to be this up close and personal with it. The overhanging thatch work is an inspiring accomplishment. It's not until I spot one slight imperfection on a wannabe tulip in the phony floral canopy when I realize, he's painted them all himself.

I knock lightly on the front door twice, then harder once. In seconds, Ang arrives and lets me in, smiling weakly.

"Hey," he says. "Thanks for coming."

"Thanks for having me," I answer, brutally aware of the awkward formalities between us.

"You painted your tulips purple," I blurt.

"Lilacs, violet," he corrects me, and shrugs. "Same difference. Here, let me take that from you. Yum." Ang takes the apple crumb pie and moves it into the living room where his dad is sitting in a black leather recliner (new since last I was here).

He is staring off into space.

"Hey, Mr. Finnegan. It's Rain." I feel like such an ass walking on eggshells, but how else should I approach him?

"Rain?" he asks, then turns his head to the window. "Nah, snow more likely. It's so cold."

"He's right about that," Ang says. I help myself to a seat on the couch. "You remember Rain, Dad. From next door? She brought us your favorite."

"I baked you an apple crumb pie, Mr. Finnegan. You used to gush about how much you liked my baking. You were always so nice to me." I lean in and make hard eye contact with the man who, I'm pretty sure is out to lunch right now.

"Is it snowing out?" he asks.

"No, Dad. It's not supposed to. Not today."

"Ah," he says. "Feels like snow."

I dare to move closer to his recliner, placing my right hand on top of his. "Maybe you're right. You never know," I tell him. For a moment, a brief light shines in his eyes, as if he's seeing me at last. But then it goes out as fast as it came, and he turns to face the warmth of the natural, slowly fading afternoon sunlight, perhaps looking for the day's first snowflake. It won't come.

Ang clears his throat and indicates with a motion over his shoulder for me to join him. We go to the kitchen where he sets the pie down on the table, unsheathes a great big knife from a block, and digs in.

"You want a slice?" he offers.

"No thanks. Not without vanilla ice cream, anyway."

"Sorry, we're all out. Who's the old woman that came tearing into your driveway?"

"Spying are we?" I don't care that he was. "That's Grandma. I snuck out the back—left her alone with Mom to sort through their garbage."

Ang is quiet. It's as if he has something to say on the matter but knows to keep his mouth shut. He puts the slice of still-warm pie on a plate, brings it to his dad, then returns. "It's nice that you came over. But there's no sense in staying, really. He'll be out of it for hours, maybe until bedtime."

"He doesn't seem all that bad. Is he—" I wonder if I should ask this; but despite the distance I've forced between us, I feel we're back where we left off, friendship-wise, and that was a good place, pre-Craig. "He's not a danger to himself, is he?"

"Naw. He won't go to see doctors anymore. But the last time, they didn't recommend in-home care or seem overly concerned about his general well-being; which, in retrospect, seems like maybe his doctors suck." I laugh out loud at this. "It's good to hear you laugh again. It's good, you know, just to see you."

"You too," I agree, feeling our earlier courtesies creeping back.

"Aliens!" Ang's dad hollers from the living room. The indistinguishable sound of breaking ceramic immediately follows his robust pronouncement. Ang simultaneously runs into the living room and gives me a pleading look to stay put. I will, of course, do no such thing.

"They're coming back to end the world!" he exclaims, glassy-eyed and distant. "It's written in the stars. They will walk on the dust of our bones."

"That's brilliant, Dad. You're half right, anyway. The world *is* kaput, but it's an asteroid, not aliens."

"I thought you said he knew about Vesta?" I whisper, picking up shards of plate with Ang. Save for a few crumbs lying nearby, Mr. Finnegan consumed the whole of his slice.

"He knew at one point. But nothing sticks. He gets everything mixed up. He'll forget again tomorrow." As if suddenly understanding his son is mocking him, Mr. Finnegan shoots Ang a nasty glare that quickly melts to desperation.

"Angus," he pleads. "Angus, my boy." He stands and wobbles over. Stumbling and unsteady, he falls—Ang is quick to catch him and set him right.

"Don't get too stressed out now, Dad," he says, trying unsuccessfully to coax him back into his chair.

"Mr. Finnegan, maybe you should—"

"You're one of them!" he accuses me, and lunges. Ang remains in between us, saving me from… I don't even know what. Is his dad that far gone that he sees me as one of his alien figments?

"This is Rain, Dad. She's my friend. You know her." Mr. Finnegan takes the better part of a minute to work out whatever misfired neurons are crisscrossing in his brain. The whole while, Ang's arm is rigid as a plywood barrier, blocking him from me.

"I think I'm gonna jet," I say, because things are getting weird. The far-from-subtle hint is not lost on Ang. I'm not at all nervous about flying with him. In fact, I gotta admit, I'm a little excited.

"Wait, I'm coming with you." He hands me the keys to his car, asking me without asking me to go warm it up. "I'll be right behind you."

"It was nice to see you again, Mr. Finnegan. I hope you feel better." That probably isn't an appropriate thing to say in this situation, but it's all I've got, and my weak pleasantry seems to land well. Mr. Finnegan's tense muscles relax and his hard scowl recoils.

"Rain," he says my name, and for a moment, he's here.

"Dad?" Ang sees him clearly, too. The whites of his eyes have washed away, bringing back that human light.

"Be careful out there. They're coming for you."

I smile as best I can, trying to reignite that oddly appropriate cordiality I expressed with his son earlier. Faced with all the awkwardness, I think I'm half-successful.

I show myself through the kitchen and out the porch door, leaving the pie and Mom's plate on the table. Outside, I cinch my winter jacket up over my shoulders, regretting that I didn't have the opportunity (or the mindset) to remove it inside and stay awhile.

They're coming for you.

"What the hell?" I ask the horizon. My overly apropos statement has too many rhetorical answers. For the first full day of pre-apocalypsia, there's way too much to process.

My family and Ang's used to be tight. Long before I had my bout of teenage psychosis dating Craig, my mother slammed the friendship door shut with Mr. Finnegan. It's hard to say exactly when it happened or why (the forever-remembered beach incident was just the tipping point); but sometime shortly before I turned five, Dad disappeared with (we believe) Mrs. Finnegan.

Yeah, that happened.

Mom and Mr. Finnegan never spoke about it, not after the police told them what they didn't want to hear. The two of them likely snuck off in the middle of the night together, they said. "Secret lovers," was a phrase I heard way too often. Though I never believed it. I still don't.

Neither me nor Ang are privy to the extramarital details, and I don't even know how much Mom knows about it. But when they vanished from the face of our Earth, that was the end of our neighborly backyard barbecues.

Come to think of it, that was right around the time Mom's relationship with Grandma blew up, too.

"What happened, Mom?" I ask the space between me and her window. Her curtains don't move, and she doesn't answer.

I walk down the back steps and pause by Ang's car. Someone is watching me.

I won't look up. The eyes (I know because I feel them) peer down from our guest bedroom. I'd rather not acknowledge those eyes at this juncture. Instead, I open Ang's passenger door and slide inside. I only want to get out of here—ride off into the sunset with the only person in this world, besides Mom, I've ever felt safe with. Yeah, Leash is my best friend and all, but you couldn't *count* on that girl to rescue a person out of a paper bag.

Ang comes out through the front, walks down his pretty walkway, and gets behind the wheel. His entire mood is off. Frustration emanates from his pores, making for an uncomfortable start to our unhinged adventure.

"So... he's gonna be okay by himself?" I ask, just trying to open a line of conversation.

"He's fine," says Ang. "He's harmless." Although there's much more to say on the matter, I change the subject.

"You sure about flying, Ang? I mean... really sure? We shouldn't go up there if you're not in your right mind, or whatever."

At the intersection at the end of our street, he stops the car, turns to me, and slips on a maniacal smile. "You can trust me, Rain." The Joker, he is not.

* * *

The small craft airport where Mr. Finnegan keeps his plane is a little over a ten-minute drive up Route One. There are cars, but way fewer than we're used to. Not only that, but most are speeding, and some are reckless.

"Everyone's in a hurry today," Ang says when a third car crosses the solid yellow line, illegally passing us. It's not like Ang's doing the speed limit either; he's edging close to sixty-five in a fifty.

"It's pre-apocalypsia," I mention, half-hoping my dumb, albeit harmless term for our current era will stick. "The beginning of the end."

"We probably shouldn't be on the road," Ang says, ignoring my dark harbinger reality check.

"We'll be in the air soon enough." This relaxes him, even as a pickup truck zooms by on our left, nearly clipping his side-view mirror.

"Animals!"

Ang slows at the top of the hill, and turns right on to Old Holstein Road, a bizarre sounding name for an airport entrance, but there it is.

With no apprehension whatsoever, he drives through the open gate and up to the nearly abandoned parking lot. There's just one other car here. Is there another not-quite-yet-a-pilot flying the friendly skies? Or, more likely, does this beat up old Chevy belong to the employee of the year, the only employee too dedicated to his job to take a day off in the face of all the doom and gloom? It might be more of an issue for Ang to fly, what with some do-goody good inside, still sticking to the rules.

"Don't worry about it," Ang says, side eyeing my thoughts. "That's Johnny's car. He's cool."

"Phew. Well, as long as Johnny's cool with us potentially crashing into a mountain, then by all means, let's go."

"I'm not holding a gun to your head, you know. You don't have to come if you're not into it. Or if you're scared."

Oh, no he did not. The jerk flower knows me too well. "You'd better watch yourself," I tell him, unsure what my next words might be. "Or I might just take over the controls when we're up there."

"I'd love to see you try," he says, then pops open his door and steps out into the late afternoon sun. There's a vicious chill in the air that would just kill to end us.

The wind picks up as soon as I'm out, trying to slam me back inside Ang's car. Forget about having one, last, fun-filled spring and glorious hurrah of a summer. Frigid February's out to freeze our blood. I push through the sudden onslaught and follow Ang on a sprint to the front door.

It's unlocked. Good for us, but what's the commentary on humanity here?

Inside, it's not much warmer, and there's no sign of the mysterious Johnny.

"Where's Johnny?" Ang doesn't bother to address my rhetorical question. Instead, he hops over the counter and snatches a set of keys off one of at least a hundred hooks. Twirling them on his finger, he slides back over the counter, grabs my hand, and leads me through the room. We're running like escaped convicts down a long, floor-to-ceiling, window-lined hall, until we come to a couple large doors that open to the tarmac. Outside, we hoof it past plane after parked plane. When we come to his dad's aircraft, Ang hops up and opens the passenger side for me. If I've a reluctant bone left in my body, I tell it to calm the hell down and get in.

The cockpit is the only space in the tiny airplane, not counting the small, indentured cargo space behind it.

Ang hands me a headset disguised as earmuffs and signals for me to put them on. He keys the engine, flips a lot of switches, pushes a few buttons, and the next thing I know, the propeller sputters and roars. It rotates around itself so fast it becomes almost invisible. Even with the protective gear covering my ears, it's loud.

"Talk normal," he says, tapping his headset. "I'll be able to hear you just fine. We should give her a sec, though," Ang explains. "With this cold, it won't hurt to let her warm up."

"How long is a 'sec,'" I ask, goading him. He either didn't hear me, or he's in the zone, preparing himself mentally to fly.

"Just wanna make sure she kicks out any latent frost."

"Oh." I gulp. "Right on."

"All right. That's good enough, I guess?" Was that a question? "You ready?" Ang's voice is clear as static in my ears. I adjust my headset, and have a momentary premonition of Johnny (or the cops!) racing onto the tarmac, and chasing us down as we fly off into the air.

I shake Johnny from my meandering mind's wing, and give Ang a thumbs up. He winks back.

"Let's do it," I say. And we're off.

I don't know whether he stepped on a gas pedal, pulled back on his steering wheel, or waved a magic wand, but suddenly, the airplane is trolling away from the building. And it is exhilarating. We aren't even in the air yet, and I'm wetting my pants. I don't mean literally. It's a mental, emotional, philosophical, spiritual peeing. Nevermind.

"You're not worried you'll get in trouble? I mean, you didn't sign out the plane or anything. What if Johnny comes back from the bathroom or wherever and thinks someone's stealing it? Will the Air

Force intercept us and shoot us down?" I'm really not as naïve as I sound, am I?

"It's my dad's plane, Rain. It's fine. Besides, he's not the only one who's out to lunch today. Just sit back and enjoy the ride."

I resolve to do so as Ang leans into the steering wheel a little, forcing the plane to lurch forward. It's like he's just learning how to drive stick on an old car, and grinding the gears.

"Oops," he apologizes.

"What?!"

"No biggie. Here we go." The plane speeds up, and I brace myself for the worst. My heart beats wildly as the wheels beneath us find air. At a slightly hitching angle, we shoot off into the sky. And we're flying.

"Waaaaa!" I scream out the excited jitters. The old, familiar intensity shoots through my veins as I remember… back when we were young, I went up once with Mr. Finnegan.

The past soars into the past, and I gaze out into the darkening blue. "It's beautiful," I say. My insides are still doing somersaults all over when the plane levels off, but at least I'm conscious and can appreciate the glory of what lies before us.

"Where to, co-pilot?" Ang asks. Even though we were lucky enough to get clear of his rinky dink airport, I doubt we'd have the same fortune landing somewhere else.

"Set 'er down yonder, at Boston Logan, one-niner."

"One-niner?" He laughs loudly. "This ain't no eighteen-wheeler."

"Roger that."

"Besides, I haven't mastered the art of *landing* just yet. Like I said, I still have a couple more classes to go."

"That's not funny," I say, even though it kinda is.

"I'm serious," he says, even though he's not, and we settle into a very serene mood as the horizon blazes with the first bright oranges of a pending sunset.

"Landing this thing is a lot harder in the dark," Ang continues. I toss him a glare, and he shrugs. "It's fine. Chill out. I got this."

Regretfully, I soak up the last bits of bliss as Ang takes us into a final climb before our descent. The city below has gotta be Portland, though it's hard to say for certain from this height. The spotty clouds conceal—

"What is that?" I ask, spying what looks to be a big, black bird flying straight for us from the west. Ang peers forward and around me, as I lean back for him to get a better look.

And then I see the unidentified flying thing for what it truly is.

"Ang—!"

He yanks the wheel hard left; my body clutches to the taut shoulder strap. The menacing aircraft spirals by, and we dive.

Ang recovers, leveling, while the other plane does a spastic jelly-barrel roll, somehow back in our direction. Ang, recognizing the returning danger, maneuvers, and the insane plane just misses clipping our right wing. It spirals off into madness as Ang levels us yet again, then angles down to watch the inevitable crash.

"Why doesn't he pull out of it?" I say.

"He could," Ang answers, watching. "He doesn't want to. Damn it, Johnny."

The nose of Johnny's plane strikes the Atlantic, and it skips across the surface of the water for a second or two. Even from this height, the wreckage is incredible.

Ang switches frequencies and calls "Mayday!" three times, cupping the headset's mouthpiece for clarity, pleading for someone, anyone to answer while lowering us slowly back to Earth. The crackle-thumping of a nearby disaster muffles the hollow static in my ears, mutilating the serenity of an otherwise beautiful sunset.

Chapter Five

We land safely enough, though I had my eyes clasped tight as soon as we neared the tarmac. I do have some blind faith in Ang's abilities, but after witnessing Johnny's horrific end, it's hard to think of anything other than becoming a flaming pile of metal rubble.

But we're fine.

It's only after we're parked and stable that Ang can finally reach someone over the radio. An air traffic controller from Bangor answers, telling us the skies have been shut down for all non-essential, personal aircraft. Didn't we get the memo?

Ang shuts him up fast, telling the guy to alert the coast guard of a downed plane. He relays the last known coordinates, his own name, plane number, etc.

"Well, that's the end of my esteemed flying career," he says, as we traipse into his car.

"You'll fly again," I tell him, kinda distantly. "The rules are changing. There are no limits. If we want to, we can do anything."

"What makes you say that?" I can't tell if he's being sarcastic.

"Well," I say, secretly pleased by the adrenaline rush of our near-death experience. "We just did."

"So did Johnny." And like the stench of low tide on a muggy day, Ang's statement lingers with us all the way home.

Ang turns into his driveway and cuts the engine. Neither of us moves.

"He was a good guy. Johnny. Friendly, knowledgeable about planes and—" Ang trails off with a legitimate sigh. "Why would he do that?"

"Vesta is the answer," I say. "To every question we'll have until it's done."

"Damn, Roche, when did you get so melancholy?"

I get out of Ang's car and cross over to him. Instinctually, I give my lost-and-found neighbor a hug.

I feel like I should say something here. I didn't know Johnny, and it's clear Ang didn't know him well. Although his death is the first (that we know of) to come out of pre-apocalypsia, it would be naïve to think it will be the last.

"I have to tell Dad what happened. I don't know if he'll even understand… or if I even want him to understand. The cops will want to question me soon enough. I should probably go down there." For the first time since the near mid-air collision and tragedy, I realize I'm bound to be in some trouble for this as well.

"It'll be okay," I tell him, summoning a source of optimism I didn't know I had. "There's nothing you can do to change what happened. Going to the police won't matter. Take care of your dad."

Ang is pensive, like he's going to say something else, something profound and personal. But then he chuffs it.

"Don't watch too much TV," he says, chucks me on the shoulder, then turns and walks away.

He'll always be there for you, Rain.

Yeah. I know.

* * *

Back inside our brightly lit home, Mom and Grandma are sitting at the kitchen table, drinking coffee. Have they been hashing out their issues this whole time? God, I hope so.

"Well, there she is," Mom says. "You left your phone behind, Rain. In the apocalypse! Honestly, what is wrong with you?"

"There are no rules in pre-apocalypsia, Mom." She doesn't flinch at my dead-on-arrival term. "Besides, cell service is spotty at best. And I was with Angus. You know... perfect, strong, handsome, protective Angus?" Mocking her is going to get me nowhere fast, but it's just too easy, especially in the presence of this stone cold woman sitting beside her.

Mom lowers her eyes and wags her finger.

"Everything okay, here?" I ask. Grandma still hasn't looked up from her mug.

Is she dead?

"I assume you had something to eat wherever the two of you were?"

"Yeah," I lie. "Mr. Finnegan made a lasagna." This gets a noticeable reaction from Mom. She raises an eyebrow, disliking the obvious lie.

"Don't make fun," she says. "Mr. Finnegan is sick." Is today the day we eradicate all grudges? As far as I know, Mom never visited Mr. Finnegan over the course of his steady decline. Not once.

You're one to talk.

"How are you, Grandma?" I dare address the unreadable stoic in the room.

"I'm about as right as rain, dear. Given the circumstances."

"Oh," I say, startled by her pleasant tenor. Was I wrong to think this was going to be hard? Maybe the two of them really have sorted everything out while Ang and I were narrowly escaping airborne death.

"Your mother has something to tell you, Rain."

"No," Mom asserts herself. "Rain, go to your room."

"Argh! What now?" I ask, then think better of it. These two aren't yet done sorting themselves out. "You know what? It's late. Whatever it is—tell me in the morning. Or maybe don't. I'd be fine with that, too. I've had enough change for one day. Two days, really. Let's save your crap for tomorrow."

"Rain!"

"I look forward to dying with you, dear." Grandma raises her mug and mouths the word *cheers*.

As soon as I'm in my room, I dismiss the entire encounter. They're getting along, or not murdering each other, anyway. That's a plus.

I assume what Grandma wants to share has something to do with why she's been absent from our lives all these years. And though I hate to admit it, it's one hundred percent Mom's fault. She's the one with the long-standing track record of excommunicating people from our sheepish tribe of two.

It can be lonely here in your isolation tower.

Ang told me not to watch too much T.V. Because my weak, premature, girly mind can't handle the news? Man, he is so outdated.

My phone battery is at just five percent. Angry at myself for not charging it, I plug it in behind my desk. I spend the next hour tethered to the thing, getting lost in well-wishes via texts and *SelfLife*. I glaze over comments from everyone I've ever known (and some I haven't).

It's surprising that, though there's literally never been a darker time in human history, so many have reached out. I respond to a few, with standard variations on a platitude: "Thank you for your kindness. We're all in this together."

I'm sure no one really cares that much about my breakup. It's not like I even talk to them in school. But I try to give the more sincere sounding ones the benefit of the doubt, pretending they didn't have some ulterior motive.

The whole thing was stupid madness, anyway. My entire relationship with Craig was a sham. And everyone knows it.

I read some of the follow-up messages that come in, but for the most part, I don't respond. The Wi-Fi is still down, but I've never had such stellar reception from the 5G. It's lightning fast and surprising. Maybe someone out there is trying to improve the network for the sake of humankind?

Or maybe it's just a dumb coincidence.

I have a draining back-and-forth with Leash who, God love her, only wants what's best for me. I swear, though, sometimes I think she feeds off of my drama.

— I can come over if you want. I'll bring a scary movie and we can forget all our troubles.

— What troubles do you have?

— You know, not much. Just the end of the world. LOL?

— Oh right. I keep forgetting. Are we still concerned about that?

— Should I come over?

I love her. I do. But Alicia's needy. And I hate that I'm judging her right now. Having a near-death experience tonight (and realizing that's what it was) kind of put things in perspective. I'm actually totally fine with the whole Craig thing. I'm glad it's behind me.

— No thanks. I'm pretty tired.

— Are you going to the big town meeting tomorrow at the church?

— Hadn't heard about it. But probably. If everyone's going. Why's it at the church?

— I think the mayor doesn't want all of Scarborough showing up at Town Hall. And the church is the biggest space in town.

I want to tell Leash about Grandma, or about Johnny. But it's not exactly what I'd imagine as a text conversation.

— See you tomorrow, Rain. XOXO!

Oh. Okay, then.

— Night, Leash. Love you, too.

I put down my phone and set it to ignore future notifications, feeling a bit like I inherited a slice of Ang's anti-technology notions. That kid never had any desire to own a phone. He "never saw the need." Then again, Ang doesn't have any friends—none that I know of, anyway. He's been homeschooled all his life, and I've never understood (or pressed him) about it.

Until now, I'd never thought to "go dark." And if I had my feet to a fire, I couldn't tell you why I left my phone home tonight.

That's a blatant lie. It's because you find everything so tedious and unimportant now. Especially such inane novelties as SelfLife.

With these rattling thoughts drowning my relaxation, I take off my clothes and get into the shower.

But what about the news, Rain?

I beat myself silly with that one.

Shouldn't you tune in to see what the global temperature is?

Maybe. Probably. But Mom didn't report seeing any news about mass hysteria or a downed plane—I imagine she was too busy hashing it out with Grandma to tune in. Plus, Mom likes to hide her head in the sand when it comes to the news. She takes an innocent, kinda selfish, family-centric approach to life. Which is fine.

Unless that's the thing Grandma wanted me to hear—that there's been a horrible development. The timetable's been moved up, and the asteroid is going to hit next week… or tomorrow!

No, nothing like that. Whatever it is Grandma wants me to hear has gotta be directly related to her excommunication. If I care enough tomorrow, I'll wheedle out their big secret.

Aliens.

Mr. Finnegan's unfounded, unexplored psychosis echoes in my head as steaming hot water rains on my body. I put his poor, misguided, and diseased speculation aside and try to make my mind go blank. Because this is what I need: blessed silence in the shower.

After spending an exorbitant amount of time in my bathroom, primping and making myself ready for bed, an unabashed hunger comes calling. A quick glance at the clock tells me Mom's surely tucked away in her bed. Who knows about Grandma? Is it worth the gamble?

My tummy rumbles then gurgles, angry with me for not feeding it dinner, and my decision is made. Quietly, I crack open my door, snake down the stairs, and make a fast turkey sandwich before anyone is the wiser. Do I feel guilty for feeling smug that I've sidestepped them all night? It is what it is. We'll be one lying, distorted family again in the morning, just in time for fake church.

It will be a wonder if the town meeting is anything less than a supreme shitshow.

* * *

I dream of a fleet of shiny, silver spaceships loitering in the evening sky, right outside my window.

* * *

I wake at the crack of 9:15 to an empty house, a useless brick of a phone, and a note on the fridge.

Didn't want to wake you. Your sleep is more important than the silly town meeting. Stay put. Eat. Take out the trash. Love you. — Mom

"Rude." My perturbed voice in the vacant room hums on *ude*. Mom couldn't text, so I've no idea when she wrote this. Has the meeting started already?

I check my phone again, with fleeting hopes the Wi-Fi and 5G network isn't down. But nope. They're shutdown still. Did I experience the last burst of connectivity last night? If the Internet doesn't come back, will that be the first stage of societal breakdown? The idea of a dead (or still dying?) worldwide web doesn't bode well for the power grid.

Making up my mind to move, I inhale a Pop Tart, dress in my Sunday's best (which, in this case, is a pair of smart jeans and a nondescript, cozy pullover), grab my keys, and get behind the wheel of my trusty, yet admittedly ancient, Toyota Tercel.

In minutes, I arrive as close to the church as I can—a full three blocks away. It would appear that every person in town (and probably a spattering of out of towners) are here for whatever false hope Scarborough officials intend to preach on this less-than-ideal February morning.

I make a point of shrouding my face as I walk down the street. I see a few kids from school, but they don't see me. I know no one is thinking of me and Craig, but if they saw me… I just couldn't deal with the potential fakeness.

It's a non-issue. No one sees me. Or if they do, I'm unrecognizable, mainly because mostly they're stuck in the rut of casting their eyes downward. It doesn't matter that their phones are useless paperweights now, they're still clinging to hope that maybe a bar or two of service will pop up. Not that I'm much better. Two days ago, pre-Vesta, you couldn't drag me from my phone, not with a thousand horses. I was stupidly, embarrassingly, pointlessly waiting on Craig.

No more of that now, Rain.

I arrive at the front of the church just as the clock chimes ten. I guess some things still work without Internet.

There's a cluster of folks milling around, huddled together or apart, unsure of what to do with themselves. Still others make their way in. I've always prided myself on turning inconspicuous on a dime; but today I test the limits of my strength by pushing boldly through various family units, into the deceptive warming glow of the church lights.

I spy the back of Mom's indistinguishable, retro-inspired hairdo, halfway up the pews, and make a beeline for her beehive. She's sitting there, quiet as a mouse next to Grandma, who looks like a cowed hostage making peace with her captivity.

Everyone present is in a tizzy. That's a nice way of putting it. Conversations run wild, slowly molding into whisper-shouting matches. In every corner, in front of stained glass windows showcasing the stations of the cross, and throughout, tensions are rising.

What is everyone arguing about? Aren't we all in this thing together?

I scoot my way through the aisles, at last arriving at Mom and Grandma's pew.

"Rain," Mom's flushed, likely thinking I might burn up just for being in this holy place.

"Rain—" Grandma tries to speak, but Mom butts in over her.

"I wanted you to sleep in, honey. Things are so crazy right now. You need all the rest you can get."

Why is she being so weird?

The pastor enters from the rectory up front. As I recall, during mass, a host of altar boys always preceded him; but today, the priest stands alone.

Seeing Father Delaney in his golden garb does something for me I can't put my finger on—his holiness, accentuated by the natural light coming in, is a hundred percent manufactured by man. But his presence (his aura, if you will), is ordained by God.

You don't even believe in God anymore, Rain. Remember?

Well, that's another story.

"Grandma," I say. I've had enough of my inner monologue and decided to begin the confrontation here. Church is as inappropriate a place as any. "What was it you wanted Mom to tell me last night?"

Mom coughs so loud that at least a dozen heads turn our way. It is just the distraction she needs to stall Grandma long enough for Father Delaney to raise his long, robed arms. I pan the crowd and see Leash in the back, far left, waving. I nod and smile at her, wishing she were by my side.

"Friends, neighbors, those who have found your way back to the church after some time, welcome." That last bit was a little catty for a priest. "It's so nice to see all your friendly faces. Though I wish it was under better circumstances."

A murmur arises, but Father Delaney cuts it off with another raise of his arms, before his flock shifts to a stampede.

Someone, somewhere, lets out a nervous laugh. Father Delaney pretends not to hear it (or maybe he doesn't actually hear it) and continues. "I know many of us are still in the depths of denial right now, and I couldn't possibly put a timeframe on how long I, nor any of you, might reckon with that. The important thing to remember, as always, is that as we move forward into our uncertain future, we must continue to honor, respect, and love one another. Now more than ever, we must live as God intended. Jesus said, 'Love one another as I have loved you.' And that, my friends, is what we were put on this Earth to do."

Mayor Johnson appears from the rectory, followed closely by two security guards and several police. Father Delaney steps to the side, to give him the floor. Needing no formal introduction, the mayor immediately takes control of the room, which is his usual style.

"Thank you all for coming." Mayor Johnson projects so that his voice resonates to the cathedral's rooftop. His natural command of any room he steps foot in is a big reason he was elected. "I'm pleased that so many of our fine town's constituents could make it here this morning despite the recent Internet outage and other, incomprehensible events. The very fact that this sacred ground is packed to standing-room-only capacity speaks multitudes of our blessed Maine community."

"Enough prologue and get on with it," I mutter under my breath.

"Rain, shh!" Mom shoots me a wicked look that does not have the intended consequence she was seeking. Rather than be silenced, I am all the more annoyed at her for ditching me, not telling me what's going on, and about a hundred other reasons.

I scan the pews and aisles again, searching for Ang. I'm not at all surprised that I don't find him among us.

The mayor continues, "Since the news of the approaching asteroid broke on Friday afternoon, there has been worldwide panic. I am sorry to report, Scarborough has not been immune to the growing sense of dread and fear."

The mayor goes on to report a few incidents in town that are almost as unbelievable as Vesta. People have looted stores in town, and some have hurt others. He mentions Johnny's plane crash over the Atlantic, but doesn't disclose his name. Nor does he go into any details about a pending investigation. Not that I'd expect him to do so in a setting like this. For a few minutes there, I'd nearly forgotten the near-death experience we brushed elbows with last night. It's just the new normal, I suppose. How awful.

"I stand here this morning, as mayor of our fine town, to tell you all that we are going to pull together as a community. We will carry on as the God-fearing, peace-loving society we've always been. We are going to enjoy life and all its splendor, help one another, rejoice in our triumphs, console each other with our losses, and do our best to keep our humanity intact, until the very last breath we take."

Is Mayor Johnson expecting thunderous applause? There's nothing to campaign for anymore.

I am beside myself with bewilderment over how to process every single thing. The feeling, apparently is mutual. No one claps. Some weep and hold each other. Others shout their perspectives into the void. Nothing productive will come out of this.

"Rain," Grandma mouths my name, leaning behind Mom's ridiculous hair. The crook of Grandma's neck is such that, at her age, it must be uncomfortable for her to be in that position for long. I lean casually back to meet her eye while Mom's distracted with the mayor's continuing attempts to silence the angry crowd.

"Rain," Grandma speaks, and Mom's ears perk up a split second too late. "Your father—"

"No! Not here!" Mom tries to stop her, but Grandma cannot be silenced. Not anymore.

"He's an alien, Rainbow. God help you. God help us all."

Mom shakes her head vehemently, trying to explain away the impossible statement with her wordless, pitiful expression.

Mayor Johnson prattles on, unheard. The gentler men, women, and children in various pews cringe away from the few fights breaking out among us. And somewhere off the coast, Johnny's body is soaking up the salt water, decomposing into a tasty treat for the fish.

"I feel sick," I say. I cannot understand the inexplicable thing my estranged grandmother just presented.

"Excuse me." I stand and head for the exit. Mom's calling me to return to them, but I won't go. If she wants to come after me she can come after me. Or I'll see her later at home. Or I won't. I honestly don't care about anything anymore.

All I know is either Mom's been lying to me my whole life, or Grandma's a raving lunatic. The latter being likely, the former being a gross impossibility. Mom's been hiding the fact that dad's an alien? Please. It's too dumb to even consider.

I wish Vesta would just annihilate us now.

No, you don't.

I brush past a man whose face, simply put, lights up as his phone dings. All around me, people are realizing the network's back up and running. They look down, see what they see, and turn back to their comfortable zombie-esque existence, for however brief.

You aren't this cynical, Rain.

If these church doors were closed, I would bust them open, satisfactorily swooping out like an action movie heroine, with the doves of morning swooping all around. It's probably best the throngs of townspeople are holding the church doors wide. This way, I don't have to make a scene with my exit. Hardly anyone notices me leaving. Only, my sweet Alicia.

She's raced her way through to reach me. She grabs my arm and holds me back.

"Rain, where are you going?" she pleads.

"I don't know, Leash," I say honestly, then break free from her weak grip. "I don't know anything."

Outside, I catch a solid breath, but the frigid February air has malicious intent, choking me from the inside.

"You son of a bitch! I'll kill you!"

I try to locate where the source of the loud-spoken accusation came from. But it is impossible to discern among the clamor of sudden shouting.

Punches are being thrown. The town is turning in on itself. Chaos has broken free.

A wave of bodies tumbles out of the church. Some people are pulling ferociously at their hair. Others yank on others.

"No hope no hope no hope!" cries Abigail Johannsen, a wilting dandelion of a sophomore. She tears off into the street like a wild animal.

What is happening?

I reach into my pocket, searching madly for my phone. Nothing. I must have dropped it bumbling through the church.

"Damn it," I curse. I'm not brave enough to tempt fate and head back in to the increasingly terrifying melee.

A stranger in a heavy silver coat passes me by on the sidewalk. His face is covered in shadow, beneath his cloaked forehead. He passes me by without a look, unconcerned with the insinuating debacle inside.

He stops.

He turns. And for an instant, he catches my eye. His face is a mask of malcontent. With his coat wafting behind him, the man disappears into the heart of the church.

"Mom," I speak her name. I have to go get her out.

"Rain!" My sweet Leash's uncharacteristic yell from God's doorstep stops me dead in my tracks. "I'll kill you! I'll cut your throat!"

"What?"

"DELIVER US FROM EVIL!" A man's voice bellows from inside the church. I have a split second to contemplate the ominous line of the Lord's prayer, when a massive, ground-shaking explosion steals me of my few remaining senses.

I'm on the ground, hurt and smoldering, deaf to all sounds, and clearly blown out of my shoes.

I roll onto my side to see what little remains of the church is consumed in hell-brought fire.

"Mom." I eek out a weak cry for her. And for Leash. And for them all.

And that is all.

Chapter Six

I dream of reindeer.

I would have thought (what with the Christmas season being shoved down our throats from Halloween to New Year's), that by now my psyche would be exhausted of all things North Pole related. But nope. There they are—dozens of them, prancing through my unconscious mind, led by good ol' bloated nose himself.

You're not unconscious. Get up.

Rudolph is here to guide me through the dark cave. The many harnessed reindeer line the drippy, moss-covered walls of my subconscious.

You are not your subconscious. Get up.

His light is my beacon. He wants me to untie his reins and release him from the others. He promises to show me some truth.

But Rudolph is not real. Aliens are not real. Bombs (and now moms) are no longer real.

Open your eyes, Rain. Carry on.

The fiery rubble that was once Scarborough Church forms, as

Rudolph retreats. His blinking beacon dims, and he pulls back from the still-exploding flames. The cinders and the stench and the death of it all come sharply into focus.

"Mom?" I squeak, repeatedly.

"Reindeer!" a voice speaks to me from beyond; and in a panic, Rudolph leads the other manifestations of my comfortable coma into an unfollowable direction—into the sky.

"Reindeer!" Someone knows.

My eyelids flutter. My arms are being pulled away. I cannot feel the right side of my face.

"Rain, dear! Get up!"

Connie Blackburn's face, covered in grit and/or soot, blocks the world. "Oh," she says. "Thank God, you're alive!"

Connie Blackburn, a girl who never paid more attention to me than was absolutely necessary, kneels to help me sit. Don't worry if I have a spinal injury or anything, Connie.

"Mom," I either say or don't say.

Connie's rattling off information. She was late for the meeting and her parents were in the church. She's a complete mess, clearly in shock.

I stand. Somehow, I am standing now.

"Leash." I wobble on unsteady legs, but Connie keeps me vertical, holding on to me so I won't fall. "Mom."

There are sirens, but not enough.

Connie's gone. I don't know where she went or if she was even really here. Maybe I dreamed she dragged me away from the church before it collapsed under its own inferno.

No, Connie was real. But I did dream of some clown with a bright red nose. I think?

"Do you have pain anywhere else?" someone is asking. An EMT, I gather. Her stethoscope is getting friendly with my chest. I'm only wearing a bra beneath this medical blanket they've placed on me. If you held a gun to my head, I couldn't tell you where my third favorite sweater ran off to.

"Do you know what day today is, Rain?" she asks. I must have told her my name, though I don't remember doing so—neither can I recall whether I climbed up on to this gurney, or if I was lifted onto it.

"V-Day," I tell her. But that's wrong. Valentine's was two days ago. "No. It's the sixteenth. February. T-Minus eight months, two days…" I trail off, because the countdown's irrelevant.

On hearing my snide reiteration of the doomsday clock, the EMT expresses an inappropriate smirk, then erases it from her face.

"We're going to take you to Bay City Medical. You have a second, possibly third-degree burn on your face." My hand goes there, but the EMT pulls it back. "Where are your parents? Were they in the church? Is there someone you'd like us to call?"

Her gurney-side manner leaves much to be desired, but she's sprung free a memory from the moments leading up to the explosion.

"Aliens," I say, resisting the urge to scream in the blind face of irony. The EMT doesn't have a response to that, so she ignores it, and keeps talking, to test my level of consciousness, I suppose.

"You weren't in the church," she says. It's a statement, not a question, leading me to believe that had I been inside, I'd be toast just like everyone else. Like Mom. Like Leash. Like Grandma. The truth of the tragedy is festering, but I can't accept it. I'm not ready to let it in.

"I'm going to be sick."

The EMT attempts to hold me back, but when she sees I'm determined to get off her gurney, she lends a hand to help me ease on down. It can't be protocol to let a kid do that—to stave off further medical treatment (do I need it?)—but we're in the end times now. Churches are exploding. Aliens and asteroids are all the rage. There are no rules. Never again. Whatever used to pass for normal is yesterday's news.

Standing helpless in the street, a couple of police officers take their eyes from the blaze to study me from afar. Six or seven firefighters shoot their engines' water cannons in the face of grave hopelessness.

How are there only two firetrucks?

Rain!

Through the tempered mayhem, Imaginary Dad comes charging. ID throws his ghostly arms around me.

Oh my God, Chicken, he says, then repeats my real name again and again. Is there anything more soothing than a father's love? I wouldn't know. Real Dad was an alien, and I don't remember him.

No, you do. You remember just fine.

ID's non-existent touch fades, and he's gone, perhaps spooked by my innermost reflections.

"You need to go to the hospital for precautionary measures," the EMT is saying, just as a police officer bellies up to our curb. Attempting to comprehend the ghastly scene, he comes up short. He's certainly no detective. Just a beat cop whose days Vesta's numbered; he may or may not care for the law anymore. Everyone's a potential deserter (or worse) in pre-apocalypsia.

At last, more fire trucks come, screeching and wailing. The church is long past being the scene of any rescue mission. I don't think anyone inside could have been saved, not even if they'd been here at the moment of the explosion.

"You were here?" the officer asks with his hand placed on the butt of his service revolver. "Did you see anything suspicious? Anyone out of place?"

I turn to him. He looks at my burned face, something I've yet to see or feel. The EMT sidles in between us and administers a bandage. I recoil from her touch, but she's so quick and tender, and the bandage is so strong that it's fastened before I can jerk away.

"You'll be okay," the EMT lies, apparently forgetting she'd just seconds ago recommended I was to go to the hospital. I catch her staring at her phone. Someone is texting her nonstop and her notifications are blowing up. "What the— Adam?!"

The officer and I watch her walk, then run off. He does nothing to stop the lone EMT as she gets into the ambulance, hits the sirens, and peels away. Is it possible there's a worse emergency than this? Or did she simply decide that everyone here is a goner and the lone survivor doesn't need her?

Oh God, am I the only survivor?

"There was a man," I tell the officer, because rehashing the tragedy is easier than reckoning with my uncertain future. "He had on a heavy silver coat."

"What about him?" The officer continues to create a new job description for himself, using amateur interrogation techniques. "Did you know him? Was he carrying anything beneath this heavy, silver coat?"

"No," I answer honestly. "I don't know him. His face was in shadows. Cloaked, I mean. I don't know what he was carrying, if anything." I don't mention that the man shrouded in evil looked directly at me. I won't dwell on his face. He's there, eager to haunt, but I won't let him. There's no point.

"Someone inside—I don't know if it was this man—they shouted something just before the church blew up."

"What did he shout?" the officer wants to know, because why wouldn't he?

"Deliver us from evil," I repeat the cursed words, half expecting to be blown to smithereens just for allowing them to pass over my lips.

"I think you'd better come with me," the officer says, and I pull away from him.

"My entire family was in there," I say, quick to count Leash and Grandma as kin. "Unless you want to arrest me, I'm not going anywhere with you."

"I only want to help you, kid." He can see in my eyes that, even if I don't know where to go from here, I won't be leaving with him. "Where did those EMTs rush off to?" he asks, turning to face an easy distraction. He's slow to realize what I've known for some time, that our actions don't have the same consequences anymore.

We're dead. Every single one of us. We have nothing left to lose.

The cop's phone goes crazy. He looks at it. More texts.

"I'm sorry for your unimaginable loss," the officer apologizes, distantly. "I have my own family to tend to." He hurries away without so much as a *Come by the precinct tomorrow.*

The officer who never told me his name crosses the street, gets into his cruiser, and drives away. This, along with every instance of life now, apparently, is remarkably defeating.

"Where the hell's Denansky going?" one of two remaining officers asks the other. The other cop shrugs his shoulders, turns his face from the flames, and cries.

"Dad?" I speak his name into the wind. But he won't come again.

I am alone.

* * *

I somehow shuffle home—if it can even be called *home* anymore. I busy myself, going through the asinine motions of making hot chocolate.

I wait patiently at the kitchen table for the milk to simmer. It's so dreadfully quiet. I want to scream a blood-curdling scream, just to ease my mind. But I hold myself back. It wouldn't do any good.

When the bubbles rise, I lower the heat and add the bag of chocolate. I must have opened the pantry doors, because I'm standing inside of it now, staring blankly at all the food.

Mom bought everything in here. I tried, a couple times in the past year, to do the shopping. But I inevitably always bought the wrong things, and she would rip me for it.

"All your baking supplies, Mom," I tell her absent ghost. I will never bake again.

The pot of milk and chocolate bubbles over onto the stove, and I couldn't care less. I'm stuck in a trance of random memories, punctuated by the morning's unspeakable horror.

I turn the flame to a dull low, then off. We must self-protect and thrive, marching steadily toward Doomsday.

Don't cry. Don't do it.

Mom's bright red kettle on the back burner reveals a distorted reflection of my face. The bandage I'd all but forgotten is firmly fastened to my cheek.

I wander into the downstairs bathroom, flick on the light switch, and peel. The bandage comes off easily, revealing a fresh burn in the shape of a distorted anvil. It covers a quarter of the right side of my face.

Lightly, I touch the redness with my fingertips, and feel nothing. Before tonight, I honestly couldn't say when I was last injured. I've been accustomed to a painless existence.

Mind the crushing weight of your heart.

I was born with Congenital Insensitivity to Pain and Anhydrosis, or CIPA for short. It's a hereditary disease that can be extremely dangerous if you aren't on the lookout for injury. Over the course of my life, I've either been extremely lucky to have avoided being hurt or I've become so numb to minor pricks and bruises that I stopped taking precautionary measures of extreme carefulness.

Also, I don't perspire. It's one of the few perks of having CIPA. I literally could be on fire and I wouldn't feel it, but I can get through a soccer game at school without stinking or sticking to my shorts. So win-win?

The burn itself isn't terrible. The scar will probably never heal. And since I don't need to put any salve or ointment on it to alleviate unknown phantom pain, I'll just let nature take its course... until we all die.

Mom's dead.

Leash's dead.

Grandma's dead, too.

And me, and every human, will join them soon enough. At least I won't feel it.

Minutes or centuries later, I'm standing in front of the big screen T.V. in our (it's just *mine* now) living room. A cup of hot chocolate is in my hands. I sip it. It's lukewarm.

I take the remote from the coffee table and bring the T.V. to life. A news anchor sits alone at his enormous desk, saying that his co-anchor "appears to be a no-show for the broadcast."

"In cities and small towns across the country," the anchor continues. He draws from notes strewn about his desk, doing a decent impression of a man trying desperately to retain his professionalism. "In cities and small towns across the country, perhaps even the world," he flusters again, "society is breaking down."

"So much for keeping editorializing out of the news." It's neither a relief nor a burden to hear myself speak in this empty house. I am numb to it. "This guy looks about one horrifying story away from throwing up his hands and walking off set." Or maybe he'll just pull out a gun and blow his brains out on air. Why not? I'm sure plenty of others around the world are doing it.

You are so dark now, Rain!

The countdown clock on the screen doesn't make any sense. It's a quarter to eight already? Where did the day go?

Up in smoke.

"Since the widespread loss of the Internet earlier," the anchor continues, "information has been, as one might imagine, scarce." So the Internet's down again? I wonder if it's only temporary, or could this be the Big One?

"Here at Channel 30, we have only the best and smartest people working to deliver you the whole truth. Or at least... we had those people." The anchorman—I don't know his name, or care to—is despondent. He's lost his train of thought; he stares into the camera, zonked by pending devastation.

Somebody off-screen calls out, "Chuck—the church."

"Right," Chuck says. "This morning's explosion at Scarborough Church claimed an estimated one hundred and twenty-five souls. That is... That's according to an earlier report from an unnamed source on the scene. I want to reiterate... excuse me. That number has not been confirmed. But authorities—those who would talk to us—

have told us that the one hundred and twenty-five human death toll projection... is likely low."

I plant myself on the couch. I may not leave this spot. Not ever. Were I to concentrate, I could recall a handful of other nights Mom wasn't here with me, under our roof, as bedtime approached. But they are too harsh—those empty thoughts—and I'm counting on the weight of the loneliness to crush me tonight.

Chuck is saying that one of their reporters has more information, "Okay now, this is just coming in... breaking... News 30's own, Gary Benchley, who is on the scene, recently reported the number of *missing* people is one hundred and twenty-five. That was the mistake, okay. However, the number of the counted dead stands at—" Chuck holds it to himself for a moment, "—two hundred and sixty-eight."

Were there *that* many people in the church? Yes, I suppose there were.

Chuck, having corrected his previous statement, apologizes. The guy is an obvious wreck. He puts his index finger to his ear, putting pressure on his earpiece like a seasoned journalist playing the part.

"I'm hearing we have Gary Benchley live via telephone now. Unfortunately, we don't have images to show you. Our entire on-scene film crew and production team have been unreachable most of the day.

"We're going to speak to Gary on a landline. We were able to dig one up, somewhere in the bowels of our studio, and connect it to—. Okay, I'm now being told the technical aspects of our refined organization aren't important."

"You think?" Two mugs of hot cocoa sit on the coffee table by my knees. I must have made one for Mom. I stick my finger in the cocoa I've been drinking. It is cold now. (Cold like Mom. Or is she still burning?) The marshmallows I don't remember adding are perfect, fluffy chunks, as if they're right out of the package. I extract three from Mom's mug and hurl them across the room and into the kitchen. This pointless act does nothing for me, emotionally speaking. I'm just going to have to pick them up later. Maybe tomorrow. Maybe never.

"Gary, have we got you?"

"Yes, Chuck. I'm here. I am coming to you live from Dino's Donuts, an eatery approximately two and a half blocks south of St. Christopher's Church."

A slovenly looking picture of Gary Benchley appears on screen. He is standing in the middle of a rainstorm, on the beach, looking frothy. I wonder if this guy was a weatherman who, by other reporters' apathy today, got promoted? His wannabe heroic photo shrinks to an eighth the size of the screen; it's been superimposed over a map of Downtown Scarborough. Somebody on the visual effects team showed up to work tonight, anyway.

"What can you tell us about the situation there, Gary?"

"From what I've learned, two hundred and sixty-eight people are confirmed *dead*, one hundred and twenty-five are still *missing*, and one has been reported as *injured*. Now, the police officer I spoke with stressed that those who are missing are exactly just that: *missing*. But from what I've personally witnessed here, Chuck, it does not look good."

Why are you watching this, Rain? Are you a glutton for punishment?

"It's just awful, Gary. Did you learn anything about the injured person?"

I lay two fingers on my burnt anvil. I should be one of the dead.

"Yes, Chuck." Gary pauses, I assume to check his notes. I pray he does not have my name in there somewhere. But how could he? Both the EMT and the cop we interacted with fled the scene.

"Gary, are you still there?"

"Yes, sorry. I'm here, Chuck. The injured survivor is here with me now. Her name is Connie Blackburn, and she's a seventeen-year-old student at John J. Wilkins High School. I'm going to ask some questions, and then hand her the phone to respond."

I can't change the channel fast enough. But the stupid remote has other plans. Either the batteries are on the fritz or God's just having a laugh.

"What can you tell us about the explosion, Connie?"

I scream and hurl the remote at the television, miss, hit the wall, and the channel magically changes to the Nightly News Network.

There's no logical reason I should hate Connie. Not for this, anyway. But I don't need to watch her act the hero or the savior or the guilty survivor or whatever role she's bound to soak up.

Bill Miller, a much more serious-looking NNN anchorman, is holding a discussion with a panel of guests. They appear overtired, overworked, and overwrought. Maybe those are all the same thing. Maybe I'm all three myself.

Bombs, murders, suicides, rapes, break-ins, looting—it's all happening. All over the world, they say. People are losing their minds on a global scale. Vesta won't destroy the world until October, but such is our vile human nature that we're already destroying ourselves.

"Her trajectory is definite," a male talking head says; and the sole female of the group rises to attack.

"I'm sorry, when did we decide Vesta was a woman? I must have missed that memo."

"Well, I just assumed," he replies. "Because of the feminine A at the end."

The sole female on the panel looks down at something under her desk. Her face changes to horror as she unclips her microphone from her lapel and walks off set, dropping her phone behind her. The discarded mic clearly picks up her last muttering, "... kill them all!"

The four male panelists and Bill Miller sit staring at each other for a good ten seconds. For the first time in perhaps the history of the National News Network, nobody breathes a word.

At the bottom of the scream, a ticker explains all:

Time Until Impact: 244 days, 21 hours, 32 minutes, 43 seconds...

They changed it from months to Ang's way. Probably because it feels more real if you know the exact number of days. I watch the ticker tick.

...39.

...38.

...37.

And on and on it goes. Downward into our darkest depths, until death do we part.

Part Two

June

Everything will be okay in the end. If it's not okay, it's not the end.

— John Lennon

Chapter Seven

Hail! Hail! The unshed moon!
All hail space on the twentieth of June.
Gray-note duets composed of wrath and ruin,
To feed the global disharmony.

Hail! Hail! The rabid June!
The piper sings a time-worn tune,
Grating lives from night 'til noon,
Her secret lives in an unwritten encore.

Wail! Oh wail! The untold end!
Where everything we know spills and bends
Into the place we know will rend
Us gone, but also forgotten.

I've never had an inkling to write poetry. Mom used to tell me all the time how creative I was, with no evidence whatsoever. Though I appreciated the classic poets my English classes exposed me to, I would have never ventured to try it myself. The old masters are gone, and their words remain. What right do I have to contribute a verse?

Four months past V-Day and I'm the semi-proud owner of a couple dozen Rain Originals. I never wrote them down, I kept them tucked away in my head. The rhyming beats and words grounded me in my stasis.

I'm thinking of titling my favorite poem of the admittedly amateur attempts, simply, *Hail*. But I won't bestow it a final title until it's complete. I could probably stand to come up with a few more stanzas. Whether the thing will take an affirming turn in the as yet unwritten lines remains to be seen. For now, *Hail: A Work in Progress*, will have to do.

I am waking now. It's been a long time. The countdown has progressed, or regressed, if you will. We lost all T.V. and media shortly after Mom died. And that was just the start.

Things happened. None of them good.

Society broke down rapidly in the days and weeks that followed unprecedented worldwide tragedies. The church bombing that claimed over ninety percent of the Scarborough population was just a blip on the global travesty scale.

It was impossible to know what was happening. No single group claimed responsibility for the countless atrocities, though many individuals who carried out the attacks had no fanatic background. It was almost as if the news of the asteroid poisoned their minds and opened up something sinister within them. That's what we thought at first, anyway.

Reports were scarce in those first days, what with the Internet being one of Vesta's early casualties.

No one could rightly explain what happened to the Web. The best theory posed—before the NNN was the last of so-called "prestigious news outlets" to go dark—was that a conspiracy at the highest level had occurred. The richest one percent of the most influential one percent shut down humanity's greatest news delivery system.

Why? How? The truth was lurking, somewhere in the darkest of online shadows.

I had my theories, and they had to do with a rogue, poisonous signal that spread like a supercharged pandemic across the informational highway.

I didn't have Internet access that fateful night. The last televised broadcast I witnessed warned people not to look at their phones. There was no further information available, and the NNN went dark.

It's been four months since pre-apocalypsia ended—four months since my sweet, naïve way of life came screeching to a halt.

Imaginary Dad would sneak into my dreams occasionally. And some of those times, I wasn't even sleeping.

One thing ID would repeat, in his random spectral appearances, was that I could come see him. And I should, *"Go to Vesta. Meet me at the end of the world. Be ready."* But I heard the echo so frequently that it just became extraneous noise in my head. Because truly, aren't we all going to Vesta?

Shortly after the NNN went down, so did the power. And it never returned. I've no clue how many people were senselessly slaughtered, nor how many became the slaughterers.

I would have died alone with my mourning, if not for Ang. I stopped eating, stopped caring, stopped trying to survive at all. Because what was the point?

I had two options, stay indoors and die of heartbreak, or go out into the world to be murdered by marauding humans. I opted for Door Number One, and I fell into a deep, black hole inside myself.

When the far off gunshots and occasional screams tapered from constant to infrequent, Ang upped his visits, dividing his time between his invalid dad and his invalid neighbor.

When the food shortage became a food wasteland and the stores were entirely picked over, vandalized, and/or set ablaze, people became even more desperate. Those who didn't initially go wild from the mysterious cell phone signals the NNN purported to be the cause, turned on each other, ransacking homes and doing despicable things to one another.

Ang came through for me in a way that few others could for themselves. He fished off the still standing 39th Street pier every day. Then he cooked on an open flame in our adjoining backyard, always with a close eye on the lookout for danger.

He would tell me, in my less-talkative days, that he'd thought people living by the ocean would have more of a desire to cast a line for dinner. There are always plenty of fish in the sea. Folks just weren't interested in that sort of thing anymore. So many people starved to death, I guess.

"It's like something snapped in everyone," he mentioned during one of my clearer-headed moments at the beginning. He'd been trying to make sense of the last news broadcast we'd both watched separately. One particularly gruesome scene had morphed into another. They did not even mention the names and the faces of the victims. There were too many to fathom.

"It doesn't make sense," Ang went on as he nailed a final board up over my kitchen windows. "Why did everyone go berserk like that? Because of a cell phone signal? Gimme a break."

"You've never been a proponent for them," I underplayed his disdain for cell phones. Ang showed no surprise as I climbed up out of my grievous, self-pity hole to point out what he was too gracious to admit: that he'd been right all along.

"It just seems like a remarkable coincidence. First Vesta, then a worldwide attack through phones? I'm not buying they're unrelated."

"What does it matter?"

"It doesn't," he says, and seems defeated.

"How do you know *you* won't snap still? It's never too late. Maybe they've got it all wrong. Maybe it's in the water."

"Exactly my point," he said. And I sunk into and became a part of the couch.

At some point, I got up to take a silent inventory of all the food I had left in the house. For whatever reason (she took it to her fiery grave), Mom had recently stocked up on canned beans and dry oatmeal. The tin and cardboard canisters containing these and other non-perishable goods lined the south facing basement wall of our cozy, two-floor, "beach-adjacent" cottage.

I wondered how long I could survive on the supplies I had? A month? Two? I doubted I'd ever leave the house, except maybe to sit in my backyard on a cloudless, starry night. If I was ever to feel bold again.

There wasn't a part of me that wanted to keep on living. It was just the natural thing to do—go through the motions of survival. The fear of death was enough to force the food into my mouth. Feeding myself also kept Ang's mouth shut about it. He was so irritating, always saying how thin I was getting. "You need to eat more, Rain," he would worry, like he was my long lost Grandma... or something.

The misplaced months that followed were dark times indeed.

In retrospect, I could have gone outside more. Probably there was nothing out there to be truly afraid of anymore. I could have banded together with other survivors to try to make sense of things. But for what? I had enough trouble trying to make sense of anything on my own. Beyond the humans killing humans thing (which Ang oft reported was still definitely occurring), I still had the whole alien heritage mystery to either unravel or forget.

It couldn't be true. It was pointless to give Grandma's last words any credence. She had been a distraught old broad, upset about whatever ancient rift forged its way between her and Mom. It took an asteroid careening to Earth for her to return to us, but their mutual grudge never died... 'til they did.

But why take it out on me? What cause would she have to lie? And why, if she *had* been lying, would Grandma pose such an uproarious, egregious lie?

"*He's an alien, Rainbow. God help you. God help us all.*"

I guess there's always the chance she'd used the word *alien* as in, someone from another country? If so, then wow. Grandma was a racist. Still, I find it wondrously peculiar that an *alien* can either be a person from another country or an extraterrestrial from another planet... or universe.

It's been well documented by our less-than-truthful government that there's no intelligent life on other planets within our solar system. But no one can know for certain, right? Isn't our limited view just one of forced perspective?

There's an infinite amount of space out there, beyond what we can pretend to know. Somewhere in my tragically cut short education, I learned Earth is but an infinitesimal speck on the galactic map —and that the entirety of everything that's out there is actually too expansive and impossible for the human brain to fathom. It's egocentric and idiotic to believe we are alone in the vast, vast, swirling cosmos. So how strange would it be, really, if aliens were real? Not strange at all. But it's beyond the pale to consider that I might have sprouted from the loins of some slender, green being.

Just for argument's sake, if it's true my father was an alien, then doesn't that make me an alien, too? Or, at the very least, an intergalactic, half-breed space mutt?

I played the repetitive thoughts in my head on repeat. I played them backwards and forwards and sideways and byways. Time slipped over and in on itself, and it crumbled. Winter broke away, and the Earth warmed; still, I sat in the dark of my basement where Ang claimed it was most safe. There, I wondered, daydreamed, nightdreamed, and sulked. I pined for a life I would never have again and wept for the one I was barely still living. To put it mildly: my mental state was collapsing into molten lead.

I lost a lot of time, and I have no clue where it went.

Occasionally, I would hear the distant (or close) sounds of gunfire. When that rat-a-tat-tat rang out in the streets, I would shiver in the shadows of the darkest corner of the cellar, feeling a fraction of safety among my cans of beans, boxes of oatmeal, and gossamer web of multi-sized spiders. After minutes or hours, I'd slowly come back out, wondering if it'd ever be truly safe to enjoy anything again.

The first time I went out back, Ang told me it was spring, though you couldn't tell by the still-chilled air. In southern Maine, you count yourself lucky if you see a sixty degree day before May. It's a cruel trick of Mother Nature to put on us, when we have the most gorgeous beaches at our disposal and can't fully use them 'til summer's hit its stride.

But all of that picturesque, storybook beauty will be gone soon enough.

Here it comes—the "woe is me" stuff.

Vesta's gonna wreak irreparable havoc. The only solace I can take in picturing the destruction—the seas running dry or catching fire, the majestic mountains incinerating and turning to ash, the dewy mornings, the sun-stroked Sunday afternoons, the melted sky—is that I won't be around to witness their ultimate undoing.

And 'round and 'round I went. My fragile brain was a never-ending spiral of manic thoughts. At some point along the way, I decided I couldn't carry on in the shape of the Me I'd become. I needed to escape my self-made prison. Half-alien or not, I would feel a sea breeze on my face before that sea breeze is eliminated.

I'll try a little less unraveling today.

"Will there still be wind?" I ask Ang, who's standing by what used to be the front window of my living room, checking his weight against the boards to make sure they still stick. He does this often, and I think a big part of it is just because he has nothing better to do here.

"Wind?" he asks, once again unalarmed by the oft unused, squeaky, dry sound of my voice. "You mean, after Vesta?" I nod. "Well, you gotta figure that some day, natural wind'll return. Probably not at first. Or maybe there will be so much wind that the ground itself will blow away into the stratosphere. Hard to say. I'm no apocalypse scholar."

"Aren't you, though?" I don't know what came over me to question his self-doubt. It's just that something about Ang Finnegan has always screamed, "post world survivor."

A harrumph escapes him. Neither of us would realistically

pretend to know the science behind an asteroid roughly twice the size of Boston hitting the Earth. For all we know, Vesta could explode our planet on impact, shattering a billion trillion (I don't know big numbers) particles across the galaxy, upsetting the rotation of Mars, Jupiter, and all the other planets, moons, and extraneous space matter, causing an imbalance that wrecks our entire universe for multiple eternities.

You don't know the difference between a universe and a galaxy, do you, Rain? It's okay. You'll learn.

Before we lost contact with the outside world, before our generator beat itself to death providing the last chilled soda I'll ever enjoy, before I withdrew into my introspective, self-involved zombie state of grief and acceptance, the NNN reported renowned astrologists and scientists were in agreement—Vesta's projected landfall would be in and/or near a town called Melford, Indiana.

Go to Vesta. Meet me at the end of the world. Be ready.

ID's ominous words echo in my head. It's not so much an ultimatum as it is a well-delivered command.

It was widely reported that Vesta's ensuing blast—the one ID would have me suffer firsthand—would "incinerate all matter within a twelve hundred-mile radius instantly upon impact." That's the killer stat that's stuck with me. The radius will include the entire eastern seaboard. That's us!

Shortly after impact, what's briefly left of the United States of America will be consumed by multiple, unknowable atomic blasts, the likes of which will be equivalent to a grossly conservative minimum of ten thousand Hiroshimas. The term *Hell on Earth* has never been more appropriate.

No one is going to have to concern themselves with the aftereffects of radiation. No man, woman, child, nor beast will escape the burn of Vesta's destruction. Not even the ever-resolute cockroach.

One day, it must've been May, Ang took it upon himself to remove the wall calendar from the pantry door. It took me all of three hours to find where he'd hidden it—behind a suitcase in the back of

Mom's closet. I never asked him why he'd done that, nor did I get angry with him for the random act of Time prejudice. I simply dug out another pushpin from the drawer and tacked the calendar back up. I continued to cross off the days between March and June because some rituals, no matter how grim, are crucial to keeping whatever is left of my sanity. The simple act of counting down our remaining days is therapeutic. It shouldn't be, but it is. If I had to venture a guess, I'd say it has something to do with the certainty of the end of the world. It's a sure bet. Everyone in Vegas is smiling.

Today is June 20, 2025. There are three months and twenty-eight days left, give or take some neglected hours. It is the first day of summer, and the sun is warm against this boarded wall. It's a good a day as any to step out and breathe.

"Is it nice outside?" I ask Ang.

"It is," he says. "There's an easy going heat rolling in off the sand."

"That sounds nice." I stand, brushing some harmless basement dust off my shorts. "I'm going for a swim."

Chapter Eight

Ang's fed me more than just food over the last four months. Despite my unwillingness to do much (other than mourn), he has occasionally attempted to explain the world outside my walls. I all but stuck my fingers in my ears and hummed the national anthem when he went on about the horrible things he'd witnessed. Mentally, I was checked out. Even so, some of his warnings seeped through my denial.

The first time he talked about it was after the church bombing. I was so out of it then that nothing he said could have resonated. His mouth moved, but I couldn't understand the sounds. It wasn't just his words—it was the entire language he was speaking.

Ang was frantic, disjointed, and he moved so fast around my house that even if I was in any shape to absorb the information he was spouting, his unstable energy blocked his message from getting across.

What I gathered, however, was that the outside world was bad. As the meteor came into view, politicians argued about ways they might destroy it. All were fruitless schemes that never came to fruition.

The scientists gave up trying to convince politicians. There was no nuke big enough to destroy Vesta. Even if there were, an explosion that size would set a devastating nuclear winter on our planet for centuries.

That was about the extent of my understanding. Maybe I figured Ang was being overly cautious or protective from expounding any of the truly gruesome details of Scarborough life outside these walls. Or, had I any strength left from crying, I might have assumed Ang was hammering boards against every door and window to inflate his own ego. What I do know is I felt safe when he was there, no matter what stupid thing he was doing. Even in my deepest doldrums, I've always been thankful for Ang.

"Do you remember everything I've told you?" he asks. His hand is on the cellar storm door handle, ready to push it open and shed sunlight on my grief-stricken hibernation—breaking it apart to glom some semblance of my former self. He's studying me—searching my face; looking for what? I don't know.

"Sure," I say. It's not the correct answer. He's always known me better than myself. And the four months I've been holed up in here haven't changed that.

He lets go the handle and comes back down the short stairs. "Rain," he says, trying to be gentle with me. "It's dangerous."

"Oh, is that all? And here I thought all this time you were joking."

"It's not safe out there, Rain," he says, probably for the billionth time. "Even a walk across your backyard could have disastrous results. Be aware of your surroundings at all times. You got it?"

"Are there zombies lying in wait for us out there, Ang?"

"Not zombies. Not exactly." He freezes, and I can't ignore the chanting in my head—*everyone is feral and no one is friend.*

"I know what you've said," I try, unconvincingly, to convince him. "But I'm sorry, I just can't imagine it."

"You don't have to imagine it. You'll see it with your own eyes soon enough."

He shuffles over to the western window, stands on a stool, holds a board, and peers out through a well-placed eye-hole.

I should blow out the candles on Mom's sewing table before we go. I'd never forgive myself if I burned down my childhood home. Even if there's going to be nothing left of it, come October, this place is my heart. This house is my sanctuary.

"You also said," I say, "that it's mostly settled out there. Right? That everyone who went crazy (for whatever reason) has disappeared?"

"Pretty much, yeah. I only assume that's because they've murdered each other in their homes." As disturbing as it should be to hear, I'm barely phased by his agreement of my uneducated analysis. "But I haven't heard any screams or crying or gunshots for weeks. We might be the last people left in Scarborough." He doesn't believe that. After all, he's still got his dad.

"So what's kept *you* from going on a murder spree? Or me? Or your dad?" The mention of Ang's father causes him to flinch. It's slight, but I caught his uncomfortable reaction in the candlelight's glow.

"Dad's another story," he says. "Everything he says now is unintelligible. He's so far gone, Rain. I almost wish he'd just slip away in his sleep. That would save him the suffering."

And what about you, Ang? What about your suffering?

"The way I see it—if you and I are still relatively sane—"

"That's debatable."

"If we are, then there must be others out there who haven't lost their minds. I refuse to believe the entire world's gone mad. This—" I sweep an arc with my arm to indicate the sheltered madness of my recent existence. "This is no way to live. People need people."

Ang scoffs, then shrugs his shoulders. "If nothing else, Rain, I'm glad you're starting to sound like your old self."

"Yeah," I say, unsure I'll ever be that level-headed girl again. "I've missed me, too."

I start up the stairs to the cellar door, but Ang pulls me back, saying, "No, seriously. You go after me. I insist."

Ang moves past me and opens the latch. The door creaks loudly, alerting any zombies, aliens, or giant, three-headed serpents that might be waiting for us.

The sunlight pours in, and I have to shield my eyes as I climb into it. The warmth on my face reminds me of the days I won't get back. At the top of the steps, Ang holds out his hand, and I take it. "It might take a minute for your eyes to adjust," he says. "We'll wait here. The coast is clear."

For now, I feel he's left out.

Squinting hurts, and it does take at least a full minute for my eyes to adjust to the afternoon sun. In this moment, I am suddenly aware how disheveled and corpse-like I must seem. I've no cause to be vain, but my self-absorbed teenage mind is wondering how bad I must smell. When was the last time I changed? Or for God's sake, bathed?!

Unphased by my odor (however bad it might be) or my appearance, Ang walks me through our conjoined backyards. When we reach his back porch, my eyesight has returned to its original glory, and I don't feel like a ghoul anymore. Not as much, anyway.

"Your house isn't boarded up." It's the first thing I notice with fresh, sunlit eyes.

"No," he says, leaning the right side of his body away from me. I turn him my way and see what he's been concealing.

"You have a gun?" My inflection poses a question, when clearly, there is indeed a weapon in his possession.

"It's not the only one," he mentions, opening the patio door. "Dad racked up a small arsenal a couple years back. What no one knew about him—he was an amateur doomsday prepper when he first, you know, started to slip.

"You've been out of it a long time, Rain. But you must have heard the gunshots coming from over here."

I tried to think. I'd been stuck in such a downward spiral of my own making, I probably wouldn't have noticed if Vesta came early, let alone a few bang bangs coming from next door.

"Well, maybe not," Ang says, reading my thoughts. "I haven't actually had to kill anyone. Thank God. But I've scared enough potential threats away with my marksman's expertise."

"Still, I'd think you'd want your house boarded up. For when you're sleeping, anyway."

Or when he leaves his dad alone to come and take care of you, Rain.

"We've made it this far with what we're doing," he says, ignoring the fact he's the only one of the three of us who's actually done anything in the line of protection.

Upon stepping foot in Ang's home, I'm overcome by a pungent stench. I have to put my hand against the wall to steady myself. In this effort, I've likely failed to keep my outward disgust at bay.

"Yeah, well," Ang says. "It's only slightly worse than your place. You get used to it, like anything else."

So he *has* noticed my smell, but was too polite to mention. Well, all our stinky cards are laid out on the table now.

"I bathe in the ocean whenever I get a chance, but Dad is as invalid as they come." He's said this in the way of an apology. It breaks my heart a little that I've forced him into this corner.

"I'm sorry," I say, as if that's a cure-all for everything, then take an accidentally deep, noxious inhale of Ang's dwelling. That was a mistake. I cough and even wretch a little at the backfiring motion. Ang laughs at the unfunniness of our situation and opens a window.

"I guess a little fresh air couldn't hurt. We can't keep it open for too long, though. I don't want anyone still out there to think we're alive in here."

Could our combined reek alert the monsters who used to be our neighbors? Are there even any of them left to smell us?

"Is your dad in his room?"

"It's where he always is."

"Can I see him?" The moment I've been putting off for months is here at last. I don't expect much from Mr. Finnegan, and Ang tells me as such.

"He's so far gone, Rain. I really wish you'd been able to visit earlier."

That seems a little unfair.

"If it's answers you're looking for, he's all nonsense now. That is, if he says anything at all, which is rare." Ang hides in Shame's shadow.

"You have nothing to be embarrassed about," I assure him. "I know you've done everything you could to take care of him—just as you took care of me." I send him a smile that hurts my cheeks, having not used those muscles for some time.

"Up the stairs, first door on the left," Ang says. I nod and make my way to Mr. Finnegan's room. About halfway up, the smell hits me like a cow fart steam train doing a buck eighty through Reek Valley. Ang likely washes his dad, or tries to, with a cloth once every few days; but it hasn't helped. The sheets on his bed alone must be worn to Hell and back. There's no such thing as laundry in the apocalypse.

I enter the open door at the top of the stairs and see Mr. Finnegan. He's on top of the comforter, which is surprising. I don't know why I expected him to be fully undercover. His hands are folded on his chest as he looks blankly up at the ceiling. Realizing I'm holding my breath, I let it out and notice he too has been clinging to some air in his lungs. We both breathe freely as our unpleasant aromas intermingle, becoming one.

"Mr. Finnegan?" I squeak. "It's Rain, from next door."

The man doesn't move. He doesn't budge. He appears to me as a recently dead and stuffed corpse on morbid display at a funeral parlor. I don't know what chemicals they use in those places, but I imagine a recently deceased person might smell just as bad, prior to an embalming.

I edge closer to the bed, careful not to knock over scattered short stacks of magazines. My eye catches a few *Sports Illustrateds* near a leaning stack of *National Enquirers*. I suppose I never really knew

Mr. Finnegan—not that I ever pretended to. But if I'd known he was an alien conspiracist/baseball enthusiast, I doubt that would have changed my early childhood impressions of the man.

"Rain," he whispers, and I come close. Mr. Finnegan pulls himself up into a sitting position with some effort. I reach out a hand to help him, but the proud shell of the man he used to be returns briefly, shunning my aid. Already, I have to wonder why Ang downplayed his dad's condition. The man seems to be perfectly capable of—

"Have they come for you yet? Have you seen them? The aliens?"

We're just gonna jump right in then. Super.

Mr. Finnegan stares at me with his big, bloodshot eyes, and I suddenly find myself curious as to what other physical and/or mental ailments he might have brewing? Ang's only ever mentioned his dad's mental disabilities, but there could very well be something else going on inside of him.

"If they'd come, you'd be gone, I suppose," he says plainly.

"Mr. Finnegan," I begin again. "What do you know about my family? About me?" I never dance around the subject when I make up my mind to comprehend a thing.

No, but you'll stew in your own self-doubt and wonder for four, bloody months!

I help myself to a seat on the bed beside him, sensing Ang's presence in the doorway. Let him watch. As long as it doesn't shut his dad down, Ang can hear whatever it is he's got to say.

"We were good friends, your dad and I," says Mr. Finnegan. "I don't know how much of it you remember."

"Not much," I admit.

"Back when Judy was alive—" Ang shivers at the mention of his mom. "We were quite the foursome. That's how you and Angus got to be so close, you know. You kids were inseparable, right from the get-go."

"Dad," Ang says, entering the room, trying his best not to choke on gentle, harmless words. "Where you been?"

"I told you I just needed a little sunlight. But maybe what I needed was a little rain." It's damn near impossible not to roll my eyes at that; even though he intended it as a sweet compliment, it was so very saccharine. "You think you can help me to the living room? I can't stand the smell in here."

We each take hold of an arm, and together, Ang and I help his dad slowly down the stairs and onto the couch where he proceeds to drink a cup of water.

"Is it still the end of the world out there?" he asks with his tongue in his cheek.

"It's not good, Dad."

"And the aliens haven't made themselves known yet?"

"What does that mean exactly, Mr. Finnegan." After four long months of pretending the subject was a fantasy I'd invented, I'm ready to go full throttle on it now. Especially since Ang's dad could just zonk out again at any moment. By Ang's wide-eyed reaction to Mr. Finnegan's return, I'm guessing he doesn't see his real father all too often anymore. Welcome to the club, neighbor.

"When you were both very young, I saw your father for who he really was," he says. I sit on the edge of the recliner next to him, holding my breath for glimpses of truth. "What happened was not his fault. You must understand, Rain." I don't, but I nod and take his hands in mine, anyway.

"Please tell me," I say.

"We were sleeping," Mr. Finnegan recalls, making eye contact with his son. "Your mother and I. Or at least I thought we both were. A noise from out behind the house woke me. Normally, I wouldn't have gone to investigate, but your mother wasn't by my side. And that sound was like nothing I'd ever heard—a mix between a coyote's howl and a whale's yelp."

"Whales don't yelp, Dad." Ang scoffs, dejected and annoyed. "He's going off into make-believe land again."

"I burst out of bed and ran to the window," he continues. Becoming all the more animated with each word.

"Did you throw open the sash? Did the moon on the breast of the new-fallen snow give a lustre of midday to objects below?"

"Shut up!" I tell him. And what to my wondering ears did appear, Ang listens.

"I believed my eyes were playing tricks on me," Mr. Finnegan continues. "Or, more likely, that I was still dreaming."

"What did you see?"

"There was a green, dome-shaped glow between our two yards, Rain. Your father saw me coming." Mr. Finnegan pauses, not for effect, I don't think, but because he's reliving his fright. "But he wasn't your father."

"What?"

"That's not what I mean. He was—of course he was—still your dad, but in a different form. His body was sleek and silver. His head, like a football standing on end, was shaped that way to accentuate those eyes. They were two large, horizontal, shining white ovals on his face."

"An alien," I say.

"What else could he be?"

"What happened next?"

"You shouldn't indulge him, Rain. We should have never helped him out of bed."

"He summoned me to him. I don't know how he did it. It was like he was in my mind, telling me to come closer. And when I did, when I passed through the outer rim of that green orb, I felt utter peace and tremendous fear all at once."

Mr. Finnegan stops and lets go of my hands. This next part, whatever it is, must be hard for him to relate. He visibly shies away from the memory, approaches it once more, and presses on.

"Your mother," he says to Ang, who has slunk over to the window. He perks up and turns now; his interest's ebbed and flowed.

"What about Mom?"

"She didn't leave us, Angus. Not on purpose. I'm so sorry."

"Sorry about what?"

"She was there. With him. Struggling. Rain, your father was abducting her."

"No."

"I had grabbed my .44, son, as I rushed out. I didn't even remember taking it. It was like I was living someone else's life—some science fiction fantasy. And just before they elevated to the stars, I swear I had him in my sights. It was clear as a fog-free morning. But… the shot, it must have ricocheted off him… and God help me, it struck your poor mother in the chest."

"I don't need to hear this crap." Ang tries to leave, but I'm standing in his way. Tears of rage well in his eyes as I've halted his escape attempt.

Mr. Finnegan is panting, struggling to recover.

"I'm sorry I never told you the truth, son. And I'm eternally sorry that this *is* the truth. It's all I know, and it's all I've grappled with for fourteen years."

I'm standing and pacing and biting my nails. I figured Mr. Finnegan would peddle some line of nonsense, but this is beyond the pale. Did he just admit to accidentally murdering Ang's mom by way of my alien dad's bullet-proof, transformed body?!

Do I believe him? Could anybody? Yet still… Why would Grandma have mentioned aliens at all if it wasn't true? And why would she and Mom have been on the outs all these years if it wasn't true? And and and—

"What happened after that?" I ask, somewhat callously. Damn everyone's feelings. All I want to know is the truth, or whatever version of it I might be able to swallow.

"I ran off the back porch, through the green dome, and into the impossible reality of it all. I picked your mother off of the ground and held her in my arms for as long as I could. I kept expecting to hear police sirens, but none came.

"And your father was standing over us, Rain. He was wearing his human face and body again. He spoke to me, in a comforting way, inside my mind. He told me he could save my Judy, but he had to take her far, far away."

"So she didn't die, then?!" Ang is one reveal away from a full-blown meltdown.

"He was so strong, your dad. He picked her up and he held her, and then a bright, yellow light shot down upon them from above. I tried to pass through it, but he shook his head."

"Oh."

"And they were gone."

If what he's said isn't true, then it's the wildest tall tale I've ever heard. I want so badly to believe it, as proof that my dad and Ang's mom might still be alive somewhere out there.

"That's why you and Mom had a falling out?" I ask Mr. Finnegan. Clinging to Earthly matters—the ones that have human emotions around them—is all that makes sense right now.

"It wasn't a falling out. Not exactly. Your mom never knew what happened. I don't even know if she knew who your dad really was."

"Is," I correct him, and suddenly realize in my gut that that's what I am choosing to believe—that he's really alive, and not imaginary, somewhere out there among the stars.

"I don't know what happened to them after that night, Rain. But I could never look your mother in the face again after that. I'm so sorry. None of it was her fault. Nor yours, of course. I just couldn't bring myself to be around either of you."

"And now?" I ask. Judgmental of his friendship failures and neighborly neglect, I throw rocks right through our mutual glass houses.

"And now we're running out of time," he answers. "That's all the information I have. It has tortured me. I have no more answers for you. Either of you."

"Yeah," I mumble. I can't look at him right now. Neither can Ang.

"I'm outta here," he says. Before the front door shuts closed behind him, I grab it and chase after him.

Chapter Nine

I walk side by side with Ang, though he is not the least bit interested in my company. I allow him the benefit of silence as we head to the beach. Even though we've both got a serious amount of baggage, he's content in keeping his anger bottled.

His stride is long, and at first it's difficult to keep pace. As I step up my angry walking game, he slows his own to match mine. I know that's what he's thinking—that if he were to leave me in his dust out of sheer, misplaced anger, and were I to fall victim to whatever diabolical monsters dwell in the hearts of our not-yet-dead neighbors, he'd never forgive himself. Never.

On the short trek to the ocean, I've yet to see anyone befitting Ang's unflattering, paranoid descriptions. In fact, I don't see anyone at all. It's just us out here with the wind blowing hard on an overcast summer afternoon. It is hard to comprehend how I spent so much time in my home.

We reach the boardwalk, and Ang sidesteps the planks to walk through the protected dunes. I would mention that we shouldn't disturb the fragile vegetation here, except that nothing matters anymore. Our measly footprints in the sand and grass will not change

Vesta's course. All apologies, Mother Nature, but you too are in for the reckoning.

I have to be careful; I don't want to oblige a doomed worldview. There is still time to sort out the alien issue. If there's anything real to sort out. Mr. Finnegan laid it out for us pretty plainly. If we are to believe his seemingly coherent story, then I am indeed a product of an intergalactic lifeform. Am I grasping at straws?

Ang bends at his knees and snatches a long, whittled spear from the folds of an otherwise insignificant shrub among the sand weeds. On our quiet, pensive power walk, I hadn't considered we'd be fishing.

"You're going to use *that*?" I say, breaking the silence just as a wave breaks against the shoreline.

"There's a lot you don't know about me, Rain," he says. But is there? Is there really?

Down at the water's edge, Ang kicks off his shoes and wades in. He gets to about hip-level when he stops, scans, and fires. From my comfortable, dry position on the beach, I watch as his sharpened weapon disappears beneath the surface. Ang curses, having missed some unseen prey; he strides in a few feet, retrieves his spear. I consider mocking him for his lack of manliness, but then think better of it. This is not the time to push Ang's buttons. Besides, I'm still working on coming out of my long, selfish slumber.

Now is the time for rumination.

When it came to Ang's mom and my dad, I never put two and two together—never cared to do the math. But I do now. It's impossible to avoid the ticking truth bomb.

Ang's mom vanished the same night as my dad. I was far too young and undoubtedly wrapped in my loss that I couldn't feel Ang's silent suffering from next door. I should have. Also... we, the children, were told the "official" answer given by local and state authorities.

They ran off together.

The simplest answer was the only answer. Any alien alibis were entirely ignored.

Ang steadies himself in the water, spear clutched tight in his hand. He homes in on a particular spot and lets loose his misguided fury once more. This time, he hoots with justification as he pulls a freshly pierced, good-sized trout from the sea. It flaps helplessly on Ang's pointy edge.

"Holy sh—." The wind takes my fully formed surprise from me, but the sentiment is loud and clear. "How'd you do that?" I ask when he returns from the waves.

"Practice, patience, more practice, and more patience," he says, kinda Zen master-esque. His fish stops vibrating and meets the end of its suffering. Ang places his spear on the ground and sits in the sand, far enough so that the coming tide won't get him.

"You must be cold," I say, watching him hold his knees, attempting not to shake.

"I don't know what I am," he says. "Or you." It's not a rebuke or a dig. He's just hurt, and maybe broken, is all.

You relate.

"In another four months, it won't matter anyway, right?" My attempt at dark humor is squashed when Ang doesn't feign a snicker.

"One hundred and twenty days," he says.

"Really, is that all? Crap, why didn't you wake me from my self-pity void sooner?" He gives me a look that reads deeply, *Don't you know I tried?* "Has everyone in town really offed each other?"

"There are some, like us, who remain untainted by the virus," Ang says, scanning the beach and finding none. "There must be. They're in their holes or their boarded-up homes, parsing out what's left of their beans, suffering their own private hells."

"That's poetic," I razz him.

Ang picks his bloodied fish spear off the beach and spins it softly in his hands. The poor, dead, pierced thing on the end does a pirouette in the air, and I am suddenly starving.

"Do you believe him?" Ang asks, out of the blue.

"Your dad?" I stall, staring out at the unknowing sea. "I don't know what to believe. Did you ever question it? The so-called truth we were told? That they... ran away togeth—."

"It's fine," he interrupts, when clearly nothing is. "We should head back. Gut this thing." He shows off the fish at the end of his spear. I can't help but feel we've both been gutted today, too.

I've forever taken advantage of the beach. Granted, life here in coastal Maine is not always sunshine and balmy rays. It's actually quite cold for about eight or nine months out of the year. By the time June rolls around (mid to late-May if you're lucky), you're so sick of the weather that the promise of a good beach day is naturally a gratifying welcome.

With our backs to the Atlantic, I make a promise to myself to appreciate the beach for what it is—how vast its secrets, how close its inviting waters, how expansive and deep its untold mysteries. Or maybe that's just the hack poet in me, whining to get out.

We encounter not a soul on the walk back. Could the roaming marauders Ang's warned about have canceled themselves out? Have the baddies of this world gone extinct?

I'm once again humbled by how lucky I have had it. I would have surely expired in the early weeks of the blackout if not for Ang. As he scans the perimeter of his property before walking up to his front door, I note the hard lines in his face, especially around his eyes. I can't recall ever seeing him this intense—my forever friend and partner in pre-apocalypsia is a stone cold survivalist.

"Where's your dad?" I ask as we enter to a quiet home. But then I spy Mr. Finnegan sitting as cozy as can be on the back porch. Ang goes through the kitchen and out the sliding door, to chastise him.

"Get inside, Dad. It's not safe out here."

"Yeah," Mr. Finnegan says. "So you keep saying."

"Oh, so you've heard me this whole time? Why didn't you

mention the key to unlocking your saner side was sitting right next door in her own cozy coma?"

I must flinch or lower my eyes, because Ang shifts gears toward an apology when he sees me.

"No, don't." I tell him. "I've been a selfish wreck of a person. Without you, I wouldn't have made it. Neither of us would have."

Mr. Finnegan is a stubborn man who looks to the distance for some unknown answer. Ang's about to lay into him some more, or maybe assault him with his dead fish, but a loud banging at the front door stops the bickering. Ang's hand goes immediately to his waistband. He pulls a well-concealed pistol from his pants. Did he have that gun on our excursion to the beach? Surely he wouldn't have waded into the waves with it on his hip.

The banging continues, louder and more pressing. My pointless concerns will have to be put on hold.

Ang scans the backyard. Satisfied by the vacant land, he snatches his father by the collar and drags him through the opened, sliding glass door and back into the kitchen. I don't wait for an invitation. I'm in, albeit tentatively.

"Get down," Ang demands. And we do. I throw my body to the ground behind the island, separating the dirty kitchen tile from the filthy living room rug.

Ang walks cautiously to the front of his house to get a closer look at the surprising visitor/would-be intruder.

"Be careful," I say from my crouched, cowardly position.

Slowly, Ang moves to his front window and peers out from behind the curtain where one of the few boards he's put up bends back a smidge.

"It's for you," Ang says with zero fanfare, then opens the door to reveal a version of Connie Blackburn who is a far cry from her former self. The only recognizable thing about her is her diamond studded watch. A coat of grime and impenetrable layers of trauma hide her striking blue eyes.

Connie's face is wet with tears, her clothes are ripped and torn, her hair is a god-awful mess, and she's shaking like a shaved pup in a snowbank. She might as well have Marauder Victim scrawled in black, permanent marker on her forehead.

"Connie?" I say dumbly, and rush to help her inside. Her very presence reminds me of the world we once knew, not too long ago, when such a thing as society and popular kids existed. It's impossible to say who's survived and who hasn't.

"Water," she begs, falling forward. Ang catches her and helps her to the couch while I pour her a half-full glass from a jug on the counter. Suddenly it hits me—all this time, Ang's been giving me water from his family's well. I don't know how such things work, but there can't be an endless supply down there. He's the only person I've ever known that didn't have city water.

And it's been months.

How has anyone survived?

Connie chugs, haphazardly spilling some out the corner of her mouth. I'd be angry with her, but she's a fright to look at; I can't begin to imagine what she's been through.

"More?" she begs.

Ang nods, and I go back to the kitchen and fill her a proper amount. This time, Connie takes smaller sips, shaking; she's clearly on edge. Pulling herself up over the back of the couch, Connie peeks out the window, terrified of ghosts that aren't there.

Or are they?

When she breaks down, she hides her head in her lap but still holds on to the water glass as if it's her one touchstone to what's left of a mostly dead humanity. Ang gently takes it from her and places it on the coffee table. I go to her, put my hand on her arm, and rub gently.

"There's no one left out there. Not anyone recognizable—" She pauses, reliving some tragedy. "They're not human. Not anymore."

Connie glimpses Ang's weapon tucked into his pants, and she recoils from him.

"I'm not going to hurt you," he tells her, which is not enough.

Being a homeschooled kid, I know other kids considered Ang an unknown entity, someone to be leery of.

"He won't hurt you, Connie," I assure her.

"Do you have food?" She's starving. I can see that now. Am I looking at my future?

"Fish," Ang offers little in line of an explanation, then heads back to the kitchen to slice and dice his catch of the day.

"You look a'fright, you poor thing." Mr. Finnegan, who has carefully made his presence known, goes to Connie and takes her hand. It's astounding, really, how different a person he is, now that all demented talk of aliens is in the past. "You are safe here, be assured."

"I don't understand why it's come to this." Connie shifts in her seat, looks out the window again, then comes back down and takes a deep breath before continuing. "They killed my mom, and they—"

Connie's horrors, written all over her face, paint an unspeakable picture. I put my arm around her as if to say, *It's okay*. But nothing is. Nothing will be. Not until it's all over and Vesta starts this world anew. May Earth's next inhabitants know peace.

"I know you lost your family too, Rain. But at least you didn't have to... watch it happen."

When the church blew up, I was standing right there. I felt the heat of the flames (but was spared the pain) when they permanently scarred my face. I spent far too long absorbed in denial and doldrums. But no, I didn't actually *see* Mom die. I could argue with Connie, but I won't. What would be the point?

"They ransacked our house, tied me up, kept me a prisoner in my own home, and killed Mom dead. Right there in her bedroom."

"Oh, Connie." Whatever I thought of this girl in years past is gone. We are sisters in a decomposing world.

"They were going to kill me, too. But I seduced one of the weaker ones when the alpha went scavenging. I asked him to untie me so I could 'treat him like the man I knew he was.'" She looks to me, being sure to make hard eye contact, as if she wants to justify her actions. "I killed him with his own bowie knife, and I ran. I knocked on doors that didn't open. Found empty houses with no food. Ran as far as I could, looking for someone, anyone who was still… human."

Connie scans my face, then turns to Ang. Something in her eyes tells me there's more to her story than she's sharing.

"Where was your phone?" I ask, point blank.

"My phone? What?"

"Before the Internet went down, before the power went out, the news was warning people not to look at their phones. Did you see that?"

"Why are you asking me about my phone? My parents were killed in front of me. You have no idea what I've been through."

Maybe. Or maybe they went insane like everyone else who received the mystery signal, and maybe you killed them, Connie. Maybe you had to. Maybe it was you or them. Still, that doesn't explain how you're standing here. No one at John J. Wilkins High was more tethered to their phone than Connie Blackburn. She would have been one of the very first to receive the menacing call to kill. If, in fact, it had been an actual threat.

"You can stay with us, Connie." I don't even think about it. I just offer. Because if the old adage of *mi casa es su casa* ever applied, it should apply today. Even if this isn't technically mi casa; and even if she's lying about where she's come from or how she got here. What else can we do but try to stay human for as long as we can?

"Rain." Ang makes no attempt to hide his concern. He's thinking of his short supply of water, among other things, no doubt.

"We aren't planning on staying much longer," I hedge. Though Ang and I haven't discussed this, I know it to be true. Imaginary Dad told me to meet him at the end of the world. And that's what I intend to do. Because when in doubt, always listen to your ID. He knows best.

"At some point soon, we'll have to abandon this place and seek water," Ang says. He's backing my play without knowing I have a destination in mind—Melford, Indiana—where Vesta's supposed to make first contact with Earth.

"There's a small pond," Ang continues, "a couple miles out of town—"

"It's been drained," Connie interrupts him.

"Drained?"

"I've been a bunch of times. It was a mud pit in May. I'm sure it's an oasis by now."

Ang gets up and goes to the door for another peek outside. "An oasis is an area of fresh water in the desert," he says with disdain. Connie shrugs, as if to say the annoying nuances of English vocabulary were never her strong suit. She didn't care for them before, and she certainly doesn't now.

Ang, seeing no other movement outside the house, returns to the kitchen and makes quick work of gutting his fish. It's a bony striper we would have had to throw back if such a thing as game wardens still roamed the beaches.

I remember when I first learned what "cleaning" a fish entailed. It's much less "clean" than you might imagine. After slitting the animal from throat to tail, you rip the dead fish apart at the seams and claw out its insides. So sanitary! As if you were pouring liquid detergent down its mouth and scrubbing with a dish brush.

Perhaps expecting some repulsive girl talk, Ang carries his fish out to the backyard to grill. The door slides shut behind him, and I take Connie to the bathroom. There, the tub is as clean as end-of-the-world circumstances will permit, and a little less than a quarter-full of water.

Back at my house, Ang hung my washed clothes over the shower rod to dry, and was extremely strict with handing me bars of soap. I shuffled around as a zombie, but still made a point to bathe every few weeks.

For my hair, I'd been using just a dab of shampoo per bath. I've still got six full bottles of Pert Plus at my disposal. If I had the mental capacity to do some bath math, I'd likely discover I've got more than enough of the stuff to splurge on a palm-full every once in a while. You know, given the limited time we have left.

I explain to Connie the rules of the house, as Ang related them to me in my house. Despite my aforementioned zombie-esque state, I guess I picked up a thing or two after all.

I tell her first; the toilet is off-limits. She says she figured as much and managed a gross existence thus far. To clean, I told Connie she should lay a towel on the tiles to drip bathe, standing atop it. "And when I say drip bathe, I mean wet yourself, scrub yourself, but please don't soak more than is necessary."

She starts to remove her tattered shirt, but it pains her to do so. Taking pity, I help her pull it up and over her head, unveiling many healing scars and fresh sores.

"I tripped and fell in the woods, running from wolves at night," she says, pointing to a grouping of bruises I've been eyeing.

"Wolves?" I question the unlikelihood of her story. "There aren't wolves around here, Connie."

"Maybe they were coyotes, I don't know. I didn't stick around to take a picture." As I'm trying to square her brief explanation with her sudden defensive attitude, I notice she's covered her breasts by crossing her arms. I'm intruding.

"Sorry," I tell her, and turn from her naked, beaten mid-section. I just feel so bad for her, which is saying a lot, considering what I've suffered. But that was an emotional, familial pain—something else Connie is familiar with, in addition to her physical wounds.

"There's two towels on the sink. Stand on one, dry with the other. I'll bring you some clean clothes when you're done. Just give a holler."

I go, leaving her in peace, but not before stalling for another two seconds in anticipation of a *thank you* that doesn't come. I wanted to think this new world would have changed her, but it seems as if Connie's still the same ill-mannered girl she always was.

Ill-mannered? Is that what you're calling her now? You used to think she was a cold-hearted bitch.

Well, if nothing else, Connie did help me out that night. Who's to say if I would have survived if she hadn't pulled me back from the church inferno? Besides, we're all afforded the benefit of the doubt these days, right?

Ang's out back, laying his catch on the grill above the outdoor fire pit. I watch as he lights a match, then the coals. I lean against the blood, bone, and gut-soaked kitchen counter. The smell does not phase me. Maybe nothing will again.

I walk out to meet him. The slow warmth emanating from the coals feels good. There's a slight wind bringing a pre-summer chill, and I put my hands close to the hidden flame.

"Summer begins at 10:45 tonight, if I remember correctly," I mention.

"How would you possibly remember that?" Ang asks.

"I've always loved summer," I answer him with a non-answer. It's the best I've got.

"What do you know about that girl in my bathroom?" he wonders aloud after several awkward moments of silence.

"I didn't like her very much... before. She seems harmless now. Given the unimaginable circumstances."

"Unimaginable circumstances," he echoes. "That's one way of putting it."

Off west, toward the bay, what I can only interpret as a shotgun blast reports a haunting echo. It is impossible to judge how far away the noise was; but it wasn't close. Thank God for that.

A rat, fat and fast, dashes through Ang's overgrown lawn. I used to jump and scream when I saw them in my basement, but now I only wonder where they've come from. Pre-V-Day, I can't recall having ever once spotted any such vermin in our area.

For whatever waft Ang's freshly cooked catch emitted, it doesn't fly far from the fire. His coals somehow don't burn off any smoke.

"We can't stay here anymore," Ang backs my earlier call. "Our potable water's gonna dry up in a few days, maybe a week. We have to move on. We've been lucky so far—beyond lucky, I guess—but we'll die if we stay."

"We'll die if we go," Mr. Finnegan cheerily reminds us of his presence.

"You're good, Dad. You can make a trip. Yesterday, I never would have suggested it. But look at you. You're a changed man."

Some of that is surely Ang attempting to build his dad up again in his own mind. Just because Mr. Finnegan's been coherent for a few hours doesn't mean he won't be gone the way of alien conspiracies in a few more. For as long as Ang's dad is coherent, the three of us watching each other's backs will be—

"I'm all set in here!"

Make that a party of four.

Connie's careless holler bursting from the weathered cracks in the bathroom window boards proves she's unafraid of the secret dangers outside. How can she be so dense after surviving her ordeal?

She's not dense, Rain. Not in the way you think.

"Rain, dear, you got those clothes for me?" Connie calls. Crap, I'd already forgotten I promised her something to wear.

"On it!" I call to her, then dash over to my house. I make quick work of clawing out the hidden handle outside the storm door. A stranger giving that thing but a cursory glance would be enough to reveal it. Then again, I have to assume Ang had it locked while I was in there.

Hurrying inside, I rush through the basement and continue up two sets of stairs through the house. I try not to think how long it's been since last I'd seen my bedroom.

Forty-Two days, three hours, twenty-seven minutes, but who's counting? I didn't realize I was.

In my closet, I uncover a tee I just know the old Connie would despise, and pile on as many more relatively clean ones as I can hold.

On second thought...

I yank everything down and shove all that will fit into my big duffle sack. My initials, emblazoned in silver, flowing cursive, give me pause: RR. I shake off the bewildering sense of self and make like an English muffin and split. I'm once again right as Rain.

Connie's reaction to the shirt is both annoyed and thankful. She's getting harder to read, here in the land of the undead.

With the vote and the boat still out on Connie Blackwood, I'll help her to a point, all the while keeping one eye on her unestablished intentions.

Chapter Ten

What it boils down to: I might not have what it takes to survive. I lack the magic ingredients—a mixture of confidence, fighting skills, and self-perseverance that Ang embodies so well. That I've made it this far in pre-apocalypsia is incredible. I'm alive solely because I've yet to be put to any tests. I've yet to be forced to claw my way out of a hopeless situation (like Connie), nor known genuine fear. At the bombing, and well after, my instincts resorted to shock; I was incapable of cowardice and heroism in the moment, and suffered crippling mental debilitation in the subsequent months. Not that I could have lifted a helping finger to save anyone that long-gone morning. Not that it would have mattered.

I've yet to be tested. I've faced no substantial threats—discounting the death of everyone I loved and my resulting, paralyzing identity crisis. Fading into the darkness is kind of my thing, I suppose. I may not have what it takes to survive.

And while we're tacking on the self-pity (a dreadful trait that flirts with all of us), I'm a coward when it comes to my emotions. The only person I ever let in was Leash. She was the one and only who knew the feral me.

"I miss you, girl." I praise the thought of her.

The faded, frayed Sailor Swyft concert tee clinging to Connie sends a flash of sorrow through my bones. The end of live music was a significant blow I've not considered, until now. I'd only been to see Sailor once, but I had had severe plans to attend several outdoor music festivals this summer. I guess everyone had plans, though. Once upon a time when the world was a virgin, we had spectacular concerts and events. But it's pointless to wish for pretty things we'll never experience again.

"I was at this show, you know?" Connie's pointing at the date on the shirt. July 8, 2023. It's been nearly two years already. Imagine it. And this girl wears my tee better than I ever did. Annoying, albeit predictable.

"Oh, yeah?" I say. Of course we attended the same show. It was the hottest event of the summer. "I didn't see you there."

"Well, there *were* fifty thousand screaming Saylorites, Rain. The odds of us bumping into each other would have been pretty slim."

"And if we had, you would have snubbed me," I say. She shrugs her shoulders. There's no sense in her denying it. "Bygones." I let the past die.

"How come I don't know you?" Connie interrogates Ang with a harsh look. Acting as inconspicuous as he actually is, Ang cleans one of his (apparently) many guns at the kitchen countertop. "You live here? Right next door to Rain? Did you go to public school?"

"I was homeschooled," Ang offers more than I would've given him credit for. "My dad taught me everything I know."

"What about your mom?" Connie asks with zero concern for his privacy. "She not around?"

"She died giving birth to me," Ang lies, bold and cold. "Anything else you want to know?"

We sit in silence, each heavy with the burden of our thoughts. At some point, Mr. Finnegan makes a grunt from his place on the couch, catching himself from falling victim to a late afternoon nap.

Ang announces he's going to gather supplies for our upcoming trip. I follow him to the basement while Connie goes out to the back porch and Ang's dad continues a losing battle with his eyelids.

Is it just me, or are we slacking? If the threat is so great outside the sanctity of this house, why do we continue the freewheeling lifestyle of the un-damned?

I've been staring too long at the light streaming through those sliding glass doors. The boards Ang secured on his formerly screened-in porch could probably withstand a lot—maybe not a tank or anyone curious enough to approach the loosely concealed exit with an inkling to find the relatively obvious door handle.

"You're worried about my dad going out back?" Ang asks from the bottom of the stairs, watching me stare back through the kitchen. "Don't worry. He's packing."

"Packing?" I ask, then realize. Ang gave his alien-obsessed father a gun. Sure, why not arm a man who's only been semi-self-aware for a couple of hours? What could possibly go wrong?

In the basement, I help Ang transfer six buckets of clean(ish) water into many empty plastic jugs he's got lying around for just this purpose. All in all, there are eighteen gallons.

Ang drags out two big duffel bags from behind the stairs, and I find and haul out a third. Between the four of us, with one person being relieved at a time, we'll be able to carry all the water gallons, but not much else.

"Maybe we should just stay put?" he wonders aloud. It's not cowardice he's showcasing—not by any means—but a general concern for his father's overall welfare (and to a lesser extent, maybe mine).

"No," I tell him. "This water *might* last another week and a half here—two if we really conserve, but then we'll have nothing left when we do decide to go. We won't make it very far without it. It's now or never."

He paces from the useless furnace to the rusting, weight-bearing pole to the base of his storm door steps.

"I never listened to him," he says. "He's been spouting nonsense for so long—if he ever admitted anything remotely like what he told us earlier, I dismissed it."

"So what makes today different?" I ask. "You believe his ramblings now?"

"They're not ramblings. Not anymore. The glaze over his pupils lifted as soon as he saw you, Rain. You set him at ease. His entire demeanor changes with you here. This is the most coherent he has been in a long time."

From upstairs, there's a scuffle accompanied by muffled shouting.

"Run, Angus!" Mr. Finnegan yells. I'm three steps up the stairs when Ang snags my shirt and pulls me back.

The open door at the top of the staircase swings wide, and the indistinguishable sound of a body hitting the floor thumps some ancient dust down on the washer and dryer.

"Yoohoo? Anybody down there?" A menacing male voice beckons. Silently, we duck into shadows. Ang holds me tight to his chest. I try to remain still in his arms, but several sets of slow footsteps just overhead inflict an unavoidable trembling in my bones.

"Shh," Ang soothes, barely audible. He's being incredibly clear-headed for someone whose dad could be in mortal danger.

Seconds tick by without a sound, maybe minutes. I can't hear Ang's breathing, though his mouth is only an inch from my ear.

"We only want the water," the one doing the talking says. "We know you've got some. Come and show us where you're hiding it, and we'll let you and your daddy here go."

Ang shakes his head slowly, then whispers, "Wait three minutes, then go up."

Quick and noiseless as a newborn kitten, he skits away from me, pops open the storm door, and swiftly walks out into the sunlight, causing me to wonder why he didn't have that thing locked from the outside.

He locks it now. It's hard to ignore the sound of the bar's mechanism sliding into place. If anyone in this marauder's gang has stayed near the back porch to monitor things, they'll spot Ang right away.

Then again, Ang's been sneaking up on me since the two of us have been crawling. Sixteen years later, I still can't see (or hear) him coming. He's a natural born creeper with a heart of gold.

"Rain, dear?" Connie sends her sweet-talk down. Nothing in her tone reveals she's afraid for her life, and she most certainly should be, especially given all she's been through already. Or maybe her experience hardened her into some new species? Maybe the new Connie Blackburn is unbreakable.

"Rain, if you come up on your own, maybe I can persuade them to not defile you."

"Fat chance of that!" A hyena's voice brays.

She sold us out.

I don't know why I'm so hurt by the realization. I suppose I should have listened to my instincts concerning the duplicitous Connie Blackburn. Then again, if I'd been in Connie's shoes, having survived God knows what at the mercy of this (or some other) gang, how can I say I wouldn't be a callous slug of a backstabber, too?

"We took you in, Connie!" I stall for time. How long has Ang been gone? Has it been three minutes yet? What is he planning to do? "Was your story even true?" I screech. I don't want her to answer. The truth might force me to take a difficult look at my gullibility factors. Like... Is Mr. Finnegan also playing me with his wild alien abduction story? If so, to what end?

Connie doesn't answer. In a way, that *is* an answer.

"Enough of these yapping birdies!" The hyena's done with both of us. I hear two other mouth breathers, distinctly. Could that be all of them? They don't sound like serious men. In fact, they don't sound that much older than me. They *aren't* seasoned murderers or thieves. They're newbie miscreants, playing the part Vesta has assigned them. And yet, if they received the mysterious cell signal, why haven't they killed each other? From my loose understanding of the supposed phone signal virus (if it's even real), the psychotic frequency instantaneously turned anyone who heard it into murderous monsters. Are the marauders in Ang's house just your run-of-the-mill, pre-apocalypsia opportunists?

Whatever they might be, it doesn't change the fact that they are here, and they are serious.

"Squawk squawk!" one of the hyena's pups calls, then coughs multiple times in succession. He's sick, and probably dying of lack of nutrition or untreated cancer or something. Aren't we all?

"I'm gonna count to three," the hyena declares. "And then I'm gonna cut this dude up with this here bowie knife."

I double over at the thought of it—Connie's tale included a bowie knife, but she claimed she'd used it to kill the leader.

Whether it's been a minute or two, I can't be sure. There's no way it's been three. Regardless, I approach the stairs with a shaky resolve.

One thing we have going for us—if the hyena's got a blade he's proud of, then there's a pretty good chance they don't have guns.

"One..."

Mr. Finnegan's packing!

"Two..."

Did they disarm him? There's no way to know.

"Two and a hallllllf..."

"I'm here," I say, pushing the cellar door open. Mr. Finnegan's lying at the other end of the hall, unconscious in a pool of blood. I run to him, but an arm snatches out and grabs me around the waist. Crusted, vile lips plaster my neck, and then a warty tongue. With everything I have, I elbow the bastard in the stomach. His grip loosens just enough, so my flailing feet hit the floor, and I tumble forward. I back crawl fast and away from him, colliding into Mr. Finnegan's side. He's breathing. My force of impact startles him awake.

It's his mouth that's bleeding most—his teeth or his gums? From what I can tell, his wound appears superficial.

"Rain," he mutters. "Rain," he says my name again, trying to focus. Carefully, I feel for his weapon and locate it tucked into the back of his pants.

"You should have listened to your daddy," says the chief intruder hyena. The other looks on with malicious anticipation. He's drooling at the mouth and razor focused on what's coming.

"He's not my father," I tell them, which is nothing but another stall tactic.

"I was going to go easy on you." The head hyena ignores my failed tactic, slinking forward. "Now, not so much."

I curl away from him, shielding Mr. Finnegan with as much of my body as I can. The sticky wetness beneath his shirt and on the floor soaks me.

"C'mere." I will kill him. I will try. "I'm your daddy now."

I can't yank free Mr. Finnegan's gun, not out from under the unmovable weight of his body. I'm straining, and it's obvious. The hyena advances even faster, recognizing my potential.

Two blasts erupt in the hall, and both intruders go down. Connie screams from the kitchen, but she's unhurt. Ang, holding a smoking gun, tromps over a twitching body. He kneels, doesn't say a word, but watches as the boy's life washes from his eyes.

And he *is* just a boy. I see that now. Probably younger than me—fourteen or fifteen, maybe. I don't know him. All I know is the danger they brought into Ang's house has been extinguished.

Only too late.

Ang rushes to his dad's side. Mr. Finnegan is bleeding out. That is clear. You don't have to be a doctor to know what's happening here. He's dying. His countdown's been cut short dramatically. Maybe he's got one minute more.

Maybe three.

"Dad," Ang says, entirely unable to hold back the emotion. Mr. Finnegan coughs, tries to speak, coughs again, and more blood spews out of his mouth.

"Can—"

"Anything. Dad?" Ang is entirely unable to control the quivering in his voice.

I wish there was something I could do. I wish I had some magic spell that could stop time, reverse it, or prolong the inevitable.

"Protect... each other." Mr. Finnegan makes a last ditch effort to speak. "Protect Rain." I don't take lightly the fact that my name is the last word on his lips.

Mr. Finnegan squeezes Ang's hand. His eyes roll up in his head, and his body goes limp. Ang lowers his father to the ground. I swear, I can feel his spirit wash over me as he goes to some eternal, ethereal plain.

"Ang," I whisper after some time has passed. "Ang, what do you want to—"

"Give me a minute. Please."

Another minute goes by. Then another.

Connie is crying in the kitchen, and I can't bear the sound of it. What right does she have to feel? She's the one responsible for this.

I stand and deliberately march to where she is. Not knowing where else to put all my anger, confusion, and desperate frustration, I slap Connie across the face as hard as I am able. She cringe-crawls away from me as far as she can go, which is only as far as Ang's non-functioning oven. Her poor, femme fatale disposition is enough to make me want to cut her to pieces with the hyena's dropped bowie knife.

"I had to do it," Connie says through watershed tears. "I had no choice! They made me!"

"You killed him," I tell her, even though she knows it. I want her to feel the weight of what she has caused.

I make good on my innermost desire and scoop the bowie knife from the bloodied ground. I reach back my arm to get a good slice in, but just when I'm about to do some actual damage to that once-pretty face of hers, Ang halts my vengeance.

"Don't," he says. "It's not her fault. It's the world."

My muscles relax. Shocked that I might have had it in me, I put down the knife. Then, with a swiftness I didn't know I was capable, I punch Connie Blackburn in her lying, traitorous, bitch nose, and smile at the thunk her body makes against the kitchen tile.

I look back to Ang. He's rolled his father over and retrieved the gun. Except it's not a gun, is it? Not any gun I've ever seen. Not that I've seen a lot of guns in my time. But this is…

It's so foreign, vibrant, spectacular, and strange that it can be nothing other than an alien weapon.

Chapter Eleven

Gunshots from maybe a couple of streets over offer an urgency to our current situation. There is an intrinsic need for us to get moving. But Ang's in sudden mourning, Connie's a perpetual phony, and I'm disoriented and vague in the presence of an alien pistol.

It's not a pistol, though. Pistols are much smaller. You're thinking of derringers, those little guns that were fired before the west was won. No, Rainbow. This is no pistol. This weapon has heft and purpose. It is a blaster. You will come to know it well.

Imaginary Dad's voice reverberates in my head. At least his ghost image isn't here to accompany his words with an ill-timed haunting.

Connie struggles to sit up as I head toward the basement door. "Where are you going?"

"To get the water." I keep it simple. The plan is still the plan.

The sun is dramatically close to dipping below the basement windows; the last vestiges of dim, late afternoon light threaten darkness. I reach up to the shelf above Ang's dryer and fumble over a flashlight. I click it to on, marveling at how fast everything in this world turned to crap—that D batteries are one of the last remnants of civilized society. But these batteries are dying. The flashlight flickers long enough for me to glimpse the bright white beam's path.

Ang descends into the dying light. The depths of his eyes hold his heart's heavy hurt.

"You killed them," I say, perhaps in an effort to take his mind off his loss. I'm not afraid of Ang. But the sheer, precise, callous way he took out those intruders gives me pause. "Like it was nothing. How?"

"They were going to hurt you," Ang says, calm and collected. "I wasn't going to let that happen." Maybe not, but was his plan intended to involve me as a distraction?

"Did you use me as bait?"

"Rain—"

"You told me to wait three minutes and then go upstairs."

"Rain—"

"You knew they'd be preoccupied with me. You knew their backs would be turned."

"I knew nothing. I just got lucky. Look, I didn't enjoy killing them, if that's what you think. It was them or you. If I had to do it again, a thousand times over, I would. Only sooner."

"Ang—"

"My dad's dead, Rain," he speaks his new reality. "And so is this whole town, as far as I'm concerned. The plan doesn't change, okay? I don't care if you're an alien or—"

"You think I am?"

"Honestly? It doesn't matter. Not to me. You're the same girl I've always known." He reaches into the back waistband of his pants and holds out the blaster, palm up. "This is yours," he says. I make no movements. "Just take it," he says, and places the weapon on the dead, useless furnace. "The crazy thing won't fire, anyway. I'm like fifty percent sure it's a fake."

"Only fifty percent sure, huh? What's the other fifty?"

"That it's one hundred percent out of this world. Maybe from another galaxy. But then you would be, too."

"Because this is mine?" I say, unsure of anything. I pick it from a thin layer of dust and am immediately impressed by the weight. For a small thing, its mass is significant. I've previously referred to it as a *blaster*, because the bullhorn-shaped opening at the end of the gun's shaft gives it the appearance of how a blaster would look, in my humble, terrestrial opinion.

I'm not sure what I'm expecting to happen as I hold it. The gun doesn't light up or turn a neon shade of hot yellow from my touch. If I'm an alien after all, and if this be an alien's weapon, it sure doesn't recognize me as its owner.

The bulbous blaster has no firing mechanism to speak of. There's a space where one's index finger should naturally go to bring the business. That curved space could (and should) accommodate a slight trigger. Maybe it'll pop out when the time's right and I'll—

"Hey," Ang says, ducking. "Watch where you point that thing."

How long have my arms been extended in this hunter's pose? I lower them, feeling as if there *was* a hot neon yellow shade after all, but in me, not my blaster.

Maybe you're symbiotic?

"Let's go." Ang takes hold of the biggest duffel and I grab a second. I hate to leave the third, but neither of us can carry it.

"Wait a minute," I say, then drop the bag to clunk up the stairs. I've placed the blaster snug against my waistline; it holds firm there, steady despite my awkward climb. Whether or not it blasts, Ang's right, she's mine. I should probably name her.

I make a mental note to press Ang on the story behind how his father came into possession of it, and wonder how long my alien ancestry's plot will thicken. How long has Ang known about the blaster? How long has he believed it to be mine?

I find Connie where I left her, crouched in the kitchen corner, holding her knees and rocking back and forth, traumatized by what went down. Or if not, she's pre-apocalypsia's greatest actor.

"You can't stay here, Connie." She looks up, confusion written all over her face.

"I didn't have a choice," she croaks what passes for sincerity.

"They were going to kill me. They used me instead, and I let them. For that, I am at fault." She shakes her head in disgust. "Water and food. That's everything now. No one has it anymore. You'd do anything, too."

"They wanted more than that." Ang drops the heavy duffel in the hall, across from the kitchen entrance. "Carry this. And if you cross us again, I'll kill you myself." I don't know how true that statement is, but it gets her moving.

"No way," I say, dropping the duffel I've lugged up the stairs. How can Ang be willing to take her along? His father's killer! "She can't be trusted."

"We can't leave her here," Ang says. He lifts his shirt to show he's strapped. These revolvers, if I had to guess, are magnums—don't ask me about the caliber. Ang wears them in holsters on a belt made for a different breed of cowboy.

"They're loaded. And there's three boxes of ammo in my bag. If she pulls anything—and I mean anything at all—" Ang whips out his left hip piece and does a flashy twirl. He holsters the gun as fast as it came out, then gauges Connie's face for any reaction. If she has one, it's the same as mine: incredulity.

"Just stay close to me for now," Ang tells me. "You can aim that alien blaster of yours at someone if we get into trouble. That might scare them off. If it's dark enough, maybe. But let me do the shooting. At least until we can have some time for a crash course."

"In killing?" I ask. Ang chooses not to answer. Instead, he goes back to his dad. If not for the terrible amount of pooled blood beneath him, I might trick my mind into pretending he's just sleeping.

I leave the Finnegan family to their sad farewells, snag Connie by the collar, and drag her to her feet.

We step out onto the back porch and into the newly come night.

"How many were there, Connie?" I ask, because every bone in my body *wants* to forgive her. If Ang's seen past her heinous actions to empathize with her compromised motivations, I should get there, too.

"I don't know, a dozen?" she answers. "I doubt their pack mentality will last much longer. They're starting to turn on one another. They're desperate and dying."

Beneath a cloudless, pre-starry sky, Connie turns to me, asks where we're going. I ignore her with ease, opting to look fondly on my home one last time.

When Ang emerges, he walks past us without a word. We follow him, duffels in hand, toward the quick path through the woods. Before reaching the low reeds of the beach beyond the trail, I turn back to see the harshest check of our reality: Ang's house is ablaze.

"I couldn't leave him to rot in there," Ang mentions. With no fire department and no available water, I imagine my house will go up in flames, too. Farewell, gentle youth.

We tread on.

It's a little over four miles to the airport by roads. I haven't mapped out our exact distance, but I guess it would be near to a five-mile hike up the beach. I don't think I've ever walked five miles before. Not in a row, anyway. And definitely not on sand.

There's not another living person in sight. It's as if the ocean's cleansed the beach of all. If Mother Nature has a sense of humor (and I like to think she does), she's probably tickled all shades of pink, knowing we'll be extinct soon. Well, you've got a rude awakening coming for you, Mother N. This all-destructing asteroid is gonna smite you, too. That'll be our esteemed planet's final chapter in the incinerated history books.

Epilogue: Oblivion For All

The sun goes down, and the horizon alights with an awakened summer night's majesty. Connie can't see the beauty directly ahead. She's exerting all her effort, dragging her heavy sack. She's like a slow-dying slug, unable to carry a simple weight through her tracks of her own slime. I snicker at the growing, grotesque image.

I can imagine a lot.

Ang isn't rushing, but he's not slowing for Connie either.

Suddenly, it's my job to keep the distance between them equal. When I fall back far enough, Ang takes the hint and slows to me.

"What's the holdup?" he asks, arriving at my heels.

"I can't lug this thing any further," Connie calls, dropping her duffel. "There are literally hundreds of empty houses all along the beach up there." She points to the multi-million dollar homes. "They're all empty. Trust me, I've checked. We could pick any of them and stay safe for the night. Or take one house each, if you need your space. I call that gorgeous three-story mansion!"

"You're free to do whatever you want," Ang says, snatching her discarded load and rushing away. Does he expect me to follow dutifully at his hurried pace?

"He's got an airplane," I half-explain. "That's Destination One." Am I trying to make a friend out of Connie? Maybe. How sick would that be?

Then again, would it be so bad to have another friend? Even one as treacherous as her? I miss Leash like I would miss the moon if it up and disappeared... or was brutally murdered in an epic space explosion.

No, that's a poor comparison, because without the moon, I'd still have the stars. Without Leash, I've been utterly alone.

There's been so much to absorb these past few months. I almost didn't have the bandwidth to allow for Leash mourning.

Alicia and her sister, her mom and her dad, and their three cats lived on the other side of town. I say *lived*, but maybe Leash's family is still there. I didn't see them in the church, though that doesn't mean much. The pews were packed, and everyone was so crowded and frenzied...

About a month ago, during one of my few and far between "awakenings," I went to check on Leash's family. I like to think that was the one night they decided to stay at the campground down the street from their house. Cats and all.

The trip to Silo Street was uneventful. In retrospect, I likely just got lucky I wasn't murdered in cold blood. If Ang knew I'd ventured out on my own, he'd have had my head. But I wasn't thinking straight for four months, was I?

The emptiness of Leash's home was brutal. Her bed had been made to a fine degree. Her sheets were tucked in, taut tight and commanding. Her pillows—all twelve of them—were lined up and stacked just so. The whole of her room, in fact, was dolled up to give the appearance that some fairy-tale princess had lived in it.

Leash was no fairy-tale princess.

Her house was clean as a whale's tooth. Spic and span to the extreme. Wherever Leash's family went, they did not leave in a hurry, which has always worried me. Did it mean Leash's Mom kept the place tidy prior to going to the fateful church meeting? Did she clean like a mad person after learning her child was lost in the explosion? And if so, where did she and Leash's dad go after that? Did they receive the supposed cell phone signal? If they did, they didn't kill each other in the nice, immaculate house.

Questions without answers—that's all I'll ever have.

If Leash was here now, she'd be more supportive of the whole "alien dad" thing than Ang's proved to be. He's said little of anything during our long trek up the beach. He's a man on a mission; and that mission does not involve idle chatter about impossible things. Then again, what is there to say? I'm sure he's brain-deep on reliving his dad's death.

Connie, on the other hand, won't shut up about Vesta. She claims she can see it in the dead of night. She says she would often sit outside, staring up into infinity, watching our coming death get brighter as the hours peeled on.

It was a trick of Connie's eye, I'm sure. Either that, or she's lying. As fast as Vesta is approaching—roughly 85,000 space miles per hour if you're to believe the old news reports—that's still not speedy enough to have it be visible in our night sky until July.

It's nearly July already, Rain. How quickly you forget your unhelpful hibernation.

"Most times," Connie says, "I wish upon several stars—as many as I can. I ask the first to disintegrate the asteroid, and when that doesn't work, I ask the next star I see to hurry Vesta along. Because enough with all this pointless waiting around, right? Let's get on with it already. We've got a date with the dinosaurs."

She is perfectly content hearing herself talk and not receiving any response. If I spoke, she'd probably plow right over me with another question, anyway.

"You haven't changed at all, Connie," is what I eventually get in edgewise. Ang slows to a stop up ahead.

"This is not a rest. Just a break," he says, commanding his self-imposed leadership position. I'm not sure I like this version of Ang. I kind of want the old one back—the Ang who was actually fun to be around.

"Look." I wave my arm over the empty sands surrounding us in every direction except for the sea. "The coast is a ghost land. Anyone who might still pose a threat is holed up inside their homes, dying or dead." I take a long chug of an open gallon, choosing to believe in my unscientific hypothesis. "There's no threat out here. Maybe there never was. We should have left months ago."

"I would have," Ang explains. "But when I broached the subject of relocating somewhere nice to live out our last months, Dad said, in a rare moment of clarity, 'We stay. Watch over the neighbors.'"

"Meaning me?" It hurts to think Ang would have left me there if not for his father. But I can press that down far enough in my gut that it won't matter. I think.

"I would have taken you with us, Rain, had we gone. But you weren't yourself. And where would we even go? Where are we going now? I can get us up in the air, but beyond that, we're gonna need a destination."

I catch myself following Connie's gaze. And when she points, I know she's pointing at Vesta. She's the biggest, clearest, shiniest light in the darkening sky.

"There she is," I say, astounded by our immortal enemy's presence. "Vesta's supposed to crash in Melford, Indiana. That's where we need to be. Let's meet her head-on. What have we got to lose?"

"What did you just say?" Ang asks.

"We should go to the scene of our pending annihilation. Indiana." I don't mention that my Imaginary Dad told me to meet him at the end of the world. Maybe we'll save that tidbit of madness for some other time.

"Yeah," Ang says, suspiciously quick to agree with my destination. "Great idea."

Connie, blissfully quiet for a moment, mulls over the plan in her head. At last, she makes up her mind.

"Epic. Ride the lightning. Love it." She turns to Ang. "What makes you so sure you even have a plane anymore?"

"I scoped it out a couple of days ago. Dad's plane is still there. Unmolested and raring to go. I gassed her up. Always be prepared."

"Ooh, you're such a boy scout. It's kinda hot." You'd think a girl who had recently been ravaged and possibly raped would have zero libido. But not Connie. It makes me wonder again if that glossed-over portion of her tale was a lie. Looking at her now, she's entirely unreadable.

"We're only about a half mile from the airport. Let's get moving." Ang picks up his duffel, but then drops it immediately. He's staring at a fixed point behind us.

"Run!" he says, and Connie does. Her instincts are good, honed. Mine, however, could use a good honing. I stall, dead for a second or maybe two, then turn around to see what all the fuss is about.

A line of headlights bump and beam in the distance. "ATVs?" I wonder aloud. I'm not going to linger here to find out.

Chapter Twelve

"We'll never outrun them towing these!" Connie exclaims between panting breaths. She's finally found a legit reason to dump her duffel. As we're running near the ocean's edge (because this innermost beach section has the most efficient sole-to-sand impact), Connie's satchel makes a splash. The tide soaks Connie's duffel and wets us both to the heel.

Ang, having avoided the rogue wave and missed Connie's H2o dump, turns toward town where he patiently waits for us to catch up.

"C'mon!" he calls. I kick off my waterlogged shoes, which helps a little. My socks are also drenched, but to take the time to peel them off would be the last nail in my coffin. The ATVs are in hot pursuit, and I almost can't believe it.

I let myself believe it. Because this is the real world now. This is where we are.

I afford myself a cursory glance over my shoulder. I can readily make out six distinct, speeding sets of low headlights. Who's to say the riders are nefarious? Maybe they're desperate to help their fellow man.

I barely avoid crashing in to Connie, who is stuck in the shallows—she just stands here.

"Connie, let's go!"

"I'm done," she says, and collapses, as if every bone in her body decided to give up and fold in. Her duffel slips from her shoulder, and the rising, bubbling tide threatens to take it away.

"The hell you are." I grab her arm, yank her to her feet, and shove her forward. Whatever flashback trauma she was experiencing will have to wait. "Go!"

To my relief, she doesn't argue. Connie moves surprisingly fast in wet shoes. When we reach Ang, up on the edge of the empty street, he shoots me an easy-to-interpret look: *You should have left her in the water.*

Maybe. But I can't have Connie's death on my hands.

The ATVs turn from the ocean and chase after us. Our path ahead is lit by their bright, yellow beams. I run faster until I reach the road beyond. To the right is the blessed airport. Is it possible we've made it without being caught?

Ang turns, drops his duffel, and kneels. He fires what I assume to be a completely blind shot. They're too far away, and he can't possibly see anything enshrouded in this darkness penetrated by unsteady, distant, jagged lights—but no. There comes a guttural, mechanical scream from the center vehicle. It careens right, crashing into another. Both vehicles flip in a crunching heap, and are, for now anyway, out of commission.

"How did you—?"

"Move!" He takes my arm with less pressure than I'd grabbed Connie's, and we're running again. Speaking of Connie, she's ahead of us now, pacing in a circle, uncertain which way to go. Ang blasts past her, and Connie gets it together enough to follow him. We run like our lives depend on it. Because they might. And we race to Ang, who's standing in a nearby hanger where his father's plane sits.

"It's a miracle no one's stolen it."

"There's no such thing as miracles," Ang states. I'd rather not communicate with his darker half.

I'm not moving as fast as I should, evidenced when Ang pushes me up and into the cockpit.

"Get down!" he orders, and I throw my head as far as it will go, into my lap. Connie hops into the backseat, screaming.

In the smaller-than-I-remember plane, Ang flicks a fast switch, and the floodlights power on. They're bright enough to light the entire runway, including the remaining ATVs which are coming at us, full speed.

I duck my head low again while Ang hangs precariously from his door and rattles off gunshot after gunshot.

When the noise clears, I dare a peek over the dash to see him positioned like the expert marksman he's turned out to be. The ominous ATV lights have all halted. Whether that means he's killed our pursuers or they're just taking cover, Ang doesn't wait to know. He floats back in and slides to his captain's chair. And side note, he must see me watching him, because he's doing everything in heroic slow motion, just to mess with me.

Settle, Rain.

Mr. Finnegan's dim cockpit lighting illuminates and emphasizes the wavy curl at the front of Ang's hair. I've never taken notice of his ridiculous duster, and this is certainly the worst time to do so, but the indecent wave his hair gives is too flagrant to ignore.

Ang sets his two revolvers on the seat between us, retrieves a set of keys from his pocket, and properly starts the engine.

"They're still coming," Connie says. At first I can't explain how she can spot them in the dark, but then I see them, too. Long, tall shadows creep toward us just as Ang pulls a lever, and the propeller starts to turn. Before I know what I'm doing, I've reached down and picked up a gun. Ang, busy with getting the plane off the ground, doesn't notice my quick grab.

The windshield cracks with an explosive noise. Connie screams.

"Are you shot? Connie?!"

No. She's ducking deep down behind us, right below where the pesky bullet pierced the seat.

Lucky girl.

Ang yanks the wheel hard left; the plane jerks, and my passenger door is riddled with bullets that somehow don't cut through.

"Down, Rain!" Ang orders. I know his intentions are good—he wants me to make it through this thing alive, but I'm really getting fed up with his superior, protect-or-die attitude.

My passenger door faces our pursuers. I peek to find them aiming long, antique rifles at us. They're going to let loose a barrage of heavy artillery on us as we cruise by. The chances of all three of us not getting hit lessen with each attack.

No more Ms. Nice Roche.

I climb up onto the seat, smash the window with the butt of Ang's gun, point it blindly in the direction of the coming gunfire, and squeeze the trigger.

The blowback from the revolver is entirely unexpected. My arm recoils so violently that my elbow collides with Ang's shoulder. He flinches, recovers, and slams on the gas. These incredible, fast-moving events are nothing compared to the result of my dumb luck shot.

There is an explosion of blue fire where the ATVs once were. The men with their guns are entirely gone—obliterated. Poof. "Where'd they go? Where are the ATVs?"

Not ten feet ahead of us, I spy my answer as the fiery three-wheeler drops from the sky. Ang swerves the plane, misses the thing by a nose hair, then has to zigzag back the other way to avoid the second one, all the while rocking us queasy.

"Rain, put the blaster down!" Ang yells. I drop it. And it's hot from use. I'd only been half-aware I was firing it. In fact, I thought I'd snagged one of Ang's shooters, but it must have been mine all along. Had I drawn the weapon clean and fast? Or did sheer dumb luck bumble it out of my pants and into my hand?

What you should be asking yourself is, 'How did I fire an alien weapon with no trigger?'

I place it carefully in the glove box and attend to the surprising ringing in my ears.

"That's no ordinary gun," I murmur a worthless thought through the uncomfortable echo. My boom stick's got unearthly powers. "I think I'll call it Boo."

Once we're practically flying down the runway, Ang hands me a headset, then puts one on himself. Poor Connie's just going to go deaf, I guess.

"There should be a third headset back there," Ang yells to her, proving my previous presumption wrong. "If you can find it, you can talk normal, and you won't have to scream."

Half a minute later, our plane breaks free of the ground. No one is chasing us anymore. I incinerated them. I killed them. I did that. Me.

Me and Boo.

"Is it over yet?" Connie calls from her position low in her seat. I lean back and poke her in the ribs.

"You can come up for air now." She rises, still shaky, and gazes outside. There's not just one, but three bullet holes in the plane's windshield, letting in starlight and reverberating sky.

"Is anybody hurt?" Ang asks. Miraculously, we are not. I run my hand over every inch of my body, just to be doubly sure. I know that sometimes, adrenaline and/or shock can trick a person into thinking they're just fine. It was a common occurrence in movies, so much so that it became a cliché. It's only once the supporting characters found themselves out of danger when they'd realize—

"Ang," I say, instinctively covering my mouth. With my other hand, I point a shaking finger at his sleeve. "You're bleeding."

The bullet is nowhere to be seen, not beneath these dim cockpit lights, but Ang's flesh wound is sharp and serious.

"Nnnahh," he says, pained by the news. If I hadn't said something, how long might he have flown without knowing? Probably not long. His sleeve is getting wetter and redder by the second.

"How much blood can you lose before you pass out?" Connie

asks. That would be a good question for a doctor, or the Dead Internet, or even a relatively smart person—three things we do not have at our disposal. Well, I guess we always have the Dead Internet.

"I have to level her out," Ang says. It takes a moment for me to understand he's talking about the plane. With a grimace, he pulls on the wheel even further. The nose tips upward, and I settle into my seat as if I'm on the precipice of a bumpy, unpredictable rollercoaster ride.

"How high do we need to be?" I ask. He doesn't answer. Instead, Ang releases his firm hold on the aircraft, easing into a linear flight pattern. He hits a button, turns a knob, and lets go of the wheel.

"Auto pilot," Ang says, to ease any of Connie's concerns, probably. Or maybe just to preemptively stop her from asking.

Once he's free of the controls, Ang's hand goes directly to his wound. He squeezes it, holds it tight. "I'm gonna need some help here," he says. "Connie, there's a white, clasped medkit beneath your seat. There should be some gauze or bandages."

"Bandages?" I say. "Ang, you got shot. What's a bandage going to do?"

"It's just a scratch, Rain. And I'm not being tough about this. I got lucky. Look." He shifts his body to reveal the bullet lodged in his seat. "An inch or two to the left and we'd be having a much different discussion."

"An inch or two to the left and you wouldn't be talking at all," Connie yells over the plane's noises, then adds an unnecessary clarification, "You'd be dead."

"Hand me the box, Connie." He reaches back to take it, but I intervene.

"You can't do everything, Angus. Let me fix you up." I open the lid and remove the equipment while Ang removes his shirt. "It doesn't look like you'll require stitches," I say, as if I know a good damn thing about anything. Though truly, his wound doesn't appear to be much more than a bloody scrape.

I wet a cloth with a sprinkling of our precious water and wipe his wound. Though his blood slows, my anxiety peaks just pondering the job I might have had to do.

"You all right?" he asks, sensing my hesitation.

"Yeah," I tell him, and quick pat-dry his arm, then smack an appropriately sized gauze pad over the cut.

"The blaster," I say. "It didn't come from anywhere around here. Definitely not Callela's." I kid. Callela's was one of too many local gun stores on Back Bay Boulevard in town. Why were so many of our neighbors uber-obsessed with hunting? In retrospect, I have to wonder how many proud gun owners engaged in extra-curricular shooting, prior to the fallout. How many were stockpiling weapons for the apocalypse?

Enough to dwindle the population (and themselves) significantly.

"You did good, Rain," Ang says, admiring my work.

Even with our comfortable headsets, the noise of the propeller overwhelms; none of us has the voice or the energy to shout anymore, so we relax into our bullet-infested seats. With a visible wince, Ang pulls his shirt back over his head, and re-takes control of the plane. The story of how his dad came into possession of the blaster, if Ang's got one, is prolonged a little longer.

The night, as is, is angelic. Given any other circumstance (any at all!) I might be swept away by the undeniable, heavenly atmosphere as we drift through the clouds.

Ang turns the wheel to head in a westerly direction, bringing into view the bane of humanity's brief existence. Vesta's full menace blazes before us. It is undeniable.

"She's getting bigger," Connie declares. "I know that's not an actual thing asteroids can do. But she sure looks bigger than she used to."

"She?" Ang wonders aloud.

"Sure, why not? Everyone knows we're the more powerful species. If you're gonna give it a gender, it might as well be female."

Connie has a point (and one that's vaguely familiar), but I won't encourage her.

"We got enough fuel to make it to Indiana?" I ask, dozily.

"Indiana's in Kansas, right?" Connie jumps in. "What's so great about Kansas, Indiana?" The depth of her misunderstanding is mesmerizing. But for whatever reason—maybe she's too tired to pursue her stupidity—Connie doesn't press the matter. "Whatever. I've never been to Kansas before. Or Indiana, for that matter. Might as well hit up as many places we can before the end. Which one we going to first, again?"

I look out and into the sky. The first stars shine dimly behind the night, and we're flying on a wing and a prayer, toward our inevitable demise.

Is there anyone sane still out there? I'm not naïve—well, maybe I am about *some* things (I'm looking at you, Craig), but not about this. We could arrive in Melford to find there's nothing left but yet another wasteland of humanity. The only difference from where we're headed and where we're from could be mere geography. I'm not dense enough to hope for some magic solution at Vesta's future landing ground, but at this point, what could it hurt? Our destination is where everything's end is going to begin.

I can think of nowhere else I'd rather be, Dad.

Chapter Thirteen

I'm dreaming. Have to be. Because this world cannot be real.

The council of elders has just delivered their mutual prophecy. In their combined centuries, the elders have never been united in their visions. So this is huge.

"The end of civilization as we know it is upon us," cries some alien, dream-made creature. I don't read sci-fi, so it's strange I can conceive of such an image.

"It will arrive," he continues, "in the form of an almighty destroyer, in under a year. It will eradicate our species."

Panicked though the crowds who hear his words are (myself included), we do not take to the streets like feral children. We do not loot each other's stores, pillage each other's homes, or lose all sense of decorum. We remain civil, as we are a civil species.

Dream this may be, but this all happened before.

I'm in some grand palace where the walls are high and menacing —much taller, plainer, sturdier than any I've ever seen. The ceiling seems to go on forever.

As do we all.

Time shifts, and I meet more of my kind inside a massive hanger.

All scurry—their faces blurred—toward the dozens upon dozens of spacecraft docked neatly in rows and ready to be boarded.

The front wall fades to reveal the outer rim of the edge of the universe. The stars are right outside, within reach, just beyond the tip of the galactic tarmac. I can breathe this familiar, outer space just fine. I would take long, vaulting strides out into the perpetual night, if only I could know for sure I'd be safe out there. Breathing in this vacuum doesn't grant me access to the vast nothingness of the universes beyond. Does it?

A familiar aroma strikes me—the very essence of my wife.

Wife?

I turn my head to know her.

"Mom!" My exasperation is lost on the waves of dreams, and she can't hear me. She's boarding one of the ships in the hanger, beckoning me to join her. I look down and whisper, "These are the hands of an alien."

They are also the hands that touched my father's, so long ago.

I wake to the sound of Connie snoring in my headset.

"Oh good, you're up," Ang says, sliding his palm over his flopsy hair. "She talked nonstop 'til she talked herself to sleep. She's been making that obnoxious death rattle for the better part of an hour."

Ang reaches around and flips Connie's headset off of her. She doesn't move a muscle, but continues to drool and snore against the back window of Mr. Finnegan's plane.

"How long was I asleep?" I ask.

"About three hours," Ang says, surprising the hell out of me. "Feel refreshed? Cuz we're gonna have to land soon."

"How's your arm?"

He scrunches his sleeve up to show me the bleeding is but a faulty memory. "I'm a fast healer," he says, as if that explains away his removed gauze and miraculous heal.

I haven't kept track of the time of day since the clocks in our house (the last holdouts that ran on batteries) stopped working. There was no point in keeping track anymore, anyway. There was only daytime and nighttime. Any fragile point of existence adjacent to one of these two fixed worlds is pointless.

Based on the way the darkness penetrates the sky, I gather it's still well before sunrise. Sooo... is the plan to land somewhere in Bumblefart, Indiana under the cover of night, and pray we can refuel? Or will we be hoofing it to Melford?

"Where are you going to land this thing?"

"I'm not sure," Ang says. "But we might as well get low and see what we can see. You'd better buckle up."

Being that I'm usually a stickler for safety, I'm surprised I've ignored my seatbelt. Not that I was coherently concerned we might crash while I slept. I'm confident in Ang's piloting skills once he's actually in the air. It's the taking off and landing that are worrisome.

The spaceships landed, snug in their rows.

I dreamed of outer space. Did I breathe normally in a galactic vacuum?

It's lost. Gone to wherever it is dreams go.

"Connie," I shout over the noise and smack her leg with my open palm. "Wake up. Ang's gonna attempt to land this thing."

"What do you mean, *attempt?*" Ang calls. "I've got fourteen hundred, twenty-two hours in the air. I was this close to getting my license when—"

"Wait," Connie interrupts. "You don't have your pilot's license?"

"Had you fooled, huh?" Ang laughs then throws a wink my way. In the dim, artificial, bleary-eyed cockpit lighting, the shape of his face dances and shimmers. He turns away to focus on our downward trajectory. If nothing else, at least he's back to his congenial self again. There's only so much Sgt. Commander, Protector-At-Arms a girl can take.

Why is your face warm? Oh, Rainbow, are you flustered?

I scan the black heavens for a cloud. I spot one, and cherish a three-second count to behold its fluffy, shadow beauty. And then we're in it... and out of it.

Ang levels the plane at—according to his altimeter—3,550 feet and dropping. Not knowing a damn thing about Melford, Indiana (other than it is situated, I think, just south of Lake Michigan), I'm surprised by the city buildings popping up. It doesn't look like anywhere Ang can put us. Not in one piece, anyway.

And it's all dark and dead down there.

"That unlit corpse of a city is South Bend," Ang states this matter of fact, as if he's flown over Indiana before. For all I know, he might have, perhaps in another life.

Ang keeps the plane on its westerly direction, looking for what, I don't know—an unoccupied runway, a strip mall parking lot, or a crop circle-free cornfield? Although the latter would likely be difficult to set down on, what with all the stalks.

The plane hitches beneath us as we constantly descend. "It's all right," he says, anticipating our anxieties. "I'm taking her to the suburbs."

"See?" Connie chimes in. "Men call their planes, their cars, their tools, their ships—everything!—*Her*. Why not an asteroid?" Has she been stewing on Vesta's gender all this time?

I won't bother with a response, it doesn't call for one. What I *am* wondering, however, is where Ang is going to land. He has to find not only a safe place but also somewhere within a reasonable hiking distance of Melford. The chances of finding a fueled up car that's not completely dead are slim, maybe none.

"There," Ang says, pointing to a green patch of land just beyond a small, lifeless town. "I'm bringing her down."

The altimeter counter drops readily and steadily, causing my stomach to rise into my throat. The plane dips at a much sharper angle than I remember from the night Johnny died in a fiery, oceanic blaze.

"Sorry about this," Ang says. "I gotta make it on this pass or—" The bright, blinking red fuel indicator light blinks, finishing his thought for him. Rather than chastise him for not trying to land sooner, I let Ang fly. He's in serious-pilot mode now, a dangerous place for me to nag.

The altimeter numbers plummet. At 1,800, I stop watching their vital roll. I have faith in Ang's ability. I do. Just in case this is the end, though, I take one last look at the rapidly rising ground. And then I shut my eyes.

When the first bump comes, it's not so bad. We're alive and unharmed. I sneak a peek at the dead corn stalks as we destroy them in our wake. We're cutting through them like a lawnmower through a daisy patch and making our indelible marks.

I have a genuine sense of the wheels skipping off dirt, and suddenly we're hovering on low air again. We bounce two or three more times before our unlicensed pilot regains some control.

"Hold on to something!" Ang commands, smashing the brake as the wheels screech against solid ground once more. The plane skids and spins out of control. My body jolts to the left, but I'm held tight by my belt. I lose sight of the horizon and smash/crush my ribs against the determined seatbelt.

"Are we dead yet?" Connie screams just as the wing to my right clips the earth. The plane slows, but not with all its pieces intact. I watch in horror as the wing snaps clean off and smacks into the tail. I can't see, but it's clear from the bang that significant damage has been done all around.

Our crash landing's momentum finally runs out of stamina, and our miraculous, long journey to Wherever, Indiana is complete. I inhale sharply, just to make certain I still have the ability. Ang reaches to turn the key, but the propeller pops and stops before he has the chance to cut the engine.

The sudden, shocked silence in the cockpit would be impenetrable by the hollow weight of any words we might speak. I don't know about Ang and Connie, but for me—I'm content just sitting here and counting my blessings for a moment.

One: I'm alive.

Two: Well, what else is there, really? Given the state of the world, one blessing is enough. Being alive is everything.

"I don't think we're in Kansas, Indiana, Toto," Connie says, breaking us free of our silent spell with a not-so-funny, ill-timed quip.

I try my door, but it's jammed shut by debris or bullet holes or twisted metal or... I don't know what.

"Everyone okay?" Ang asks.

"I could use a hot bath and a stiff drink, if you know what I mean," Connie says.

"Yeah, Connie, we know what you mean, you blatant remnant of a dead society."

"You all right, Rain?" Ang asks me again. His eyes, tender in the early hint of dawn, scan my face for injury or worry.

"I think so," I say. "Can we please get out of here?"

"Roger that."

Ang unclips his safety belt, pushes his door open, climbs out onto the upturned footstep, and reaches his hand in for me to take. I try to move, but roll my eyes when I realize I'm being held back by my own, lifesaving seatbelt. I let it loose, ignoring any creeping embarrassment, scoot over, and allow Ang to help me up and out. He does a tremendous job of balancing on this small step as I slip, catch myself, then hop to the ground. I withstand a desire to kiss the dirt as Connie's dominating, tall figure emerges from the broken plane.

"So Indiana, huh?" She slips down, circles and assesses the damage. "I don't know much, but it looks like we're not going anywhere else. Not in this thing, anyway. And no offense, Mr. Pilot, but your landing skills suck."

"I got us here, didn't I? We're not dead."

"Oh yeah." I scoff. "You're a cause for celebration."

Ang reaches into the cockpit of his father's airplane (Connie's right, it'll never fly again), grabs the three duffels, one at a time, and drops one at my feet and one at Connie's. I unzip mine, and Connie does the same, although hers is soaked through after her shenanigans back on the beach. I'd assumed we had left her duffel there for the sea to claim. Apparently not. Ang must have doubled back in the heat of the ATV pursuit and grabbed it.

In the end, it doesn't matter. The plastic gallons in Connie's sack have spilled open in the crash. The same goes for Ang's. The only saving grace is that the contents of *my* duffel somehow remained intact, surviving our crash. Ang oversteps and hoists my bag over his shoulder. He then points toward the rising sun in the east.

"We passed a road about a mile back that way," he says. "I don't know where we go from here, but we can't stay in this field."

"Why not?" Connie says, admiring the long view. "It's a good a place to die as any. Hell, you can even have my share of the water. I'll just shrivel up over there, I think."

"Connie," I say, summoning the courage to care. "Don't you want to make it to the grand finale? Don't you owe it to yourself to spit in the face of Vesta when she comes?"

"You used *she*." Connie smiles wide, and her eyes bug out a little. She bops her head to some whimsical tune in her head. "Okay. I *would* love to flip her off. She'll be coming 'round the mountain when she comes. She'll be coming 'round the mountain when she comes."

"Yee-haw." Ang joins with an exaggerated eye roll.

"Do you think Vesta'll be ridin' six white horses when she comes? Whaddya think Rainbow, huh?"

I twirl on her—just long enough to deliver a fatal, "My name is Rain."

She gets it. My threatening gaze gives her no choice.

And so, we plod on, marching toward our imminent doom. After a quick trek through the cornfield and a few random Connie renditions of old folksongs, the sun rises, bright and potent.

"So what's your story, anyway, Ang?" Connie asks as we pull out of the drooping, black, unattended husks. "You don't mind if I call you Ang, do you?"

Ang's body language tells all. He hasn't warmed up to her, not even a little. How could you blame him? Putting aside that she's a death bringer, there's not much about Connie Blackburn to like.

When we were juniors, it was widely known that Connie would emotionally and socially torture any girl who didn't pay her homage.

I'm not saying she expected us to bow and kiss her feet when we passed her in the halls (although she carried herself as if she deserved that sort of attention), but one was definitely supposed to be in awe of Her Grace.

Sometimes a brave (or stupid) girl would get it into her head to challenge Connie's rule. It wouldn't be much of a coup—the poor thing might just earn up the courage to defend herself from a snark encounter. Connie would inevitably dig in with her razor-sharp claws, challenging her contender by pointing to her clear and present flaws. It mightn't even be an obvious blemish to the casual teen. Sure, if you had an acne problem or an ongoing difficulty with your weight, those were some of the easiest punches Connie'd throw. More often than not, though, she'd go for the jugular. She'd stare into your soul and rip at what you assumed were your own, personal inadequacies, making you feel like the worst human being ever to scrape unmanicured toes across the planet.

Am I giving her too much credit? Ha.

One of my biggest regrets of our high school years (and perhaps of my entire life) was when I didn't stand up for Gretchen Billings on the miserable day Connie crossed her path. It just so happened that, during gym one day, Connie leaped up to spike a volleyball over the net. For as short as I'll live, I'll never forget how (for whatever reason) Gretchen, who was on the opposing team, jumped at least one and a half times her body length on the other side of the net. She not only blocked Connie's attempted spike, but smashed the volleyball right back into her perfect face. The level of "oohs," "ohs," "ahhs," and stifled snickers that echoed throughout the gymnasium was a harsh ruckus.

It took a good thirty seconds before anyone bothered to see if Connie, who was lying on the floor, trying to quell the steady flow of blood rushing out of her face, was all right. I think the shock of us witnessing the queen go down hard had paralyzed us.

"What did you do?!" Billie Hainsworth shouted through the netting. Billie was Connie's first-in-command. She doted on Connie's every move, studied her, kissed up to her, hoped to *be* her someday, probably.

Gretchen, suddenly aware of what atrocity she'd committed, retreated a step or two across the hard, indifferent gym floor. If she'd gone to Connie in that moment, my end-of-the-world companion likely would have snapped Gretchen's head right off. Instead, Gretchen continued to walk quietly off the court and into the locker room. There, she waited patiently for the beating that would surely come. The one she may or may not have thought she deserved.

When the bell rang and everyone was dressed, Gretchen found herself miraculously unscathed. We would learn through the high school grapevine in the days to come, that Connie had given her faithful followers explicit instructions not to lay a hand nor a derogatory remark on Gretchen. Everyone knew Connie was just biding her time for a devastating counterstrike.

About two weeks later, after losing a lot of sleep, some hair, and biting her fingernails near to the bone, Gretchen finally received her long-expected punishment. There's not a more apropos way to say it: Connie's burn had the *potential* to inflict about as much devastation on Gretchen as an asteroid on Melford.

When a fully healed Connie Blackburn strode into the cafeteria that Thursday afternoon, she didn't stop until she came nose to nose with Gretchen, right at her table. Gretchen's close friends (of which I was not one), did nothing to stand with her; for that would have cemented them in Connie's mind as meat puppets who deserved to suffer some backsplash wrath. A few of Gretchen's friends and others even dispersed from the cafeteria as soon as they saw the popular posse approaching. Everyone knew it was going to be an emotional bloodbath.

"Gretchen, darling," Connie began, and the cafeteria went dead silent. "I forgive you for almost breaking my nose. As you can see, the bruising and swelling has gone down sufficiently." In fact, she looked even more the goddess than before, if that was possible.

"Connie," Gretchen tried. "I'm so so so so so very sorry. I never intended to—"

"Shhh. It's okay," she said. Then louder, so everyone could hear, "It's not your fault you're a half R—."

Now, first of all, the R word is the worst kind of profanity. Anyone heard spouting that obscenity (not to mention its heinous cousin, N—) would be outcast from the hierarchy of school society, and for good reason. In this case, even the mighty Connie Blackburn could not escape a full month of being a social pariah for her ill-contrived slander.

I never could figure what Connie was thinking when she said what she said to poor Gretchen. In doing so, she hurt not only Gretchen but also herself. She struggled to regain her status with a careful, coordinated campaign—the likes of which I didn't give a damn about, and so, do not know how she eventually clamored her way back to her pre R-word role as the indisputable queen of John J. Wilkins High.

But the devastating effect Connie's word left on Gretchen was permanent. Prior to that day, only a few of Gretchen's closest friends knew her father was... slow. Again, I was not one of them. But with that one, wretched curse, Gretchen's worldview shattered, as the cruel word spread like poison. She'd long believed the world was kinder in the face of her father's disability. Then again, she'd never tangled with Connie Blackburn.

"What do you think happened to everyone here?" Connie asks, bringing me back to the present. She's been prattling on for the better part of ten minutes, I gather, and I've only just tuned in.

The first houses we've passed were dark and quiet. Better for us, worse for humanity. Maybe everyone here has split, cashing in their front row seats to Vesta for a few extra seconds of alive time. I don't see how it'd be worth it. Either way, really. Stay or go. Doesn't matter.

"Did they hurt you bad, Connie? I mean, really?" I pose the question that's been bugging me since she reappeared. "Or was that all just part of your act, too?" She stops, looks me over, but doesn't speak.

"Nevermind," I tell her. Connie's silence once again tells her story better than all the words at her disposal ever could. No, she hadn't gone as far off the ranch as everyone else. Maybe she really wasn't infected by the mystery phone virus.

"There's a pickup truck on the side of the road, up ahead," says Ang. His eyes are superior by leaps and bounds. He points to my Boo blaster. "Stay alert on our approach. Be prepared for anything. And if you shoot that thing... actually, maybe don't shoot it. I'm afraid of what the blowback might do to us at close range."

"Did you find this in my house?" I ask, suddenly keen to get to the bottom of his unlikely possession of an alien artifact.

"I did a sweep early on, during your blue period. So yeah, I found it under a floorboard in your parent's closet."

"My blue period?"

"Sorry, like Picasso. Nevermind. I thought it was strange your dad would leave it behind. But I never fired it. I couldn't if I'd tried. I was saving it for you. For when I knew you'd come out of your funk, because I knew you'd need it."

I don't know what to say to any of that. If I'd been holding on to any fleeting hope that I might still be one hundred percent human, that ship has sailed. This hefty, seemingly always-loaded weapon in my hand is proof enough... of everything.

"How'd your dad get a hold of it then?" I find another worthless question.

"He took it from my room one day when I was out fishing. I tried to take it back from him. But I don't know—I think it made him feel... validated."

"Validated?"

"Yeah, like he wasn't crazy after all. Even though he couldn't verbalize much of a rational thought before you came over, I think that blaster told him it was okay to believe in his memories."

Ang holds a regular-sized Earth gun in his own hand. He takes the lead toward the (hopefully) abandoned pickup truck, and Connie and I follow close behind. He walks a wide perimeter, just to be sure, and peers inside.

"All clear," he announces after popping the tailgate. He lowers his weapon to his side, then slides it into a holster I didn't know he'd had. Once again, I have to wonder how he's able to do such things in such a casual manner—as if he were a time traveling cowboy, dispersed from his realm. I've lived next door to this boy my entire life and have never witnessed this side of him. He's dangerous, bold, mysterious, and scary. Did his survivor's personality stem from being hardened by a doomed world? In light of it all, how much have *I* changed? I can't imagine much.

The keys this truck's long-gone driver left in the ignition do nothing. Ang tries and tries, but he can't get the engine to turn over. "No gas," he proclaims after five minutes of frustration.

"What was the plan, anyway? Drive to wherever the hell Melford is? And then what? Wait to die?" Connie asks.

"You're right. There's no sense in going anywhere anymore." Ang tells Connie what she wants to hear, perhaps just to get her off our backs. It won't work. "If you want to stay here and die on the side of the road, that's your prerogative. I'm hungry."

Ang turns and walks briskly past a bullet ridden sign covered by a low-hanging tree branch. His brisk movement brushes the leaves aside, unceremoniously revealing our location.

"Welcome to Melford," I read aloud. No one balks. We just continue on, over the town line. Yet I wonder, did Ang know where he was crashing all along?

Part Three

Summer to the End of the World

All hope abandon ye who enter here.

— Dante

Chapter Fourteen

We've been holed up in this barn for eleven monotonous days. Even as I form a malformed calendar in my head, I feel the weight of Time not mattering anymore. By all of our accounts, today is the fourth of July, which means there are three months and fourteen days until the world's demise... but who's counting?

Ha. Ha?

Today, at last, we've branched out from the ghost town that is Melford to raid a few desolate houses in neighboring Wheeler Falls. In the fifth and final empty home, we've discovered a map of Indiana. It's the kind that folds out easily, sixteen different ways, but is a bear to close up pretty again.

"We're about one hundred and forty miles north of Indianapolis, and a thousand years from what used to pass as civilization," Connie says, surprising us with her grasp of latitudinal direction. "Maybe that's where everyone's fled? It makes sense, right? Go to the big city where smart people have all the answers? Maybe Indianapolis still has electricity?"

She has never said anything intelligent. That's just Connie's gift.

Still, it is a mystery where all the abandoned homes' owners have gone.

"These sparsely populated lands are where people settle to stay away from big city folk," Ang answers. "I suspect the grid being knocked out here wasn't as big a problem as it was in Maine. Some residents might have even welcomed a return to simpler times. The people here were farmers, enjoying the idyllic aspects of town life. That makes the disappearance of everyone even more disturbing. You'd think they could get by living off the land and their livestock for six months, easy." Ang stops talking abruptly, maybe realizing he's divulged too much of his own inner desire for country living. He's always seemed out-of-place back home, what with his reclusive nature and avoidance of technology and (let's be honest) humans in general. And Scarborough isn't exactly what I'd call a metropolis.

"Wherever they went, did they take their cows and chickens with them?" I ask. And since none of us can pose a plausible solution to the mystery of the disappeared animals, Connie blasts us with an impossible possibility we've been ignoring.

"Maybe they were all abducted by aliens," she mentions, blindly tapping on the door of my questionable heritage. Despite all our wandering boredom these past eleven days, neither Ang nor I have brought up the whole alien thing. I don't know about him, but I'm reluctant to discuss it, for fear that one more speculative conversation might grant the out-of-this-world theory legitimacy.

Maybe part of Connie knows about you, Rain? Maybe she's not as dumb as you think? After all, she never questioned your Boo blaster.

As Connie unwittingly stumbles near my nebulous ancestry with unintentional, exploratory innuendo, Ang's chosen to leave my questionable alien ancestry alone. To tell the truth, I prefer his silent way. Since I have no concrete answers, there's really no sense trying to workshop it. We still have three and a half months to hash it all out, to likely come up with nothing but ridiculous theories. Good for a laugh, maybe? Though I can't honestly see the benefit. It'd be like fishing for carp in the toilet. All you'd catch is crap.

That's crass.

Hours fly by like the days. That's how it is now. One moment we're here, and the next we're somewhere else. Time itself has no meaning, just as nothing we do, say, or feel has any lasting import.

I'm a Debbie Downer if ever there was one. At least I know what I am capable of, emotionally speaking.

I disassociate often when it comes to my dark thoughts and doldrums. I'll blink and I'm waist deep in Lake Michigan, reeling in an easy catch from a decent cast. Or Connie will tell me it's Tuesday, but it feels as if we just celebrated Tuesday yesterday. Was that last Tuesday already? There's nothing much to do except wander the lifeless landscape, wonder where it's all gone, and grieve for our world that's so broken.

It passes the time.

We've been staying in a two-story, sturdy barn with ample hay for sleeping in the rafters. Yeah, there are plenty of actual houses to choose from, but neither Ang nor I can see ourselves squatting in someone else's abode. Connie's been all for it—she even offered to scavenge for fresh sheets to make the beds every morning. But she'd never go alone. Not after what she's been through. Or not been through. Or whatever.

Out behind our sturdy barn, according to an adorable, child-made sign on a tree, is Elderry Pond; it is teeming with tiny fish. Or at least it was teeming with them when we first arrived. Now, I'm not so sure. We've been hooking so many of the bastards, I think they've started catching on. Just yesterday, Ang and I had to move over to the other side of the pond where a big school of lookalike anglers had gone. Of course, none of those noodle, lightbulb-headed scaly monsters could survive here. They are deep-sea divers, not idle surface dwellers. If they'd hopped over from Lake Michigan, I'd be a monkey's uncle, I suppose. They don't belong there either. But damned if they don't look exactly like anglers. Ugly things. If I caught one, I'd probably throw it into the field. Let it die in the heat of the sun.

The fish in Elderry are getting smarter, though. I'm not paranoid. The unsightly angler doppelgangers that skirt to the far edge of the pond when they see me coming is just one example. They all do it now. In another couple of days, I wouldn't be surprised if every species of fish congregated in the middle, away from mine and Ang's death sticks. Without a boat to paddle out there, we'll be plumb out of ideas and back to the verge of starvation. Good end times!

In between fishing and campfires, Ang's been teaching me how to shoot. If worse comes to worse, and we have to go hunting, I'm confident I could pick off a rabbit... if it was sitting completely still, less than thirty feet away. The trouble with pesky rabbits, though, is they never sit still. Also, we haven't seen any. So there's that. Even if the place was overrun with them, I couldn't rightfully murder one. Then again, severe hunger can change one's perspective on that sort of thing pretty quick. Or so I've heard.

I've a growing, uneasy feeling Ang's waiting for something to happen here... before the apocalypse, I mean. He's not quite as on-edge as he was back in Maine. But he tends to look over his shoulder more than is casual. The one time I called him out on it, he said, "You never can be too careful. Just because there's nobody here doesn't necessarily mean there's nobody here."

Whatever. I'm done trying to figure that kid out. If I haven't done so by now, after knowing him for most of our natural lives, then what hope do I have in getting any deeper with the little time we have left? The real Ang is just gonna have to die with him.

If there even is a "real Ang."

As far as I can tell, Connie's the only one of us who's not on permanent edge. She seems content where we are. And why wouldn't she be? Ang and I do all the work.

Summer suits Connie, as one might expect. She spends most of her days lying out in the sun, working on a tan that, at this rate, no one else will ever see. I'd chastise her for not helping with daily chores, but really, there's not much to do. And I imagine a helpful Connie would be more destructive than this current, selfish, flesh zombie. There are no threats for at least a twenty-mile perimeter in any direction, and all we need to do to survive from one day to the next is fish and cook. Ang and I have that covered; and until now, it's been a cakewalk. If there really was anyone hiding out in these sleepy towns, they would've seen our fires' smoke and come investigate. But it's just us that remain: the pre-apocalypsia trio. It's hard to imagine there's anyone left... anywhere.

"They've outsmarted us at last," Ang reminds me, as we wade our feet along the water's edge. The smallmouth bass are indeed not biting this afternoon, gone the way of the grotesque angler.

Is it still the fourth of July? I've been so many places since breakfast, I can hardly remember who I am.

A glimmer of a speedy tadpole flashes past my big toe and is gone. He's off to the center of the pond to report to his surviving friends.

Laugh it up, worms of Elderry. You'll be obliterated and gone soon enough, just like every other soul caught floundering in this sea called Earth.

"How do they know?" Ang asks. It's a rhetorical question if ever I've heard one. Still, he presses on. "Fish might be the dumbest species on the planet. Even if we had been in the same spot day in and day out for a year, used identical bait, and managed to keep our heartbeat on an even keel; and even if every single atom in the universe hummed on the same frequency; and even if nothing in their underwater realm ever changed one iota, these stupid fish wouldn't have been able to predict our extraordinarily obvious intentions to hunt and eat them. Not in the world we used to live in, anyway. Something's changed with fish and beasts."

"And us," I overstate the obvious.

Ang scratches his chin. It's as if he is mimicking a sophisticated, provoking gesture he once saw on some ancient, classy, British television show. Not that the freak watched T.V.

"Survival got amped to eleven," I tell him. "Something is in the air—a new electricity. I only wish it would lend us enough raw energy to power a freezer. Then we wouldn't have to wade in this muck, scrounging for food. Not every day, anyway."

"You'll always prefer the Atlantic to our little Elderry," Ang says, a little ominously. It's as if he's predicting my future will be spent shackled to Melford. His too, I wonder?

His shoulders hunch up and breakdown in one fluid movement while his brow furls into a decent impression of a determined but distraught grandpa. The transformation from handsome teen to ornery old man came quick, then reverted in the blink of an eye. He's back to being my strange but trusty, wholehearted neighbor with an apocalypse complex the size of... well, a very big asteroid.

"I'm goin' in," Ang says, rolling up his cuffs. He takes three long strides into the pond before realizing it has the potential to be much deeper than he'd anticipated. He retreats, doing a spinning motion with his index finger, indicating for me to turn around.

"I never figured you to be shy, Angus," I tease him. If he turns red, I don't know it, because I've flipped myself around to face the long dirt path back to the barn. Before now, I wouldn't have figured he'd be embarrassed around little 'ol me. In some ways, I suppose he's always been like a (barely) older brother. No, I take that back. I've no earthly idea what it'd be like to have a *real* brother. But it just sounds wrong about Ang.

When I turn back around, Ang's evaporated. All that's left of him is a pair of raggedy jeans and his faded black tee. If my alien ancestors are hiding in the horizon's shadows, maybe they've shot a supersonic laser down, precisely degrading my best friend to his atomic core.

He is your best friend. Isn't he? What would Leash think?

I know she would approve. Seriously though, where'd he go?

"An—?"

Ang's jet black hair reappears. His rigid face pops up too, breaking the surface near the center of the pond, proving my overactive imagination false (I'd briefly figured he'd drowned himself).

"They're all bunched up in the center," he calls. "Just like you said. I'm gonna swim around them. Try to push 'em toward you. Be ready with your line."

It'll never work. What is he thinking?

Maybe the overreaching potential of his bonehead scheme is fueled by his desire to fill our bellies for just one more night. After all, we can't go to bed hungry on America's birthday.

Ang circles the center like a tiger. Can tigers swim? It doesn't matter. His freestyle grows ever more impressive with each stroke. I hold his pole tight in anticipation, making the fishing line taut against my sweaty palm.

"Make your move, Angus," I tell no one.

What is wrong with you, Rain? Get a grip!

Ang circles and circles the sprawling fish, keeping his flutter kicks to a minimum. This has the same effect as a thousand buzzing dragonflies on the glistening surface.

He goes under again, and I discard my stolen sandals, daring to dip more than just toes in the water. Why did I expect it to be chilly? Here we are, smack dab in the heart of summer, and I think a freshwater pond the size of my backyard would be frigid. Such is not the case.

I smoosh the whole of my right foot into the murkiness, and my left foot follows. Dusky, brown muck and mud (two very different sediments) are pushed upward and out. The uncertain pond floor floats to the top, then spirals in all directions. The delightful mess is indicative, maybe, of infinite universes twisting and coiling into each other, well beyond our reach.

"I'm starting to think like your dad," I tell Ang, but he's not here. And he's no longer circling.

I snap out of my weird funk to find Ang's vanished again. This time, I don't (not for a second) believe he's in any danger. It's just silly Elderry Pond, and Ang's a champion swimmer.

The seconds tick by and there is still no sign of him.

"Ang?" I whisper. Or maybe I didn't. Maybe my breath is caught in my throat; or maybe I've been scared speechless.

A flurry of activity arises near the pond's center and a swarm of splashes ripple toward me. That's the signal, I surmise. I gain my bearings, grasp the rod even tighter, and cast away. The minutes'-dead earthworm, currently gutted on my hook, sails through the air and lands with a satisfying *ploop,* about twenty feet ahead.

Nothing tugs, though the water bubbles over there.

Those agitated splashes continue, gaining speed directly at me. Without allowing myself a moment to succumb to rational thought, I drop the fishing pole and break free out of the pond.

"What are you doing?" Ang hollers from somewhere far away. Though, I denote a tone of good humor in his disapproval. "Catch a fish, for god's sake!"

Does Ang believe in God? Do you?

I gather my wits, turn back, pick up the pole, and cast again. This time, the line soars a gentle fifteen feet. It skims along the surface once, twice—and then a fish breaks and crests over the top, opens its incredible mouth, and swallows my earthworm whole!

"Holy sh—!" I curse, unbelieving of my extraordinary dumb luck. With Ang hooting nearby, I reel the prize in, then pluck it from the sea. And yes, I know Elderry Pond is a far cry from the Atlantic Ocean, but it's human to pretend. And I have to hold on to every shred of my humanity.

I expertly remove the hook from the fish's lip (thankfully, he didn't swallow it, as I originally thought), and place him in the bucket to flop and expire. Though I'd really rather not watch his spastic death dance, it gives me something to look at while Ang puts his pants back on over his clinging, soaked boxers.

On the walk back to the barn, I tune Ang out, thinking about the poor dead fish. I've eaten hundreds of them since the lights went down on Scarborough, but this was the first I've actually been responsible for. It's different. It shouldn't be, but it is.

"That was a one and done."

"What?"

"Tomorrow they will have learned our new behavior. All of them.

Every evolving creature in Elderry Pond. Those are seriously the smartest fish I've ever come across. Maybe that's true of all beasts, great and small now." He pauses, stops, pauses again somehow, then continues. "Anyway, we'll have to try for bigger game tomorrow. We'll see if the deer have brains and guts, like our friend, Mr. Fish."

I'm not looking forward to seeing any animal's guts and/or brains. But starving to death is an unacceptable alternative.

Chapter Fifteen

We all kind of faded into our own evening last night, with nothing to celebrate. I couldn't even tell you what I did. Wandered for a while until I wound up back in the hayloft? Maybe. I remember at one point I was desperately scanning the stars for some fireworks, and spying not a one. I couldn't even conjure a silly sparkler with my spent imagination. Kinda sad.

It's at least two hours before dawn, and I'm barely functioning. Somehow, the two of us made our way out to some wooded area west of the barn.

One species unaffected by Melford's unexplained mass exodus is the deer. In Scarborough, evidence of our rotted-from-the-inside-out society was that our friends and neighbors' corpses stayed behind to stink up their houses. Animals back home either died with their owners, ate them after the fact, or high-tailed it into the wild. But we never had much deer to speak of in the streets of coastal Maine.

We carry long rifles we've "borrowed" from nearby homes. Ang's is supported by a sling he's wrapped around his shoulder. Mine, I've gotta lug.

It had crossed my mind, when Ang first presented me with this rifle at the crack of pre-morning, to bring my Boo blaster. The thought of what it would do to an animal took me out of it. I left my Boo tucked behind a crooked, cornered bail of hay.

I must admit, I do feel somewhat silly snaking through these dense trees. Every twig and leaf crackles beneath my clumsy feet.

We'd briefly considered asking Connie to come with us on the hunt. All it took was a reminder of her unhelpful, unappreciative approach to our survival efforts for us to leave that terrible idea alone. The girl has shown her worth to be worthless. The only reason she's alive is because of us, and she'd better start acknowledging that and pitching in, or she's gonna get the business end of my boot.

Ang still blames her for his dad's death—a thing that arguably could have happened with or without Connie's interference. I'm sure, like me, Ang doesn't want to see her die. We're not animals or beasts.

Not yet.

The crunching beneath my heels continues. It's so intrusive that I decide to break our silent communication protocol to ask how to lessen the noise. Ang assures me that the sound isn't that bad, and I'm overreacting.

"Maybe you're under reacting. Did you ever think of that?"

"Good one," he says, and I glimpse a smile. Then he does the sign language for (at least I assume it's true sign language) *zip your lips*. He waves a couple other nonsensical hand gestures, which I gather to mean, "There's prey up ahead."

After a dreadful long time moving slowly into the heart of the woods, Ang says that we should split up. He's convinced the same gift of intelligence bestowed upon the creatures of Elderry Pond has also been bequeathed to the deer. His plan is to forge ahead, in an opposing, circular pattern, to flush out whatever we can: deer, rabbits, squirrels.

"Squirrels?" I hiss with disgust, shining my flashlight on the ground. Just as the nasty notion crosses my lips, my belly turns itself over. I read somewhere that the human body can live for three minutes without air, three days without water, and three months without food. If that's truly the case, do I really need three square meals a day? I won't make it if those meals have to comprise (barf) squirrel. The leaves on these trees don't look poisonous. They're likely more agreeable than squirrel meat, anyway.

I shake off my disgust and try to think with a pre-apocalypsia mentality.

Protein is key, I must remember. Without it, my body might carry on for weeks and months, but I won't have much pizazz in my step.

I've never really been hungry. Nothing worth speaking of, anyway. I can't imagine what it's like, and I don't want to find out. I guess it could be worse. We could start eating each other.

No, Chicken. Yours is not that story.

We'll see.

"Just sit tight and shoot at anything that comes charging your way," Ang says, then adds an afterthought, "as long as it's not me."

"This is how you teach me to hunt?" I criticize his technique. "*Sit tight and shoot?* Is that all you got?"

"There's not much else to it, Rain. That's how my dad taught me." Remorse sweeps his face at his mere mention of his dad. It's as if *not* thinking about him brings Ang peace, and speaking his name makes the pain real. I totally get that. I do. That feeling passes.

Ang rushes off, making significant scuttle sounds as he goes. I don't think he's as skilled at this sort of thing as he thinks he is. In fact, before this day is through, I foresee the two of us shimmying off toward another town beyond our perimeters in search of proper food. And people! There must be some of both nearby. We cannot be the only humans left.

The first speckles of light make their appearance above the treetops. The shadows of distant branches evolve into well-formed outlines of oaken characteristics. I hope we have another sunny day to look forward to. In fact, I hope all our future days are sunny. We deserve that.

A nearby rustle shakes my mind free from the promise of a warm

July. The pitter patter of tiny, furry feet comes directly to my ears mere seconds before I see the nervous, little bunny. He stops, about ten or fifteen yards in front of me. I know he's a he by the way he shivers his whiskers. I figure female bunnies wouldn't be caught dead doing that.

Speaking of dead... Mr. Cute As A Bunny senses his own death is coming. He stares straight at me from his proper distance, as if welcoming the final transition he'd have me deliver.

But my finger hovers far from the trigger of Ang's gun. I'm as far back as the clip allows, and I'll creep no closer to the pull. Fishing is one thing; adorable, whisker-twitching bunnies are quite another.

Gently, and with no sudden movements, I lay my rifle on the ground. The bunny cocks his furry noggin, as if to say, "Why don't you have it in you, Rain?"

A thunderous blast echoes from the east. The ground explodes a good three feet from where my newfound friend just was. There's a hole there now with knocked up leaves raining back to Earth. In a mad flash, the bunny's darted away. His white, bushy tail zigs and zags from my view.

Ang comes clamoring through the coming sunrise, waving his arms like a madman and shouting something unintelligible. By the time he reaches me, I'm standing tall in the face of his admonishment.

"The rabbit gave you every opportunity! He was literally just sitting there, begging for you to kill him. Do you want to starve to death, Rain? Is that it?"

"I don't like your tone," I tell him, as if I'm straight out of Buckingham Palace. I kick the rifle—the one Ang unceremoniously gave me earlier this morning, in lieu of my extraterrestrial cannon. "And no, I don't want to starve to death. I want to be here for the big show. Also, you missed your target by a mile."

"Yeah right, three feet maybe."

"Whatever. I'll bet you couldn't hit an elephant with a grenade launcher."

"That's a ridiculous statement. You saw me shoot with perfect accuracy while hanging on to the plane." He scoffs, but I know I've hit a vein, so I pinch it.

"That was different. Those were bad guys you were aiming at. Face it. You're as gentle as me, Angus Finnegan. And I think you can only shoot straight when our lives depend on it. Or maybe the same spirit you claim has somehow made the animals smarter is also staying our hands, to keep them safe. Maybe we'll starve to death, after all."

He picks up my discarded weapon and slings it over his shoulder to partner his own. I'll never fire that thing again. It's pointless.

Following a brisk walk back to the barn, Connie surprises us with two heaping bowls of dry, but not stale, Frosty O's. She's placed the bowls opposite each other on the rustic, red picnic table by the silo.

"Come and sit," she says, pointing gleefully to the breakfast of champions she's harvested. "I was taking a stroll through the field at sunrise, and you'll never guess what I stumbled upon? There was a copper ring in the soil, just itching to be pulled. So I pulled it, and there was a ladder down below that. Sure enough, it led me to an honest-to-God doomsday shelter! There are rows and rows of canned goods down there, but I thought I'd treat you nice with a simple bowl of Frosty O's to get you going today. Eat 'em up, then we'll go explore the shelter together."

She's so proud of her dumb luck that her unmitigated mirth is almost contagious. And just when I was about to write her off to the wolves, too. Connie'd hit the mother load.

"Good job, Connie," I commend her. Because it looks as though she might need some encouragement. Who knows, maybe her own tide has turned.

"It's not quite rabbit stew though, is it Rain?" Ang cuts in with more than a hint of bitterness.

"It's better than nothing, ingrate." I sit at the well-balanced picnic table to chomp on some frosty oats.

"You didn't see anyone down there?" Ang asks Connie, then

spoons a mouthful of his own Os into his face. Though I'd prefer the Honey Gold variety, I'm thankful for this bounty.

"Down where?" Connie plays dumb. "In the bomb shelter?"

"You called it a doomsday shelter before," I inform her.

"Doomsday shelter, bomb shelter, storm shelter, fallout shelter, what's in a name?" Connie asks, almost sing-songy. I've never seen her in such high spirits. Not even when she was Queen of John J. Wilkins High did she shine like this. "No, Ang, I did not come across anybody down in the bowels of the Earth. I think I would have remembered bumping into someone."

"Maybe they were hiding?" Ang pushes, trying to (and succeeding at) being difficult for difficult's sake.

"If they were, then they're world class, expert-level hide and seekers. I brought a flashlight with me. And a gun. I'm not stupid. There was no one but me and the food. Okay?"

It'll have to be. We'll have to trust Connie once more and go down into the depths with her. Otherwise, between the smart ass fish, Ang's terrible, cursed aim, and my reluctance to shoot, we'll all be dead in three months.

Oh wait, we'll all be dead in three months, anyway. Right. Almost forgot about that. Three months, thirteen days, and a handful of hours. I can't help but do the mental math. No shelter, no matter what name it goes by, will save us from annihilation.

"Maybe we could—"

"No." Ang interrupts her. "It won't work."

"There's enough food down there for us to survive for years! We could ride out the asteroid undergr—"

Ang smashes his fist on the picnic table, causing his half-empty bowl of O's to splash up into his face. He stands and backs away from the mess, from the table, from us.

"Lemme know when you're ready to check it out, Rain," he says, then walks off into the barn, as if we won't need Connie to help us find the place.

"What's eating him?" Connie wants to know. She's entirely clueless of Ang's emotional background.

"He's a dead man walking," I tell her, then finish slopping up my cereal.

* * *

I don't know what it is about hope, and I'm not about to wax philosophical on the subject. Mainly because I don't have any of the fleeting stuff.

Despite Ang's outburst, Connie still appears to be in positive spirits, i.e. hopeful. With a tall, business-like smile, she leads us through the field, past our still-dead and forever unmoving plane, to a well-covered spot approximately one hundred yards from the crash site.

"Here," Connie says, surprising us without fanfare. She bends down and pulls a large copper ring out of the weeds. Ang and I would have found this place if we had more time to wander. It was just the luck of the draw that Connie uncovered it first—which is fine, since she's sharing.

Before we venture down Connie's mystery ladder, I scan every inch of the field. Ang does the same. It's not easy or foolproof. There could be threats crouching behind any of the groups of dead and droopy cornstalks, but I doubt it.

"It's not a trap," Connie gives her tainted assurance. "I promise you. We're in this together until the bitter end, you guys. I can't tell you how sorry I am for what I've done. And if I can't redeem myself in your eyes before the big bang comes, I can at least die trying."

Did this girl experience a drawn-out soul searching epiphany while Ang and I were out bickering over un-killed rabbit? Whatever the case, I have to give Connie credit for owning up to her mistakes.

What's done in duress is still done, Rain.

"Well," I say, moving toward the hole in the dirt. "We didn't come out here to stand around all day."

Ang's not as convinced of Connie's heel to face turn (if that's even what it is). Not taking any chances, he hangs back to allow me to go first. With Connie in the middle, if she turns out to be a two-time lying skank, Ang'll get the drop on her before she can drop us. His position makes sense from a callous, calculating, and unforgiving perspective. It's also extremely plausible I'm reading too much into all of this.

Climbing down the well-secured rungs, I imagine being eaten alive by some subterranean monster. If death before asteroid comes, I just pray for it to be swift. Off with my head in one quick chomp, monster!... Actually, scratch that; it sounds incredibly painful.

But what if Connie's got a group of marauders down here? What if they're lying in wait to bludgeon and eat me?

I have no acceptable answers at my disposal. I can only hope and pray my fate doesn't pan out like that. It would be a pretty dumb idea for Connie to have taken up with some nefarious others. Dumber still if they concocted some half-cocked plan to ambush us in an abandoned shelter. There's only two of us (not counting conniving Connie in this scenario); these rabid, drooling, madmen I'm imagining could have taken us at any time in the past two weeks.

So relax. There's nobody here.

I step off the last rung and plant my shoes on solid ground. However, being that we are at least thirty feet beneath the field, I should rightly refer to this footing as solid *underground*.

With my flashlight shining brightly, I make my way through a fully stacked row; racks and racks of varied canned goods line the immensely oversized space. Connie absolutely undersold the wealth of this place. There's enough food down here to last the three of us until the end of time.

Two sets of feet hit the dirt behind me. I turn to see Connie's painted-on smile. "No need to go anywhere now, huh? And before you ask, yes there are plenty of can openers. I found a box of them in the corner. Not that it would be difficult to find that particular household utensil elsewhere. This isn't that old episode of *The Twilight Zone*."

"I don't think that's accurate," Ang says, flopping out dirt as he lands. "There was never a *Twilight Zone* episode about a man at the end of the world in need of a can opener. You're thinking of the one where the last man on Earth rises from the rubble to realize he has all the time in the world to read every book. When he goes to crack the first one, he drops his glasses and they break. Oh, the ironic humanity!"

One of Ang's hands holds his flashlight, but the other balls up into a fist so he can clench it between his teeth in a mocking manner. His gun, I notice, has been holstered. If he truly thought Connie was a two-time bastard, he's holstered that idea as well (for now, anyway).

"Settle down nerd, I didn't say I was a *Twilight Zone* aficionado."

Ang's lost the happy-go-lucky vibe as he stares at the plethora of food. Is he thinking what I'm thinking?

"Sloppy," he mutters, shaking his head from side to side and confirming we're on the same page. What should be a moment of Zen is overshadowed by the disappearance of an entire town.

"What's sloppy?" Connie asks, but he refuses to answer. "Are you wondering who all would have dumped this here? The whole town's disappeared, yet they abandoned all this food? Yeah, I wondered, too. Until I decided nothing matters, anyway. Right, Rain?"

Connie's rhetorical question is sound. Since we arrived here in Melford, Future Home of Vesta's Landfall Blast, we've seen no people, alive or dead. There's been no trace of food, and no sign of the murderous rampage we survived in Scarborough. All this time, I've been afraid of stumbling into a death ditch where dozens or hundreds of corpses—women, men, and children—are huddled together in one area, clutching their plastic Solo cups with trace remnants of the poisoned Kool-Aid.

Fortunately, I haven't staggered into that grisly scene, or anything remotely like it. Yet. Pre-apocalypsia's still young.

Living in this abridged, faltering-to-decay world, who knows what one should expect around any corner?

I draw my attention to the shelves again. Casually, almost nonchalantly, I run my hand over the labels. Yes, there's the essential, stereotypical nutritional necessities you'd expect to find—the corn and jarred honey and bags and bags of rice and endless supply of peanut butter and dried beans and powdered milk and boxes stacked on top of boxes of dehydrated meat and air-sealed pickles. The home-stuffed pickle jars have been sealed tight. The lid's edges support a decorative, dainty, Chantilly lace. Someone took great pains to care for these sour delights. And there are a lot of them.

My tummy rumbles, and I take down a random jar from a higher level. Carefully, I twist the lid. When it won't budge, I use some elbow grease and really work it. Behind me, Connie works a can opener while Ang stands by, still shaking his head in deep thought... or is it disapproval?

I can't get the damn pickle jar open. I curse and have to restrain myself from chucking it against the far wall. The flashlight I thought I so carefully secured between my knees drops and rolls away.

"What—"

The beam shines on...

A man?

My flashlight reveals what is clearly a door, camouflaged to appear like the far, grungy wall. I go to it, put my hand on the sneaky knob.

"Don't," Ang says.

"What? Why not?"

"Just don't. C'mon."

I turn the knob anyway. Ang doesn't flinch, but it's locked. I shimmy and wrangle it a little, back and forth and again, but nothing budges.

Ang relaxes. He dumps out a nearby crate of uncooked pasta boxes and fills it with other foods he haphazardly snatches from shelves. I shine my flashlight on Connie who's got a handful of peanut butter and a face smacked with honey. Nice combo, queen.

I want to know what's behind Door Number One And Only, and a mere lock will not prevent me from finding out. Maybe I can break the door down if I slam my body against it while jimmying the knob?

I take one, big step forward, and my handsy neighbor has the audacity to grab my arm.

"What is wrong with you?"

"Not here," he says.

Everything comes into focus. Even in this dingy, poorly lit subterranean coffin. There's been a shift in our chemistry.

Ang's been hiding something since we crashed, maybe longer.

Maybe forever?

Whatever secret he's harboring isn't gonna stay in the dark anymore. I move back to the ladder and force him up and out.

It's time to slice Ang open and scoop out his selfish truths.

Chapter Sixteen

"Spill your guts or I'll spill 'em for you."

As soon as we're topside, I shove Ang hard in the back. He stumbles, but keeps his balance and regains a steady footing.

Connie isn't rushing up the ladder to interfere in our squabble. I couldn't care less about the mysterious, underground food she's stuffing into her face.

"Rain, maybe we should—"

"You've been walking on eggshells ever since we crashed here, Angus. And it's got nothing to do with me or Connie. You're always looking over your shoulder. And you have this air about you, like you're expecting another shoe to drop. So either tell me right here and now what's going on... or I'm outta here." I scan the horizon, plotting a lonely course west. "That way."

"All right, let me explain." He takes a deep breath, and then, for the love of all things holy, he begins. "We have allies here."

"What?" Is my hair smoking? My forehead is so hot, I might just explode all over him.

"In one of his more coherent states, my dad told me what to do at the end of the world. He said to come here, to Melford. Just like you proposed we do, Rain." Ang lowers his eyes. He can't look at me.

"What are you talking about? Don't you dare use your dad's in-and-out dementia to sidestep the truth." I draw a deep breath. "We both know what I am. There's no sense in pretending anymore. Whether you choose to believe it or not, I've accepted it. I've been communing with my alien father for most of my life. Whether we speak in dreams or in a kind of hypnotic state, he's always been there. For the longest time, I thought I was talking to myself. But it's more than that. Much more. I know it now. We're connected, Dad and me. And he's the one who directed us here. *My* dad. Not yours."

Connie pops her head up and out of the hole. She sucks the life out of a pickle, then chomps it in half. Under her other arm, she balances a crate full of canned goods.

"Hold on," I say, taking a step closer. My thoughts swirl. Why would Ang lie about his dad now? Why wouldn't he have mentioned it earlier? He's edging toward the hatch. If he doesn't explain in full soon, I might just shove him in. "What did your dad tell you about the end of the world? What do you mean by *allies*? Start from the beginning."

"Rain—"

Everything I've been and everything I am are boiling to the melting point. Sensing I'm about to lose all control of my anger, Ang smartly sidesteps the hole in the ground.

"You guys want some pickles?" Connie asks, too dense to read the room.

"Yeah, leave a jar and piss off." That was maybe a little rude, but I'm hangry, and I don't need her mussing up my argumentative gears.

She at last senses the tenseness between Ang and me, hands me one of the pickle jars, and heads to the barn with her crate full of goodies.

"Don't stay out too late, lovebirds," she taunts as she goes. I suppose, to an untrained eye, Ang and I might resemble an old married couple. But that's just how next-door neighbors act, isn't it? I dunno. I don't have much frame of reference for our sort of thing.

"So you lied," I state the unvarnished fact. My wounds are cold.

"I omitted. Rain, he's my dad." As if that's excuse enough. Maybe it is. "He's my dad, and he told me we'd be safe here. The allies would come."

"What the hell are you talking about? What allies?" I throw out my arms to encompass the vast, empty field. I can't believe I'm still standing here, entertaining his half-formed explanations. But I am.

"The allies at the end of the world." He just keeps repeating his nonsense.

"Stop circling and say what you mean!"

"He said Melford's where I'd find my mom!" Ang shouts. The wind kicks up, as if born of our mutual loss, blowing Ang's words back in his face. In the distance, Connie continues walking toward the barn, unfazed.

"Angus—"

"He said she told him she'd meet him at the end of the world. Here."

"She told him Melford? Melford, Indiana? Specifically?" His silence confirms his belief. "You must have misunderstood."

"I did not."

"Then... he must have been confused. Melford was on the news. We knew Vesta would make direct contact with the Earth here. Before we lost power, we knew. He must have known. He must have been confused. In his state."

"That's just it, Rain. He told me about Melford last year. It was just before he started obsessing over aliens. And then he got sick."

"Family's all we've got," I lay the most inane cliché on him, because it's all *I've* got—the unlikely hope I'll be reunited with my dad someday. I need a moment to comprehend what Ang's just revealed.

Is it possible his mom and my dad were *both* aliens? What really happened the night they disappeared? How much of Mr. Finnegan's story was accurate? Perhaps he didn't have all the facts.

"Why didn't you just tell me?" I ask, terrified that the answer might have to do more with my insecurities than Ang's duplicitous nature. "I could have handled it."

"Maybe so," he says, searching for my eyes behind my fallen hair. I won't allow him that luxury. "I didn't want to burden you."

"I'm a big girl. I can handle anything after what I've been through." If that isn't the colossal understatement of the century, I don't know what is. "I didn't fall apart when your dad told me I was the daughter of a friggin alien, did I?"

He smirks. "No, you didn't."

I can't handle his subtle self-aggrandizing. It starts in his face and works its way through his body. It seeps out of his bones and gives Ang a confidence he doesn't deserve. Not for this.

"Rain," he says, breathing heavily. He leans in to me. What is happening here? Is he going to kiss me?! Seriously? Now?

If he was. He's not anymore. I've pulled away. I'm barely cognizant of having done so, but I have done so.

He straightens, stretching his neck in a way that can not be comfortable, and is certainly not appealing. He stands tall on his toes to scan the entire field.

"We're not alone," he whispers.

"Of course not," I mock him. Because he's ruined any chance we might have of becoming something more than just neighbors. "There are aliens everywhere. Look! There's one right in front of you!" I flash my hands out fast and surprise him with a *Boo!* Though I'm not really feeling the tired playfulness I've exerted, it's there. The look in his eyes slowly changes my mind.

"My dad told me—" Ang kneels low for cover where the dead stalks stand half crumpled and crooked. He grabs at my arm and pulls me down.

Suddenly we're up again and running for the barn. With a couple careful glances over my shoulder, I see what he intuited. A tight militia of faceless soldiers march with purpose across our field. We've run less than ten steps when we dig in our heels.

"M-Maybe it's them. The allies?" Ang's lost cool may be irretrievable. "Where are they coming from?"

"It's like they rose out of the ground. Like ghosts." Since the moment we arrived, I have felt an intruding presence, both in my peripherals and my outer limits. In retrospect, I realize I didn't allow my conscious mind to recognize the threat; I chalked my paranoia up to an overactive imagination and probable lack of proper nutrition.

"It's them. I know it." Ang declares with just enough validity to spiral back to himself. "The allies. We're going to be fine." He slows to a stop and makes his stand. What choice do I have but to stand with him?

The militia moves swiftly, like clouds' shadows before a storm. But the shadows they carry aren't dark like ours; they're soft, like wavy fluid. The more I try to explain these entities to myself, the more they confound reality. As a unit, they are one, gliding and zigzagging through the field in impossible patterns.

"They're not human," I suggest. None of this is right. None of this can actually be happening.

Because aliens don't exist.

Yes, we do.

They reveal themselves. Right in front of us. Here in plain sight for Ang and I to behold beneath the noonday sun. We hold our unsteady ground as the tallest of them approaches.

Eight figures face us, when before I counted dozens. Did the others dissipate back into the ground whence they came? Or were their previous numbers a miscalculation of my over-stressed mind?

These humanoid beings are a pristine shade of smooth silver. They do not have elongated faces, oblong eyes, sausage fingers, or lanky bodies. They are not some film interpretation of a nightmarish alien invasion. What they are is more complex than Hollywood ever put forth on the big screen.

"It's not just my imagination, right?" I ask Ang. He's not shaking.

Why is he not more startled by what we see? Their eyes—if they *are* eyes—are two, large ovals of pearly white, and entirely unreadable. It's illogical to discern whether they intend to do us deadly harm or would care to invite us to tea.

"Just play along," he says, confirming the least of my vulnerabilities.

The one front and center moves forward, lowering his weapon and extending his arm-like appendage in Ang's direction. At the end of it is a hand-like hand. It's reaching for Ang, and he's not moving! He's going to let the alien touch him!

"Ang!" I exclaim. But he can't hear me. He's in some kind of trance. Frozen. This creature from some other planet has captivated him. It owns my friend and neighbor.

I know what's coming next. I see it with all clarity. When the alien touches Ang, Ang will die. The alien's power will be too much for a mere mortal to absorb, and he'll turn to ash on the spot. I won't let it end him. I just won't. The odds of a half-alien hybrid such as myself surviving this creature's touch is far greater than Ang's.

All my life, I've shied from risk and danger. When the world collapsed in on itself, I withdrew from it and holed up in my basement for God's sake. For months! And who was it that watched over me?

I'd be dead a hundred times over, if it wasn't for Ang.

These selfless thoughts rage through me in a nanosecond, and I see clearly my only course of action.

So I take the action.

I launch my body in-between Ang and the alien. Here in our lonesome cornfield, the interloper's slick, silver finger brushes my anvil-shaped scar.

If this be death, be unafraid.

Something unreal is happening. And yeah, I realize this entire scene is pretty unreal, but the depths of this mind-boggling alien encounter keep getting deeper.

The tingling sensation that began with my scar penetrates my pores. An interstellar signal hitches an instantaneous ride on my blood and flows through my body in a matter of microseconds. It's not a feeling, not exactly—has anyone ever *felt* their blood coursing through their veins?—but an intrinsic knowledge of one's own inner workings. If that makes any sense? One unprecedented thing the alien's touch has done—she's reversed my circulation. Just as my brain understands this being is female, it also realizes I've been internally re-routed.

The present does not move backward in a jiggly way; the Earth does not reject its orbit around the sun; Vesta's eternal death march does not cease, and nothing extra-ordinary happens outside of the realm of me. I encompass the intergalactic phenomenon within, and accept it for what it is—all mine.

Ang's look of wonder is but a fraction of my own, as there is no discernible way he can know my circulatory system's gone counter-clockwise. I certainly cannot tell him such a thing. Even if I wanted to, my mouth won't open to speak any words. Every piece of me is focused on the billions of micro-explosions occurring underneath my skin.

The alien has receded. Though she keeps her distance with the seven others, her psychic grasp remains firm. She's poisoned me forever. I just know it.

I am fifty-three thousand shades of nervous, scattered energy. But I can change that. I can mold it to suit my needs. Right now I need her to get the hell out of my business.

She's scanning you for truths.

Instinct forces my walls up, and the alien senses my resistance; she retreats even further, disappearing from our sight, and taking the seven with her. My blood stops for a millionth of a millisecond.

I die.

It feels like I die.

But then I force my organs to pump correct again and right my blood's bloody circulation in the proper direction.

The vanished alien persists with her intrusion, whispering in previously untapped areas of my brain, *"Bisectoid."*

"What?"

"Aura."

And just as fast as the alien presence came into my head, she is gone from my psychic perspective—leaving me to reflect on the otherworldly communication.

"That was them. For sure. Where did they go?" Ang insists on living out his parents' fairy tale. Although it would be very interesting to know for certain whether Mr. Finnegan's advice was based on any concrete knowledge *Mrs.* Finnegan had, or if it was merely the universe's most incredible coincidence.

"How did your mom know this would be the place to meet aliens?" I speak. For the moment (for my sanity), I am putting off any analysis of everything that's just occurred.

"Aliens?" Ang says. His eyes roll from side to side in a state of unprepared confusion. "What about that intimidating militia said *alien* to you?"

"You're kidding, right?"

"No, why? What did you see?"

On closer inspection, Ang's eyes aren't the ones doing a circular, three-ring circus trot—the mad, dizzy spell is all mine and my pupils alone.

"They—" I say, desperate to bring meaning to the conversation. "Aura."

I malfunction, and I blip. My vision explodes into a preposterously unacceptable, blinding hot, white neon blur. Then everything goes dark.

Chapter Seventeen

"Rain."

"Yeah," I answer. My head feels as if it's been split in half. The moon is a blooming onion in a sky full of stars. I'm lying in the field, and it's night? "What happened?"

"Thank God you're okay," Connie says. She's standing, looming over me and Ang.

"What happened?" I ask again.

"You zonked out," Ang explains. "I've never seen anything like it. It was right after those heavily armed intimidators headed away. I didn't want to move you." As close as the word *intimidators* is to the mark, I'm reluctant to explain the impossible-to-explain sensation of my reversed circulation.

"How long was I out?" I ask, simultaneously trying to judge the time by the stars, a skill I do not possess.

"It's nine o'clock... ish," Connie informs me. Her diamond-studded watch is still ticking strong.

"Whoa whoa. Slow and easy," Ang says, helping me to a sitting position.

"Is it true?" Connie pries. "Were they really aliens? Ang said you hallucinated you saw aliens."

"Whatever they were," Ang begins, coming around to trying my unique perspective on for size, "they're not as inviting as I'd thought they'd be. They vanished into the trees when you went down and out. I wasn't sure if you were unconscious or sleeping or having an out-of-body experience... or what? They did something to you, didn't they?"

"I don't know," I say. "I don't know what they did. I think she might have tried to read me."

"She?" Connie asks, as if it's a shock that our intergalactic visitors could be female.

"Read you?" says Ang.

"I can't explain it. I felt like she was probing me for something. Maybe she was testing my moral character or scanning my history—" They stare at me, dumbfounded. "I know how it sounds."

I wobble, and my screaming skull relents. Ang's hand on my arm steadies me. "Let's get you to bed."

"Ooh! What else did I miss? You two finally seal the deal?" I feel my face betray feelings that aren't even mine. I tap into all my worthless, tired energy to find the strength to ignore her.

"I'm exhausted," I say, barely walking beneath my heady weight. How have I been unconscious for so long? What else might be wrong with my body and/or internal organs? What else might that alien have rearranged?

"You slept half the day away. That would make anyone tired." Ang tries a warm smile to follow up his backwards statement, but it comes out looking nervous and afraid. What else isn't he telling?

I hate that I don't trust Ang anymore, but he did that to himself. Mr. Shady Secret Keeper's got too many, um, shady secrets.

I'm too wiped to think clearly.

"You're sleeping in a proper bed tonight," Ang says, leading me into the house by our barn. "No more pre-apocalypsia rules. We're far beyond being polite, law-abiding citizens."

The whole idea that we shouldn't sleep in people's homes was mine and mine alone. If our trio was a democracy, I would have been outvoted. But Connie's opinion on such matters doesn't matter. She's got a long way to go to earning her place at the decision table.

There's just something entirely personal about a bed. When you walk into someone's home, you trespass on their energy space; even if they don't live there anymore (which is the case everywhere we've been), their spirit still thrives in their kitchens and their dens. A person's own room exudes that spirit a hundred fold; and in the bed where they dream their nights away—that's the quintessential goldmine of a personal aura.

I never knew I felt this way until I lived the hobo lifestyle. But eight hours lying unconscious in the dirt will do a lot toward changing your perspective on such things.

"Fine," I say, giving in and kind of looking forward to it. "I'm too wrecked to argue."

"Finally!" Connie pops out a gasp of relief. "Thank you, space men!"

The walk back to the house is slow going. My limbs betray me, and my mind is like a newborn calf's, still working its way out of the prenatal fog and into the morning dew.

The climb up the three insignificant porch steps is grueling. Ang has to support me as I cannot hold the rail. He takes my arm gently but firm. I do not know how he manages both ends of the tightness spectrum, but he does.

The shattered window to the right of the door is still as nasty as we left it, seven days back. Glass shards spike out along the upper edges of the frame, showcasing Ang's shoddy haste to enter. This was the first home we ransacked, only to come up empty, like all the rest. And before you say anything, I do see the irony of breaking and entering with the attempt to rob vs. harboring some malformed moral code about not sleeping in somebody's home. But what are you gonna do? Hunger's a fearsome beast.

Connie lights the way with her flashlight, and somehow, I make it up the stairs to the master bedroom. I find myself in sheer Heaven, under the owner's massive bedspread, before I can register having lain down.

"Ang," I whisper to the darkened room. But he's already gone.

What was I going to say? There's so much Ang and I need to sort out. I hope to have some clarity in the fresh promise of tomorrow. Maybe then, all of this (any of this) will make sense. And while I'm wishing for impossible things, why not poof the existence of Vesta away?

If only.

* * *

"Rainbow." I know that voice. I feel his weight on the bed by my side. "You're so beautiful, baby girl. When did you get so big?"

"Dad?" I ask, blinking and sitting up. He is here—the ghostly conjuring of my alien father. I reach out to touch him, but he flinches.

"Not yet." He stands and crosses to the window. "It's not safe."

"Is it really you?"

"You're not crazy, Chicken. Well, maybe a little. After all, you're my daughter." He smiles, and it's the only sight I've ever wanted to see. Why, even now, do I forgive him for splitting?

"You left us," I accuse him. Over the years, he's manifested in dimly lit shadows. I didn't have the gall to pretend my visions of him were real; for all I figured, he was just another figment of my overactive imagination. But after all I've been through, I've nothing left to lose. I'm going to squeeze the truth out of him—whether he's actually my long-lost dad or just a phantom of my subconscious.

"Rain, I don't have much time."

"Of course not," I say with arms deliberately crossed on top of the blanket. The natural pre-dawn tinges of lighter gray beckons the dawn. Dad takes a quick peek over his ghostly shoulder, as if scanning for some intruder.

"When I left you and your mother—" He stops, choking on his

words, and changes direction mid-thought. "You aren't at home. Where is she?"

I open my mouth to blurt that she's dead, but something stops me. His eyes, so hopeful in despair, beg of me to tell him false. If I deliver the truth, it will end this surreal hallucination. I don't know how I know it, but I do. The revelation might also end him.

"We're okay." I'm a liar. There are worse things I could be. "We had to leave Scarborough in a hurry. It's a long story." At least that last part is accurate.

"You have to keep her safe, Rain. A war is coming."

"War?" I leap out of bed to face him. I won't make the mistake of getting too close, not after the cold shoulder he's previously given. "What are you talking about, *war*? There's an asteroid on its way, Dad. Wherever you are, maybe you didn't get the memo. Our days are numbered here. We're down to—" I try to do the countdown math but I've completely forgotten what day it is. "A little over three months now."

"Don't worry about that," he says, unbelievably. He kneels before me with his big eyes and holds out his hands. I want, more than anything, to forgive him. To hold him. To be held *by* him. For him to tell me everything is going to be all right. It's all just a terrible, lucid dream.

If this is a dream, it's breaking up. The man posing as my once upon a time father fades and flickers in the morning light.

"Vesta... smokescreen... the Volcrex poisoned minds... they annihilate without prejudice... take no human prisoners... Ra—"

"Volcrex?" I shake my head. The name, as ridiculous as it sounds, menaces with seething familiarity.

My alien father is somewhere out there in the great beyond, calling out to the void in-between us, shouting desperately, but is muted.

"Where are you? Dad?"

"They want the Earth!"

His image jumps into the light, then vanishes.

"Dad?"

"...Elderry!" The empty room echoes his last utterance from light years or galaxies away.

Did I hear him right? Were his final words directing me to the pond that's literally right behind the barn?

Alone, once again, I ponder the meanderings of my wavering psychosis.

After allowing myself a moment to breathe, stew, and contemplate, I go to the mirror. The glass must be composed of a magical entity from a fairytale world. Because the vision reflected is not me.

My usually ratty, dark brown hair is much lighter and straight. Did Connie give me a makeover in my sleep? Surely I would have woken at the pulling and scrimping on my scalp. Even if she'd given my mop top a solid comb-out (Ang never would have dared!), Connie couldn't have re-aligned my eyes. Those eyes I've always thought were too far apart are closer now. I'm not making this up. I run the index finger and middle finger of my left hand across my brows. They are pristine and gorgeous, curved majestically in the right places, daring to define glamor at their outer edges.

I must be dreaming still. I shake my head and slap my face a little to give myself a jolt awake. Where I've struck cheek there is something else. Or rather, the absence of a thing—my upside-down anvil-shaped burn scar is gone.

I stand tall before this perfected self-image—vain, but proud. The silver streak of hair I've always fantasized I might own falls to dangle and bounce in a perfect spiral before my eyes.

"Wake up, Rain. Wake! Up!" I pinch my taut arm skin and yelp, but I'm still here, indisputably more attractive than ever.

I blink, and my new eyes blink back. Suddenly, Ang, having heard my freakish yelp, comes charging into the room, guns in hand and ready for a fight with some unknown deviant.

"You're alone?" he asks, perplexed. "It sounded like someone was attacking you." He rushes to the window, looks out, and spotting no criminal climbing down the side wall, he turns, relieved for all of two seconds before spying the new me.

"Rain?" he asks, approaching slowly. "Is that you?"

"Yeah," I say, uncertain myself. "I guess I got my beauty sleep."

He comes closer, takes an unhurried stare-glare up and down my body. "What? How?" he stutters, unable to comprehend the incomprehensible.

"I've changed," is all I can muster. For whatever reason, I do a little twirl, just as the open window blows a breeze through my silken, silver-struck hair. "Do you like it?"

"No—" He brushes my cheek with his hand, and I let him. I'm more stunned by his unappreciative remark than his forward gesture. "I mean, yeah. You're beautiful, but—"

"Okay, so we're in agreement, then. It's an improvement."

"It's not you, Rain."

"Of course it's me," I tell him. The heat beneath my skin rises to my cheeks, and I hear my mouth saying things I don't actually believe. "The ugly duckling's turned into a swan."

"Where is this coming from? You were never ugly, Rain. Don't put on reverse airs." He lowers his eyes to the floor momentarily. When he raises them again, I see in them he's hoping I've changed back to Rain 1.0. Even if I could backpedal the alien magic (is that what this is?), I wouldn't dare. I'm going to give my new features a test run first.

"The aliens—they gave me something," I say, incredulous as to what it could be. If they *were* Volcrex, and if the Volcrex are sinister beings (as the Dad phantom seemed to be insinuating), why would they give me anything? "They've made me *more*. And not just this pretty face. I feel like I could do the impossible."

"Like what? Fly?" Ang turns in a huff. Whatever newfound powers I may have inherited may convince him of what he did not see.

"I saw my dad. I don't know if it was a dream or... some other reality, or this one. But I know it was him."

"Where? Was he with my mom?" Ang blows off that I might be three words shy of being a raving lunatic.

"No, he—" In the time it takes for me to gauge the seriousness of his previous statement, Connie enters the room, drops a half-eaten jar of kidney beans, and swallows what's left in her mouth, to make room for the gasps.

"Rain?"

Rather than go through the whole thing again, I brush past them and race down the stairs, out into the morning light. I want to be alone to sort through my thoughts, my new body, and my feelings. No doubt I've got a lot of them.

Chapter Eighteen

I sit on the bank of Elderry Pond, searching for any sign of fish. If they're smart enough to seek sustenance at the muddy edges while we're away, they've also developed some sixth sense that tells them when we're here. And even though I've no intent to pluck the little fishies from their watery homes this morning, they continue to keep their fair distance.

If the aliens can give me the power to change my appearance (for whatever grander purpose that couldn't possibly include egotistic vanity), then surely they can give the fish in the pond a bit more instinct. Maybe I got some of that, too?

My reflection shows the same gorgeous me. If this had happened four months ago, I'd be giving Connie a run for Prom Queen. Dang.

Not that that sort of thing has ever mattered to you.

No, but pretty things are nice to look at.

Though the pond's unsteady surface makes my cheekbones' chiseled-to-perfection contours wavy, the essence of my beauty is undeniable. It's my superimposed self-image I should deny.

The act of changing my physical description was my doing. It must have been. If the aliens gave me the ability to do it, they certainly didn't force my hand. Though I'm skeptical about how I wielded the alien voodoo, I know it was me. It's what I've always secretly wanted—to be good looking. And I kinda hate myself for it.

A dose of nausea hits me, and I keel over into the mud. This is not who I am. I'm stronger than this. Whoever said that *beauty is in the eye of the beholder* was probably correct; but screw that guy! And yeah, it was most assuredly some over-privileged white male who coined the phrase. The problem with his statement is that *everyone* is a beholder. And *everyone*, if you think about it, is just a sneaky word for society.

Have I always been this shallow, Elderry? Or has the recent addition of Connie Blackburn unwittingly turned me this way?

I'm projecting. Flawed as Connie might be, this is not her fault. I'm my own girl; I need to take ownership of who I am. Of me.

A fish jumps, breaking the surface. It is within casting distance. If I had my pole, I doubt I'd catch him. When he lands, the ripple effect of his tiny splash extends all the way to my feet. I let the disturbance wash over me, and decide to stop being so pigheaded. I never actually thought I was ugly. Well, maybe when I was young. But what little girl (and maybe boys feel this, too?) doesn't have self-deprecating thoughts from time to time? Were my previously unrealized, low self-esteem issues telling me I wasn't pretty enough for my gay-as-a-three-dollar-bill-boyfriend? Dear Elderry, that might be a cut too deep.

Still, despite everything that's come to pass, I hope Craig's okay.

To hell with all of this. I don't need the self-imposed drama. I don't need this new skin.

My reflection changes in the fast fish's wake.

I'm me again.

I keep the silver streak in my hair, just because it brings me unadulterated happiness. That's not excessive narcissism, right?

Okay, now that all that nonsense is settled, what else can I do with my alien powers?

With my mind, I try to raise the fish from the watery depths... to no avail. I attempt to force my will upon the sky to bring down a showering rain... to no end. I cannot open a portal to another world, teleport to kingdom come, save my dad from whatever plane of existence he's currently on, communicate with the creatures who made first contact, or conjure a simple apple in my hand. Even the smallest of magics (that I might suppose) are beyond my nascent, alien-given abilities. But I can make unconscious spells that play on my bloated sense of beauty? How stupid.

Was none of it real? I retrace my steps.

My particular madness began while Ang was muttering on about how *his* dad told him to come here, to Melford. Just the thought of Ang's audacity forces me to compartmentalize my boiling rage. Apparently, I'm still not over my weird neighbor's withholding of that information.

Ang said his dad said he'd find allies "at the end of the world," here in Melford. It stands to reason that Ang thought the door in the fallout shelter was one way in to his mysterious allies' safe house. And maybe a way in to finding his mom.

My ID—should I be referring to Imaginary Dad as just *Dad* now? After our last meeting, he feels like more than just a fragmented phantom.—He said something about Vesta. That the asteroid was a smokescreen? And then he mentioned Elderry.

I stare blankly across the pond. Riddles rarely have more obvious answers than this. Wherever he was calling from, Dad seemed to be held against his will. By the Volcrex, maybe?

Soooo, if all of it's true, then we—Dad and I—are not Volcrex natives? How many alien species can there be?

An infinite amount.

I firmly believe in my heart of hearts, that I am some species of alien. Or at least, half-alien, anyway. The vote's still out on whatever Mom is—was.

Mom was an incredibly strong woman. I realize that now. She dealt with the loss of dad, the falling out with her closest friends (the Finnegans), yet still permitted me to be friendly with Ang.

I don't remember her as ever being in mourning, although she must have suffered when dad left. Despite that, she picked her head up and carried on. She raised me the best she could, gave me all the love she had. Then she lost her own mother somewhere along the way.

Whatever Grandma's misinformed perceptions of Mom, it took a coming asteroid to slap a temporary band-aid on their relationship. A coming asteroid that may not be our doom after all? That's impossible, Dad.

I look up, and I see Vesta clearly; she's making her steady course through our universe. But not according to you, Dad.

Smokescreen.

What, if anything, is real?

I miss my old life. I miss my family. I miss not having to wake up in a town where everyone murders each other daily. I even miss the banality of school. Heh, has it really come to that?

With regrets and unanswered questions by the thousands still swirling, I strip down to my underwear and bra, and I go for a soul searching dip in Elderry Pond.

I've always been a decent swimmer, but today, I feel stronger. I will take all credit for that. Forget the unconfirmed space magic. This too, is me.

It's not long before I reach the center of the pond. With a deep inhalation, I dive, just to see how far down I can go. When half a minute or so passes, I figure the pond's brown, dreary bottom can't be much further. I pity the average human for their pain receptors. I've heard drowning is one of the most painful ways a person can die. If that is what's to occur here, I won't feel a thing.

It's been the curse of my life, since you asked. Imagine placing your hand in a fire to feel nothing. Or falling off the garage roof when you're five, breaking your leg, and relentlessly trying to stand and walk on it while Mom screams for you to stop, but you're just too stubborn to obey her. Sure, in theory, it sounds like a nifty thing to be impervious to pain. But when put into practice, a person can die from being oblivious to the body's warning signals.

Elderry Pond might very well be the death of me. I have yet to bring my absent pain's threshold to the breaking point. If I had, I wouldn't be here to tell you about any of this.

Will that last instant where my lungs suck in water be my first and last brush with physical pain? Sadly, there has been research done on an outlier group of CIPA patients who pushed themselves as far as they could go. The CIPA interviewees who survived their own stunts expressed their motivations as: willing to go to extremes so they could feel something, anything.

Nine times out of ten, those lost souls would perish at their zero hour. The ninety percent who do die don't report to the medical community on whether they suffered in their last moment.

As for the supposed scientific results published, who knows if those lucky subjects in the tenth percent survival camp were even telling the truth when asked questions of such a personal, intrusive nature. I read that study when it came out. I might have been the only person in Maine with a downloaded copy. Seventy-six percent of that surviving tenth of the sad, CIPA-inflicted described their near-death experiences similarly. "It hurt like a son of a bitch," was the general consensus.

I can see that. I have never experienced physical pain, but I can still see it. I pity my poor brothers and sisters who have so much emotional scarring from their lack of physical pain that they feel the need to resort to such measures. Some of them justify it as being "not suicidal," because (they insist) their intentions are not to "go all the way." But what about the other ninety percent who trip off that edge?

Perhaps the most important fact to come out of all of this is: I always thought I was the only one. The disease used to be so astronomically rare. But in the past twenty years, the numbers of diagnosed babies has grown, almost astronomically compared to near-zero. Yet I never could find an online community. My guess is we're all just incredibly shy. I certainly never want to talk about it.

The prescient fish swarm to encircle me and my selfish thoughts. They come near, but not near enough for me to grab one. Not that I would. I'm embracing an adventure here; I have no desire to kill anyone today, fish nor foul nor least of all myself, thank you very much.

One of the fish-eyed creatures exudes a solid white glow with his thousand-yard stare. He snuggles up next to me as I continue my descent, lighting my path, all the way down. My rational mind wonders if any of this is actually happening. So I kick my rational mind right in the nuts.

All of it and everything. It's all real, Rain. And you're a major part of it.

My lungs have had enough, and my brain's spouting nonsensical ID madness again. Intelligent, incandescent, ichtyfish or not, I must retreat before I test the absolute lengths of my crippling disease. I make a move to reverse my motion, but my shining, silver-tailed companion shakes his head, eyeing downward.

I look again. And there is the blessed bottom of Elderry Pond! Written in huge, unmovable, impossible letters cut from the muck of the Earth are six ludicrous words strung together to form a nightmare:

"Abandon all humanity, ye who enter here."

Rather than question the nature of my sanity for the billionth time today, I flip my body around, plant my feet firmly on the 'y' in 'ye,' and push off, kicking like a cocaine mule who's accidentally sniffed her own powder. Just before my lungs pop and my heart explodes, I break the surface of the water, free of the death zone, and breathe the pure, sweet air of Melford, Indiana.

My friend, the fish with the well-lit eyes, surfaces nearby. He flips his double-pronged (or is that a solo prong?) tail and dives back down. I can only assume he's rushing to report my upsetting failure to his super-intelligent fishy friends.

Ang stands at the pond's lip, surprised to spot my emerging. For a moment, I share in his astonishment. I am beside myself with buoyant emotion.

Ang came for me.

I would shout his name, but something resembling a vine just snagged me from below. And back down I go. No amount of a will to live will save me this time. Nor, come to think of it, did I have the luxury of gasping pleasure from one final breath.

The daunting (to say the absolute least) message glows below, as I slide by, carried precariously toward death, and maybe Hell.

Abandon all humanity, ye who enter here.

The rot of my current problem is Elderry's roots—their unyielding snarl is inescapable. Strangely (perhaps strangest of all), I no longer have the desperate urge to draw breath.

I am dragged to an underwater cave of sorts where a sizable, cavernous shield of a door closes fast behind me. The pond in this non-space immediately drains, and the entangling vine—my shackler—retreats.

I am alone, sopping wet on dry, impossible land, for no more than a minute when light floods the cavern. I spy no electric poles or wiring, but I imagine they could be underground. Beyond that, there are no bulbs or artificial light sources on the stalactite-filled ceiling.

It's because this light is alien-made.

The walls must be moving, because I am not. They float on a layer of thin, light wisps of air and dissipate into a quintessentially devout brightness.

"What—" is the only word that makes sense in this non-linear moment. A silver robe, just my size, hangs on a hook on a nearby wall. Against my better judgement, I put it on.

I imagine I am still sound asleep in my stolen bed inside the farmhouse. I shut my eyes and open them.

There is a new presence here, at my side. I figure it must be Ang. But I know it is not. Because I'm definitely not asleep in that bed anymore. And none of this is a dream.

This is all too real.

"You are not dead, and you are not crazy. You are not dreaming, and you are not who you were." The comforting character who is both directly next to me and distant (and also as a whisper of purple smoke in my brain), speaks in more of a lighthearted tone than I can appreciate, given the extraterrestrial circumstances of this ordeal. Though she hides her true face, I can sense she is glad I've come. But does she know I was dragged here against my will?

Who are you kidding? She sent the prickly swamp vine after you.

My thoughts are my own. My ID has been silenced. I'm on some other plane. I belong to a grander existence.

"Where have you taken me?" It seems like the most obvious question. There are others—oh so many others—that will have to wait.

"Here we are," she says. And I realize we've been moving toward this strange place for some time. We now stand in the center of a rotunda-shaped hub. I cannot discern if she is moving her mouth because—and there's no other way to explain this—I can't quite be certain if she has one.

The hustle and bustle of dozens of alien lifeforms whizz past. They are heading in and out of side-tunnels. There must be two dozen or more cutting into the circular walls of this place.

"How... How did we get here?" I ask. Whether I move my mouth is also an unknown. For all I figure, we could both be speaking telepathically. Or I could be screaming.

"It's a bit like Grand Central Terminal, I agree," she says, reading one of a bajillion thoughts plastered on my face. "But what works, works."

I recognize that none of these busy beaver aliens rushing by have the slightest interest in me. They bust so hard just to get to where they're going that anything (or anyone) standing directly in their path gets a whisk-by glance at best. Some of these fast-moving creatures—the ones who aren't lanky and gray, naked, genital-less, and otherwise pretty much exactly as Mr. Finnegan described—look like ordinary people. In fact, some of them could probably easily pass as human.

Maybe some of them are.

"My name is Jova, Rain. Come." She flits her seventy percent human hand/thirty percent baby walrus flipper in a way that can not be ignored, and I follow her into the ecosystem. Bumping and prodding my way through, I recall Ang's face once again as he was standing at Elderry's edge, witnessing as I was tugged violently back down. He did see me, right? Did he jump in and swim out to rescue me? Oh no, did Ang drown?

There's nothing I can do about his fate now. I'll have to go with whatever this is for a while. Then I can begin to formulate an escape.

Jova leads me far and wide, through many corridors and corrals. I'll never find my way out of here on my own. Even if I could, the entrance to the cave came crashing down, sealing me in.

You're not a prisoner here.

That stops me. Because clearly I am.

"I'm—I'm—" What am I? Anyone special?

"You are an Aura. You are one of us. All will be well. You'll see." That time she definitely moved the mouth she barely has.

The hall darkens, and an unwelcome jolt strikes me in the gut.

What if I never see the sky again?

I journey three hundred and sixty degrees approximately two hundred and twenty times. When I'm significantly dizzy and visibly lost, we stop.

And here I am, once again. All alone in my childhood bedroom.

Chapter Nineteen

It's been days and/or nights. Who the hell knows anymore. They're studying me, that's for sure. Jova tries to reassure me from time to time. I'm positive now that she communicates by some form of telepathy.

No matter how long they keep me here in the comforts of my own pretend home, I'm not buying any of it. The room is a near-perfect facsimile of mine. Just "near-perfect" because there's a slight graying on the outer edges and corners of the scene.

And despite Jova's voiceover through unseen speakers stating that I'm not dead, I sometimes wonder.

Since I've been chilling here in my fake bedroom, I've slept with the perfectly crumpled Somara-Somara sheets and finely crumped red wool blanket I love so well.

I've heard, "Rain, come down for dinner!" no less than three, possibly thirty, times. All in the same perfect pitch and pitch perfect cadence. The only explanation other than the implausible—that the aliens have trapped me in a memory—is that this is either Heaven or Hell or... somewhere in-between.

Abandon ye! Accept this. Accept this.

If only I could accept, except I'm stuck in a state of emotional paralysis. I can't fully appreciate the depths of this delusion. This is my memory. This is my bedroom. Two years ago (maybe three?), I kept it this way.

And Mom's alive and calling.

But I'm not buying it. Not until "somebody explains what I'm DOING HERE!" The triumphant return of my voice works as a boost to launch me upright at the edge of my bed.

The doorknob turns, and in comes Mom.

"What are you screaming in here for?" she asks, half-concerned. I'm unharmed and in one piece, that's what matters first and foremost. She stares, even comes to me, but I don't answer. Because this part never happened. This is not a memory after all. This is new.

"You're not her," I say, fighting back the take-no-prisoners tears. "Unless I really am dead?" I didn't want to believe it. Not until now. But what other explanation can there be? And hey, if it's true, I never suffered a microbe of pain.

Why would an alien race dwelling beneath a small pond in Nowhereville, Indiana want to play these twisted mind games with little ol' me?

Because you're one of them. You're Aura. They're only testing you.

"Don't talk about death, Rain. You know I hate it when you go dark." That's what Mom calls my somber moments. Dark. If that's *not* a Heavenly version of Mom, then Jova's dug way deep into my subconscious to mine that jagged diamond.

"If you don't want me to believe I'm dead," I say, looking sorely into this holographic Mom's eyes. "Then why mess with me?"

She smiles awkwardly in a way I've never seen her do, flickers, and is gone. The similarities between her anticlimactic exit and ID's are not subtle.

"Jova," I speak to the now-empty room. "Don't be unfair. I accept it. I've moved on."

I have always shied away from speaking to a person's softer side. If it translates to beseech an alien's better half, maybe I'll get somewhere. No doubt the crack research team analyzing my thoughts and reactions to every little thing must know I'm lying. How could anyone ever move on from what I've suffered?

Jova stands before me. Her random, instant materializations are quickly becoming annoying.

"You will always be tested," she says, floating across the room, an inch over my carpet. "Because you were human before you were Aura. Every day from here to the end of all worlds will be a test."

Jova looks out my window. I follow her gaze to see something moving in the grass outside. It is Ang, running straight for the house.

"Rain!" he calls as he reaches the window. Jova just stands there, her face an unreadable, blank canvas, as my neighbor and self-described, quasi-protector knocks heavily and uncouth on the windowpane. Without meaning to, he smashes with all enthusiasm and fear. Glass shards drop in and shatter on the floor beneath Jova's pale, shadowy silver, feet-like feet. She doesn't move an inch because the hologram can't hurt her. I wonder, could actual glass do the trick? Does anything cause the Aura pain?

"Rain," Ang says again, grabbing hold of me. I'm not convinced—not in the slightest—that he's real. "Where are we? What is this? Are you okay?"

"It's an apocalyptic alien bunker," I tell him, sort of distantly, as if not accepting my own words. As I speak, I try my best to humor both Ang and Jova. I wouldn't want either to think my concern for him isn't real. "They have a loose hold on my perceptions, my entire reality. Where are you?"

Though he's standing in front of me, holding my hands in his, I refuse to acknowledge any of this. At my core, where my most logical levels of reason dwell, I know everything here is a facade, and Ang won't be able to see it. Because he's as much a mirage as my Mom.

"They are testing me," I tell him, pointing. "She is."

Ang turns, sees whatever he sees, and recoils in horror, shrieking. He knocks me down as he barrels, screaming to my bed. He's slunk back tight against the headboard, hollering and squelching something awful. God, he's practically clawing at the wall.

"Stop it!" I yell to Jova. If I must bear witness to that horror for one second more, I will explode into more pointy shards than those at her toeless feet.

Thankfully, she pulls back whatever terrifying image she's projected for Ang, and he settles into a quiet, embarrassed mold of his former self.

"You are wondering what's real," Jova speaks without moving her thinnest of thin lips. If she had them before... did she? It's possible I've miscalculated her face. Or failed to mention those long, oblong eyes—how pretty though they glow so incessantly white.

"What are you going do with us?" I ask, not really sure if I want an answer. But before she can respond (if she was going to respond), Ang leaps from the bed and makes it halfway across the room where he freezes, mid-air. In his right hand, he clutches a bowie knife. It's one I've never seen. Had he hid it in the folds of his clothes?

Wait, is this really Ang?

"Unfortunate." Jova shakes her head in disapproval. With a slight wave of her hand, Ang's jagged blade jumps from his grasp. It flies through the air, right at her. Jova casually leans, and the weapon skims past her, directly out my broken window. I follow the knife as it flips off into the phony world outside.

"Can you manipulate everything?"

"In time, you will come to understand." She blinks, and an unfrozen Ang crashes to the floor. Half aware of my lunges, I'm beside him, helping him up. Whether all of this is a figment of my overwrought imagination or I'm in some ceaseless Purgatory, I don't care. He's still the only friend I've got these days, real or not.

"You may say your goodbyes," Jova says. "Make it quick."

"What?" Ang asks.

"We have other plans for you, Angus Finnegan." Jova took a beat before pronouncing his name, as if the mere sound of it was a vile thing to utter.

"I won't leave her." Ang stands tall. Does he not realize he'll have no say in the matter? Jova sighs, leaving me to wonder how many alien emotions are similar to our own.

"In time, you will understand," she reiterates her intentionally cryptic bull. She's so cold the temperature in my faux room plummets. Ang stiffens. His blood rushes from his face. He turns to a statue in a heartbeat. And then he is gone.

Jova, my cruel, alien tour guide looms over me. She's transported herself from across the room to where I am—to where Ang just was. To where I might just attempt to kill her standing.

"You are Aura, former Earth child." She puts on a soothing voice in a calm, motherly tone. But it's as if she's an AI recording of what a soothing, motherly voice should be. In other words, Jova's putting on a show. But for what purpose? What am I to them? "You know so little. You rage so much."

"You don't know me." My eyes spit fire at her. Oh, if only.

Jova lingers, perhaps weighing her next words. "Your job—your only job in here is to abandon your humanity. Leave off the part of you that is of this world and unlock the true *you* from beyond."

I have to laugh. In the face of all this redundancy, she doesn't seem to have a coherent idea what to do with me.

She's biding your time.

"You are unique," Jova continues. "With one touch from me, you've already changed your appearance."

"And changed back," I say. Jova doesn't argue the finer points, though she glances at my hair's silver streak, then seems to admire my humble, persistent scar.

"You are a mixed breed."

"I am human," I say, instinctively. "I'll never abandon that."

"Perhaps." She sighs again, this time more audibly, as if to overexaggerate. "But you did read our sign."

* * *

I blink, and I'm in a four-walled, padded cell with no apparent doors. This I can recall: I am a prisoner of an alien species called Aura. They claim I am one of them. Or "part" Aura, anyway. This seems to be of great importance and interest.

I've only met and communicated with Jova. She hides her compassion in the shadows of her ever-looming scientific curiosities. I sense she would be friendly in other, not-so-dire circumstances. But she's fascinated by my very existence and doesn't bother to conceal it.

The room (if you can call it such) is lit by that same starglow fluorescence I first encountered in the shining rotunda. If I were a betting girl, I'd say this is the same space as my faux bedroom, only shaved down to the non-essentials. I'd guess that this barest of containers, with the fine-cushioned white walls, is the "base" cell. Likely, they have the ability to manipulate the space into any shape, location, or monster's domain. Or maybe they're just super good at holograms.

I find no comfort in these thoughts. At least they had the courtesy of keeping my arms free of a straitjacket.

Maybe you're actually in one?

The last thing I remember... Ang. He was there in my not-my-bedroom. And it *was* him. I know it was him. And they took him. They've taken us both. We are Aura prisoners.

"Rain, are you coming down for dinner?"

No, Mom.

Her persistence knows no bounds. She shatters her previous record of three, penetrating my real, cubed holding cell.

"Everything a test," I say for the benefit of my silent watchers. "Fine. What's the worst that can happen?"

My bedroom door materializes. I have no second thoughts and turn the loose doorknob. It wiggles in my palm. For the longest time, Mom and I were at odds over who should fix the thing. It was a simple job, or so she claimed, but it was the principal that mattered. I can't remember exactly what my side of the argument was, but she was trying to teach me how to be a woman. I think. A woman who could be independent against all odds. A woman who could screw in a doorknob.

In retrospect, I realize how utterly stupid that is. Mom was as stubborn as me. In the end, I bore her down with my nonchalance. She tightened some simple screws and washed her hands of it. The last I'd left my actual room sixteen or nineteen days ago, this knob was still as tight as the day Mom fixed it.

This memory is at least two years old, then. Closer to three.

Following that brief and light realization blur, my muscles carry me out and into the hall. The whiteness of the blank storage space behind me fades, as does my thinly veiled bedroom door.

I've decided, albeit somewhat begrudgingly, to go along with this rouse, this farce!... at least for a while. Reliving this tinged rehashing of a time gone by, I will do my best to keep my emotions in check. Because that's what she wants to see—Jova and the rest of them. They want to break my humanity.

What's the worst that could happen if I play their stupid game better? I might feel a little sad about a time gone by? Since this whole end-of-the-world scenario started, it's safe to say I've been in a constant state of depression. I'm pretty sure that's how everyone everywhere feels all the time.

If anyone anywhere is still alive.

Entering my fake kitchen is like stepping into a dreamy past. I can't imagine what emotion or reaction Jova's attempting to elicit. I just have to keep reminding myself: none of this is real.

Ang was.

"You look tired, Rain. What's the matter?"

"Nothing," I hear myself tell my mother, though I haven't spoken. My voice, as if I was a ventriloquist's doll without a ventriloquist, came from a blind spot behind me. I turn and see I am there, sitting at the opposite end of our kitchen table, pushing some sorry-looking peas from one side of my plate to another.

"Mom?" I ask. But she can't hear me—not the real me, not the me I am now. Having assumed I would be an active participant in each charade has, perhaps, emboldened me to go through the motions. But the aliens won't allow me the luxury of being an active participant in my own life—not this time. The best I can hope for is to watch my former self play this scene out. There's nothing special about this, not that I can see. Just another night home, eating Mom's meatloaf in brooding silence.

"What's wrong with you?" I ask myself. The me of at least two and a half years' ago (given the pinpoint accuracy of the loose doorknob coupled with the general state of the place) stares fixedly at her food. She's giving Mom nothing, as I was wont do back then. I despise this version of the me I once was.

"You don't approve of this version of you. Do you?" Jova's voice, low and monotone, is piped in from above. The scene freezes with Mom standing there by the sink, plate and sponge in hand, mid-scrub. Even the water dripping from the faucet is stuck in some strange, miraculous pause. It is the strangest sensation to behold—watching your life just stop.

"I don't understand why you're showing me this." I imagine a group of alien scientists behind a one-way, see-through wall, taking vigilant notes on every move, word, or facial cue I make. If they are there, they remain silent, allowing Jova to lead the dumb show.

"It's *your* memory," Jova says. "Whether you acknowledge this common moment, it is there, in your mind."

"I was a jerk. I didn't appreciate her," I say, figuring she might want a brief insight. "You want me to shed my remorse? I can't do that."

There is a moment of silence punctuated by a flickering of images that are reminiscent of dear ol' Imaginary (*Real*) Dad. Do they know about our ghostlike communications? Do they know *everything*?

"We don't care about your feelings," Jova says. "Emotions are the weaker side of humanity's attributes." Her voice lilts at the end of each sentence, as if she doesn't believe her own sentiment. It's a hardly noticeable flaw in her sea of confidence. She appears, as if from a pop, right in front of me, blocking the drastically faded image of my dead mother.

"What are you hiding?" I dare to ask. Enough with the Little Miss Nervous routine. This alien may know me better than I know myself. She can see right through my veneers. But maybe I've got an extra little something inside that I haven't yet tapped into. "I've figured you out, you know. Whatever you've pulled out of me—these memories and visions—they aren't yours to manipulate. You're sadists. That's what you are. Do you have a word for that in your language? Or is that just what *Volcrex* means?"

Someone found her angry pants.

Unfazed and unflinching by my knowledge of their alien arch enemy, Jova leans to her right. When she does, Mom explodes into a bloody, carcassy mess behind her. Unable to help a reaction this time, I slam my eyes shut and turn away.

"Sadist is one word you may call them, if you like," Jova toys with me. "But the word *Volcrex* has no meaning. It has no life, no feeling, no soul. Volcrex is our eternal enemy. Volcrex is our reason to hate and be suspicious. These are two qualities we have in kind with your kind."

"You should brand all that on a tee shirt," I say, then dare another look at the world these aliens have showed me. Thankfully, Mom's bloodied mess of a body is gone. There's just my padded, no-windows, no-doors cell again. At this point in my evolution, I'm prepared to just live and die here, if that turns out to be the case. Today, tomorrow, Vesta Day. Whenever. So be it.

"We've analyzed your blood and—"

"My blood?"

"You are one hundred percent an anomaly. Your Aura to human ratio is split, practically down the middle."

"What does that mean? When did you take my blood?"

"All our one thousand, three hundred, thirty-nine tests are inconclusive. They do agree that you are a definitive member of both species. But the split is too close to fifty percent to be accurate."

Jove wouldn't lie. Not about this. I know we've just met and all—how long ago was that?—but I guarantee she takes that pure alien lineage stuff pretty seriously. She wants me more Aura than human, but they can't decide a consensus on which way my blood swings.

"Whatever I am, it doesn't much matter, does it? Maybe you haven't heard—being down here in the underworld—Earth is going to be annihilated. I don't know when you got here Jove... can I call you Jove?" She doesn't move a muscle, if she has muscles. Gauging her lack of reaction closely, I do my best not to cringe at my own, sudden character shift. I've never actually been this tough. "You picked the wrong planet to set up shop."

Now she smiles. Or at least, I perceive that her leathery, grayish-green face has crinkled upward, in a semi-amused manner. She leans in and whispers, "Who was it, might you suppose, that threw the rock?"

What was it ID said? He'd called Vesta a "smokescreen."

"Why?"

"If you're lucky and productive," Jova says, continuing her pattern of ignoring my questions, "we'll let you out for Armageddon. It's coming, and sooner than you might think."

"When—" At last, I'm on the cusp of sorting some minor detail. "When you took my blood. That was... so long ago."

"You are beginning to experience time as an Aura," Jova explains. "In the past, you may have misplaced large blocks of time. That is natural. It is a sign of Aura maturation."

"The months lost after Mom's death," I say. The words come out as if I'm far off, on a mountaintop.

"You are becoming," she tells me. "You will be fully Aura some day."

Jova lightly taps my forehead with her long, freaky finger, and I do not flinch. In fact, I welcome whatever new gift she might bestow.

I wobble. Because oh, she's drugged me. No alien magic here.

"Sleep will pass the loss of time."

The last thought I have, as Jova winks out of my conscious existence is:

Forget Volcrex. It's you who are the sadist.

Chapter Twenty

Most days, they leave me alone.

My best guess: we're in early August. If you held my confiscated alien blaster to my head, I'd say today is the fifth. My life (all our lives) is ticking by, and I'm stuck wasting far too many terminal breaths underground. I am trapped like a fly in the proverbial alien ointment. 'Til Vesta do we part.

It's a smokescreen.

I've had plenty of time to consider (and reconsider and reconsider) ID's words, as well as Jova's. Neither of whom have visited me in this white room, this physical carnation of my doldrums. I am not naïve enough to believe they aren't watching me, though. And I wonder at the sheer numbers of the Aura who are actually down here. In the entry rotunda, there were dozens—too many to count—passing through to get to wherever it was they were going.

Where were *they going?*

Nothing I cling to can form the perfect puzzle. There are too many pieces missing. The ones I do hold are misshapen, out of whack, or inverted.

At this point in my prelude-to-doomsday adventure, I couldn't care less about what the overall meaning (if any) of this might be. When Vesta comes, I only hope I get to view the obliteration with my own eyes. Jova gave me that pitiful hope, anyway. Maybe I can fake it 'til I make it... until the end.

I never would have guessed I'd spend the end of my life locked away in an alien cell. Having done a similar disservice to myself, after Mom and Grandma died, I've perfected the art of enclosure. My self-prescribed (and apparently, unavoidable) time lost in my basement is likely the experience responsible for keeping me sane here.

Now and then, my captors change the scenery inside these four miserable walls, just to screw with me. My favorite so far was the one where I was floating in outer space. No helmet. No space suit. Just me and my bleached white prisoner's cloak they provided. Having no sense of the universe (*galaxy*) at large, I floated aimlessly amongst those phony stars and nebulas for hours, maybe days.

Have I slept? Have I eaten much? It's easier to answer the latter. When I'm hungry, the miracle machine forms this room into a three-dimensional dining area where they provide me with a homemade meal of my choice. They know my palate's particular preferences before I do.

In every experiment, where they choose to transport me is of my inner self's choosing. Whether I'm dipping my toes in the water at Old Orchard Beach or relaxing on our backyard hammock—

But we took that hammock down after you fell out of it. You were only an infant then, Rain. I'm surprised you remember it.

I remember every lazy swing, Dad.

"She's phasing out, latching on to the past." Jova speaks to unknown entities. She's somewhere in this room with me. Are they all? "Watch her closely. Her 'Then and Now' are compounding."

I can hear you, plain and clear, Jova. Do you know it? Are you speaking in Aura? Or is that English? I can't tell. Just don't take more blood. I may be faint of mind and spirit, but I am not lost. I know exactly who I am. My name is Rainbow, and I am one and a half years old.

With Mom at the bakery day in and day out, Dad and I mostly hang out in this sweltering August heat wave. Sure, he helps at the shop whenever she needs him. He does what he can—what is within his limits. When Mom first opened her shop, Dad was more of a central figure, helping wherever he could. He only peeled away when she hired what Dad called "proper help."

"Why are you so clear to me now, Daddy?" The first words I've spoken since God knows when come out scratchy and tasteless, like roughly used steel wool sponges.

My rational mind (if I still have one) tells me these images are ones I should not know. I was too young to remember this. Yet they are as vivid and accurate as if they are happening to me, then and now.

Are they?

"She has a strong footing in both times. She'll be all right."

She is me, and I hear you loud and clear, Jova. You can't hear me?

As the scene goes, instead of becoming an inactive participant in a faux room, I'm straight and narrowly focused, unearthing a happy moment that's been buried in so much detail.

I'm becoming what the Aura want me to be. They are changing my perspectives, illuminating me, sparking my alien self. But to what end? Don't they have more important things to do with the actual end of the world on the horizon? Shouldn't Jova and her kind peace out on their alien ships before it's too late?

Or maybe… maybe they can't leave. Maybe something is holding them back, or maybe their kind stranded them here.

"She will come to it in her own, found time," Jova says.

Our hammock settles from its first violent rockings when Dad and I got in. We swing gently, under our combined weight, with me in his protective arms, getting all cozy. All is right and well in the world. A songbird sings to another.

"You gonna talk today, Rainbow?" he asks. I dare the sun's glare by staring into it, wince away the brightest rays, and catch him smiling down at me.

"Yeah," I want to tell him. But I am a speechless toddler. "Today is an excellent day to talk."

"Never think me unreal," says Dad. The hammock cuts through the low air with purpose. Each time his dangling left foot scrapes the ground, he pushes off and sends us soaring. I can't talk, no. But I can coo. I can laugh and I can love and then some.

Behind his cheap pair of gas station-bought sunglasses, Dad's eyes well up with something very much like tears. He stares into the morning sun, perhaps dreaming of a place far, far away.

"If you want, I can take you to the stars, Rainbow. Just say the word, and we'll hop a ticket to Kotaria X in the Pynastic Domain. That's the furthest destination in the ship's database. You know, Kotaria X is known for its spectacle of sparkling, raging waterfalls."

We bathe in the gentle evening sunlight. Dad's chest rises and falls beneath my cheek. My tiny body grows sleepy.

"Ma," I say, and it's my first word.

"Yeah, and your mother too, of course. We should take her, too." Dad laughs, entirely oblivious to the milestone. Then, in a blink, his demeanor changes from playful to ashen. "She's not like you and me, Rainbow. Very few are. It wouldn't be easy to get her to come along."

Dad goes silent, and soon he falls asleep in the hot breeze. I doze for a minute or two. It's all my little frame can handle, being stuck to his sleeveless gray tee shirt by my baby sweat.

But that's not a tee shirt. It's his true, alien skin.

I pretend it's all a dream and try to think instead of fireflies and rockets.

"Ahhhhh!" I scream and pound my fist against the padded wall. Nothing changes until it does. A door materializes in the middle of my white room, and Jova walks through it. I give her nothing but the sound of my exasperated breaths. If she gets close enough, I might just rip her throat out with my teeth.

"Settle," she says in as soothing a telepathic voice as she can put on. "Come." Jova makes a motion for me to follow her through a door that's just appeared. But I am hesitant. I've been locked up in here for so long that the prospect of leaving actually frightens me. Whatever the date may be, Vesta is surely a prominent figure in the sky. Have humans killed each other off completely? We were certainly headed that way.

"Where's Angus?" I choke out. My only solace has been the thought of him surviving down here. Although, given what happened the last time I saw him, I've not deluded myself into thinking he might have escaped. He's in his own Aura-made prison somewhere down here in the bowels of Earth's crust.

"Your friends are safe," Jova says, reminding me (for the first time in a long time) of the existence of Connie Blackburn. "This is the only window you will have."

Something in her eyes confirms it: I'll never get an opportunity like this again. This version of Jova is not the same one who brought me here. She is kinder, truer, and putting herself in great danger to help me.

Or I'm in for yet another theatrical illusion.

Pending any further analysis of the situation, I follow Jova out of my prison. I don't waste a glance back over my shoulder. I've been in there long enough to know every inch of the cursed place. How they were able to continuously and seamlessly transform my surroundings is a question that will probably never be answered. If I can get away from the room of many facades with just a little life left to live, then I'll have to be content with the mystery.

For now anyway, I'm history.

* * *

We go swiftly through corridors and dark passages. Jova moves fast—too fast for me to keep up, let alone get a word in edgewise. She's gone rogue, and I can only guess at her motives.

I try (and fail) to form a reliable mind map of our journey. By the time I've got half of it sort of figured out, we've reached the familiar cavern I came in through. Jova stops short of the closed exit wall, apparently unwilling (or unable) to leave with me.

"Why are you doing this?" I pose to her. "You've always been so —" What's the word I'm looking for? "—scientifically callous in your approach. What's changed?"

"It is V-Day. I won't let them use you as they intend. Get as far away from here as possible."

"V-Day?" It's all I can do just to mutter Jova's unheard words back to her. Have we time traveled to the culmination of World War II?

"I am tired," Jova says, broadcasting her weakness plain. "If I don't retire to my chambers now, I won't be of use in the first battle."

"Battle?" I am a useless shell, a repetitive, mindless machine.

"System rebooting." The robotic voice suddenly echoing through the cavern is as ominous as it is confusing.

"Maximus." Jova's large pupils dilate as her slick and slender frame blocks a brightening red eye on a wall behind her. "You have approximately one minute before he sends the alert."

"Alert! Alert!" the robotic voice shatters Jova's prediction, calling to all who might listen. "Prisoner 1463H-H has escaped Cell Forty-Two. Scanning perimeters."

"Go!" She shoves me forward, and hastily I walk until the great, moss-covered wall begins to rise, pouring Elderry Pond over my feet and ankles. I turn back to see my captor-turned-surprising savior as she speeds off in the opposite direction.

"Wait! What about Angus?"

But she is gone, and I'm too late. A deluge fills the space as the large slab continues to rise. Almost immediately, I am up to my neck in Elderry.

In a lapse of self-preservation, I consider doggy paddling back into the Aura underground. If I do, I'll have no chance of ever escaping again. I know it in my gut. I know it like I know my own name. Like I know every line on my mother's face. Like I know that my father is actually my father. Like I know he is, in fact, of an alien species called Aura. Like I know the Aura are engaged in a perpetual war with the Volcrex. Like I know they want to use me as a weapon to their advantage. Like I know none of it will matter when this world ends, and today! Like I know none of it should matter to me. Not in the slightest.

But it all does.

"Scan complete," comes the robotic voice from the depths below. The one Jova called Maximus doesn't miss a beat. "Prisoner 1463H-H has been located in the Elderry Entrance. All available personnel to Elderry Entrance. Repeat, all available personnel—"

I don't stick around to await recapture. Shutting down all logic, I allow myself fully into the pond. I push outward, leaving the secretive Aura realm behind. I'd rather not indulge in what this specific action says of me—does it make me an unfeeling wench to have left Ang? Or is my selfishness just a result of my part-Aura nature now? Would I be more apt to go back if he hadn't been so sketchy in our last days above ground?

Nothing matters! Shut up and swim! Swim to the surface to meet Vesta! Embrace the world's end!

Smokescreen.

My head crests the top of the pond. All thoughts, concerns, questions, and loyalties are dead in the water as I stare down the promise of the apocalypse.

Sunlight strains to be seen on either side of the asteroid—she owns the entirety of our sky.

"Vesta," I speak her name. The end is so near, I can almost... just... reach out and touch it.

V-Day.

What is there to do anymore? Jova said to run. But to where? There is literally nowhere to go. There's no place on Earth I could hide. Why would she submit me to this ending?

My rational mind tells me to stop, but my feet won't listen. I run all the way to the barn and climb up into the hayloft. There's a hole in the thatched roof that wasn't there before.

This entire planet will be a hole soon.

At least I'll have a decent view from the top. I hoist myself up and climb through. From here, the sky is even darker, shadowed by the doomsday rock above.

The countdown is over. The Aura have robbed me of my last months on Earth. Could there have been something between Ang and I?

"Rain!" His phantom voice is a dagger in my heart.

He is no phantom.

Across the field, I can just make out his muscular frame as he shoots through the thick of dead stalks.

Surely, this is still only pretend. Either my exhausted mind's playing tricks on me in the light of Vesta's shadow, or else I'm still back in dreadful Cell Forty-Two, dancing to the beat of whatever snare the Aura are drumming.

"Rain!" Ang calls again, getting closer.

"Angus?" I dare speak his name, as if we could have a second chance to live.

I stand precariously on this rusty, old, creaky, cracked roof to get a better look. If my eyes are truly deceiving me, they're doing a wonderful job of it as Ang comes charging right up to our barn.

"Angus?" I say again, this time a little louder so the ghost of who he might be (or not be) can hear. No gray marks suggesting falsehood lie on the borders of my periphery. "Is this real?"

Leaning forward, I can almost accept the fate of falling. Were I to shatter every bone in my body below, it would be a fitting end to my pained, pain-free existence.

Oh, stop it! You were a happy girl in the before times.

I dare not recall any of the before times.

"Hold on! Don't move!" he says, then leaps so high he clears the lip of the barn roof to come down softly behind me. "Be careful. This whole thing could come apart with one wrong step."

"You—how did you—" That jump is easily twenty-five feet if it's an inch. Ang cleared it like a little kid skipping over a bored log.

"You're okay," he says, eyeing every bit of me. It's not a question, he just knows me.

"What time is it?" It's not that I have any faith in the scientists long-dead. But if their agreed upon countdown was close to the actual thing... "It must be almost 12:02."

Ang grins in a funny kind of way. Granted, any happiness on his face would seem out of place, but this reaction has a spark to it. "Time to go, Rain. We have to move."

Ang reaches to grab my hand, but I pull away, fighting to take my eye off of Vesta. She's the closest thing to Hell on Earth, and too perfect to deny.

"We're dead, Angus," I tell him. And Vesta is burning. "It's over."

"You're wrong. Look."

The weight and magnitude of one hundred thousand atomic explosions annihilate all existence. But I chickened out and blinked, missing it, and all of everything is gone.

No, it's not. Vesta is.

"Where'd she go?" I say, staring up at the heavy cumulus clouds that have reappeared in the sky. With the sun on full display behind them, it takes my eyes and my mind a moment to adjust to the new view.

Vesta is gone, and those big, puffy clouds don't stay fully formed for long. I watch with refreshed horror as they turn to wisps of white tendrils, and those curly, cottony twists become smoke.

"I don't—"

"Look." Ang holds my shoulder steady. With his other hand, he points beyond the deformed, chopped clouds. A fleet—no—a seemingly endless line of alien spaceships hovers on high. When I squint, I can see beyond that first row to many many more.

"Your dad was right," Ang says. "Vesta was a smokescreen. For Volcrex."

I turn from the dotted sky to see Ang's put on an expression I've never seen him wear. He appears to be inwardly rejoicing. It's almost as if he sees some ultimate good that might come out of this attack.

But is it an attack? Those ships are just sitting there.

"They want the Earth," Ang says, somewhere far away. I know I've heard that exact phrase before.

"They have it," I say. Because even if humans do still survive outside of rural Maine and Melford, Indiana, we are easily defeated. We've seen that much.

That Vesta isn't actually real is going to take me a minute, though—a minute I don't think we have.

What's going to happen when those ships descend? The Volcrex are going to beam down (or walk, or whatever it is they do) and clean up any shred of humanity left, starting with us.

I won't run anymore.

"How did you get out?"

"They let me go," he says, sounding familiar. "They let me come to you."

Ang's complex, hidden-agenda is infuriating. How did he make that incredible leap? Is he—?

He's always been kind of alien, I suppose. In his unique way. His entire life, Ang's exuded an out-of-this-world-kinda outsider vibe.

"You're Aura, too." It is not a question. There's no other explanation.

"Close," Ang turns to me, away from the hypnotizing space army that hasn't moved an inch from their possibly-attack formation. "Apparently, I'm with them." He reverse nods toward our unwelcome visitors.

"You're Volcrex." I didn't want to say it out loud. But I felt the obligation to do so. It's as if the words, when spoken, make the possibility real. "Is that what the Aura told you? Then why let you go?"

"It makes sense in a one-trillion-quintillion-to-one sort of way that the galaxy's longest rivals would come together in the form of, well, us. You and me."

Romeo and Juliet, I think but do not say. There's no need to bring ridiculous comparisons into our muddled mix. Plus, those two chowderheads die.

"We're supposed to be enemies," he admits, thickening the conversational quicksand. "But they made us neighbors. They made us close."

"They took our parents from us," I say. If I doubted Ang's allegiance before, it shines in his eyes here and now.

"Never underestimate my loyalties." The bastard winks at me. With the dawn of a new oblivion rising, he has shown: *We are one.*

Chapter Twenty-One

The looming spaceships fill the entirety of our atmosphere. They hold there for the whole of the afternoon, giving Ang and I some time to reevaluate the world's near-end and to become reacquainted.

Turns out, it *was* Ang who broke the window in my holographic house, not a doppelgänger facsimile. They'd locked him away for days prior to that, he explained. When the Aura released him of what Ang called his "cage," he flew the coop, only to find himself in our shared back yard.

"I was out of my mind when I saw you, Rain. I couldn't tell which end was up. I'm sorry I couldn't do anything for you then. I couldn't do a thing for either of us." He reflects. "They broke me down to build me up, suspecting early on I was Volcrex—"

If I shiver, it is from an unexpected chill, and not from Ang's insistence on also being of alien descent. I just don't have the brain capacity to hold more shockers. So, for now anyway, my flawed nervous system focuses on the weather. From my perspective, it was July like last week; this Melford cold has me a little turned over. The fact that it's mid-October is blowing my mind.

V-Day, noonish.

"They weren't looking for us, Rain. But you found them. We don't make sense to them, you and me. We're hybrids."

"What about Connie? What happened to her?" I ask, not expecting much in line of an answer. It's a stall tactic. Eventually I will have to engage with his half-Volcrex identity—what it means, and if we should even believe in it.

"I don't know where Connie wound up. But she must be some kind of mixed breed, too."

"Why do you say that?"

"Didn't they show you?"

"Show me what?" I don't want to know. Don't tell me.

"There's really no one left out there in the world. Vesta did what she set out to do. The human race has been extinguished. And they did it all by their—"

"Wait," I stop him. "They poisoned us. The Volcrex—your kind—destroyed people's minds."

"Says who? The Aura? Rain, they tortured me down there. What makes you think it wasn't the Aura who turned humans against each other? They're certainly capable of it. Maybe you got the royal treatment, being that you aren't their mortal enemy. But I wasn't so lucky. I don't believe a word or telepathic message any of them communicate."

"But they told you you're Volcrex? And you believe that? You can't just cherry-pick whatever narrative suits you on a given day, Angus. We're human. I am, anyway. My results were split, and I didn't get exact numbers. But I like to think I'm at least fifty-one percent human. And there's gotta be more of us out there. I refuse to believe everybody's gone. We have to carry on. For them."

"Nice speech," Ang says, deciding to be a jerk. It took but a slight shift for him to get there. "But nothing changes the fact that we're sitting ducks down here. Vesta was a smokescreen. You were right about that. But the Earth is in their hands now. Both the Aura and the Volcrex. Pick a side."

"You can't be serious."

He is.

"It's the only way we can survive."

Out in the open like this, where the dead stalks lie flat, rotted by time here at crisp fall's halfway point, the front line of alien ships can surely see us. Our low cover turned "no cover" doesn't seem to phase Ang. But I'm out here, too. So there's that.

"You should go," Ang says. "I honestly don't know what they'll do to you when they come."

"Or you!" I shoot back. And suddenly I'm too self-aware of my place at Ang's side. "What are they to you?"

"When the Aura touched me," Ang tells my story. "They awoke something inside of me. I've been waiting for it my whole life. You must have felt the same?"

"What I felt was an awakening." This I know.

"I don't think it matters, Aura or Volcrex, E.T. or Superman. They're the aliens, Rain. They're the enemy. All of them. Not us."

"So you're choosing Volcrex. The cowards who hid behind Vesta."

Dear, sweet, departed R&J, hold tight to love's lost breath.

"Let's not put a label on anyone just yet," Ang says. And dear God, that awkward twinkle in his eye is his ill-timed way of flirting with me again.

The lead ship moves. It creeps low in the sky—low enough to get a better look at us, or the Earth, or both maybe. My body wants to flinch and bolt, but my brain won't let it.

"You're braver than I thought, Roche. Keep that blind courage up and we might just get a quick death out of this after all."

"Is that supposed to be a compliment?"

"No, brave can also be code for stupid."

"Code *is* stupid, Stupid. And don't call me Roche."

A beam of bright yellow luminescence burns the western edge of the field, about fifty yards away. It's there, and then it is gone, and then the dead stalks rustle on the ground. A shadowy figure materializes there. From this distance, it appears to take the shape of a female, in human form, with silky, black hair.

Now I will run. Now is the time to run. Run, Rain! Run!

You survived the Aura. You lived to tell of the Vesta smokescreen. You can take this on, too.

My frightened imagination knows no bounds. I presuppose this alien woman approaching is biding her time. Any second now this imposter will shed her cloak of human skin and morph into a gigantic, hideous, thirty-two tentacled rock monster to rip us limb from limb.

The Volcrex emissary keeps her biped frame. As she gets closer, Ang loses all sense of logic and goes charging directly at her. This invader from above is about to meet my neighbor's ill-conceived wrath.

"Mom," I hear him say. His legs fail him and he crumples at the alien's feet. All reason and understanding, if we had any before, are gone.

They embrace: Ang and the long-gone Mrs. Finnegan. But it's a trick. Because space creatures are holographic wizards. Or at least, the Aura are. If our unlocked powers aren't a shining example of symmetry across species, perhaps this mother of illusions can be.

"Not real." I try to speak to Ang, in my head. I don't reach him. "She's not real!" I repeat aloud for those in the cheap seats. He lets his faux mom go, and she faces me, and smiles.

"Oh my gosh, how you've grown," Mrs. Finnegan says. An unassuming lilt in her voice is all it takes to send me back to a time of innocence. This woman played house with me when my mother was too busy. She poured the best imaginary tea and baked the most delectable make-believe crumpets. And though this absolutely cannot be the real Mrs. Finnegan (*it just can't be, right?*), that light and refreshing swaying in her tone is one of a kind. Whether she's woman, alien, or some mixed breed like us, it's clear that both Volcrex and Aura have their most intricate of deceptions mastered.

Ang who, moments ago, was on the brink of a Vesta-sized breakdown at the sight of his mother, looks upon her with suspicious eyes.

"No tricks here, kiddo. It's me. Come on. It's now or never." She extends a hand to Ang, as if begging him to go with her. Something's off.

Ang is hesitant still. Inevitably, we'll go our separate ways. He to his Mommy and I to my grave. They'll beam up together, and I'll be blown to smithereens. Whatever is left of me (if anything) will rot out here in the pre-winter sun, just an unrecognizable pile of nameless fragments in the dust. Though I would prefer the idea of being a grumpy pile of bitter bones to Rain dust on the field.

"Don't go, Angus," I state a simple plea, then point an accusatory finger. "She exterminated humankind."

Mrs. Finnegan is responsible for over six billion deaths. I'm not letting her escape judgement on this one. Just as I hold Jova responsible for the actions of the entire Aura race, I place Volcrex's crimes squarely on Ang's mom's shoulders. When you present yourself as an alien ambassador—which is essentially what she's done—you bear the full guilt of atrocities made.

"My kind, your kind, humankind," Ang says. "What's any of it matter? I'm Volcrex, Rain."

"She's not real, Angus!" I double down on my entirely unscientific theory. "You are being manipulated! Their science is miraculous. They manufactured a planet destroyer! And we all bought into it! You think a Mom projection is beyond their capabilities? Trust me, I know."

I also know, but do not say, that when you're inside the projection's power, you really can't be certain of anything.

"If she's not my mother, then why come down here and greet us at all? Why not just annihilate us and be done with it?"

"I don't know," I say, exhausted. "Let's go back to the farmhouse, Angus. Let's live whatever life we have left on our own terms."

But his Imaginary Mom will never let him go. Congrats Ang, now we both have a phantom parent.

I find myself eager to turn away, knowing that as soon as I do, I'll likely be zapped to ashes by one thousand ships. I should put my footsteps where my stupid courage is and march. How far might I walk before they end me?

The alien posing as Mrs. Finnegan eyeballs me while her son looks on. He's trying desperately to gauge her reality. Or lack thereof.

"You've always been tenacious, Rain," she says. "You're so like him."

Don't ask who. You know who. Don't you do it. Just go. Turn and go. Elderry isn't far from here. You can outrun them if you believe in yourself. You can outrun the entire Volcrex army if you put your mind to it.

"Who?" I hear the word squeak out from my throat, and hate myself for it. The answer comes quick, and it melts me to my core.

"You know who. He's our prisoner." She nods to the array of ships.

I look up. Could it be? The lead disc in a sky full of them appears to tip its nose as a gesture of good faith. But that's just intergalactic mind games, driving more deceptions into my perceptions.

Always tricks and manipulations. What game are the Volcrex playing? I look to Ang for any guidance, but the boy is lost in his own sea of doubt.

"Come with us, Rain," the Volcrex ambassador proposes. "We know you've been in contact with the Aura. We know they're hiding like the subterranean filth that they are. Come aboard my ship. Report all you have seen and all you know, and I swear, I will let you and your father go in peace. We'll even throw in a half-decent ship for you. I know your dad's always wanted to go to Kotaria X. I've never been myself, but I understand it's lovely."

"He saved you," I tell her for no other reason than to prolong a decision. "My father saved the real Mrs. Finnegan's life. He beamed you into *his* ship and flew away. Not the other way around."

"You are entitled to your answers, of course you are. And you will have them. I promise you that."

"Why'd you annihilate us?" I shout at her. "You were our neighbor! You were human yourself! For so many years! Why?" I'm on the verge of tears, but I won't let her see me cry. I'm stronger than that. Or I can be.

"I see you are in pain, child. I realize how hard this must be. Know this—it wasn't us who poisoned humanity's hearts and minds. That was all the Aura's doing."

"I don't believe you," I spit a half-truth.

"You don't have to. You only have to believe in our strength." Mrs. Finnegan raises her arm, and all at once, half a dozen spaceships fire deadly lasers on our barn. Burning embers of hay and tinder puncture the air. The heat of the explosion is intense where we stand, though not as impressive a showing as I think Mrs. Finnegan intended.

"Stop it!" Ang yells. "This isn't who you are, Mom!"

"Oh, honey." She does a terrible job at placating him. I think she's been off planet far too long to have held a shred of motherly instincts. "We're only clearing the playing field."

The guise of Mrs. Finnegan falls away, and she sheds her human skin. Her body image flickers, and is gone, leaving her much taller, much blacker, and much more terrifying in her true flesh. Her dark and shining, bald and pointy head leans down and whispers something in Ang's ear that paralyzes him. He stands there, a prisoner in his own body.

And then I feel the full weight of consequence. At first it is a sweet tickling on my neck. That pleasantness lasts but a sliver of a moment before the crunching, suffocating truth of what's happening comes to light.

I am in pain. This is what it feels like. If there are varying degrees of suffering, I remain unfamiliar. Mrs. Finnegan's hold on me has awoken my body's receptors to torment. I am at once in incomparable agony and oddly relieved. Because at least now I know the full curse of being human.

I am choking to death.

The white of Ang's right eye turns red with determination. If he's not careful, the boy will give himself an aneurysm before his rightful death.

Mrs. Finnegan says something in her alien tongue that sounds like, "Grekken parta trulio, baccha vrrrnet," but I hear the English translation in my head as, "Come to me, half-breed of mine enemy."

Inside myself, I envision the stem of my brain lighting up like a million undersea candles. With that inner power, I expand the scope of my aura outward, reaching to Ang with silent thoughts. He meets me halfway. There, we connect and disappear.

Our own brief illusion—amateur, unsure, and untested as it is—confuses the alien just enough to put her on her heels.

In the glow of our invisible atmosphere, we hide. How long can we stay here before the sleight of mind dissipates? How long will I be able to delay another strangling? How long before she realizes we still haven't moved from—

"Eat this!"

The Volcrex formerly claiming to be Mrs. Finnegan is hit by a bright, blue blast of energy. Her shining, terrifying alien body goes flying backward, over our field.

Connie Blackburn stands, just two feet from where the Volcrex was, holding my father's smoking blaster in her steady hand.

"Deus ex machina, bitch," she says, precisely narrating her intrusion with impressive timing.

Ang falters and falls, as do I. But we hurry to pick ourselves up as the ships align for attack. The red-hot points of their laser scopes seem more than ready to blast the three of us to infinity, or beyond.

"Ang," I say. It's the only name I have strength for. Our facade falls beneath the tired slipping of our mutual power. Connie sheaths my Boo blaster in her waistband and puts both her arms around Ang and I.

"We've had enough extinction for today," Connie says. She is utterly confident and uniquely un-her. Although she's now responsible for the death of both Ang's parents, he snatches her by her shirt collar, and we fly.

In a heartbeat, with Ang clutching tightly to us both, we're airborne, leaping hundreds of feet at a time, dodging Volcrex laser after Volcrex laser. We don't stop until we splash into Elderry Pond, and even then, we keep going.

When we're significantly beneath the surface, I look back. Their advanced, alien lasers cannot penetrate the water. In fact, they bounce off and head harmlessly back into the sky.

Ang's special propulsion powers cause us to strike the Aura welcome sign too hard, pushing away just enough letters so the sign now reads: *humanity... enter*.

The cavern door rises, and we pass through. It goes back down again, sealing the three of us in the dry space safely.

A wheelless shuttle careens into the cave's foyer. A door shooms open, and out comes Jova in stunning human form. I recognize her aura instantly. She's all in her eyes.

"We had to be certain," she says in way of an apology, I suppose.

"Of what?" I ask her.

"That you wouldn't go freely to them. You're more powerful than you think. In Volcrex hands, you would be their ultimate weapon."

"If you're so concerned about me, then why'd you serve me up on a silver platter?"

"Everything ends," Jova states rather morosely. "The Aura population is but a fraction of a percent of what it once was. Someday, hopefully not soon, we will be wiped from existence. It is an inevitability. But we hold on for as long as we can. We make moves based on probable outcomes. We—"

"Did you annihilate the human race? Tell me. Was it you?"

Jova inhales deeply. "There are still some humans left," she says. "We saved as many of them as we could. They are under our protection, elsewhere."

A surprising thunder of alien lasers rains fire and brimstone from above. The Earth outside quakes. Melford, maybe all of Indiana or more, is likely gone.

"Come with me. It's not safe here. You're expected."

"Was that really my mother?" Ang interrupts with a perfectly reasonable ask.

"She was... and still is," Jova says. The cavern wall suddenly ripples and changes to show a live feed of the field where the alien ambassador struggles, but gets to her feet. Her alien form morphs back to that of Mrs. Finnegan, and she disappears in a golden beam of light, headed back to her ship.

The mother ship.

"I told you—all three of you—everything is a test. Of your humanity, and of your alien natures."

"I'm a mutt. Just found out. Got all kinds of alien DNA in me. Ain't that something?" Connie smiles obnoxiously and blows a big bubble. Where the hell did she get the gum? Forget it. I don't care.

"You're—what?" Ang expresses my restrained confusion.

"They can't say for sure. So I've got zero affiliations. And could give even less of a flying—"

"Your father is their prisoner," Jova tells me. "We've known that for some time. We're working on a rescue mission, now that the Volcrex have landed."

"Why are they here?" I ask, not yet ready to appreciate the full weight of the truth of my dad's existence. "What do they want?"

"The same thing they've always wanted," Jova explains. "They feed off of death and destruction. And we Aura are their favorite snack."

I enter Jova's shuttle with a heavy heart. I need to rest.

"You're going to be good now, right Angus?" Jova asks him. "You won't make me send you back to the tar pits?"

"She's my mom. But there's nothing human about her," he says with a stoic cadence and depressed resolve. "I am not your enemy."

Ang sits in the seat next to me and holds my hand. I put no meaning behind it. We're just two survivors of a world gone mad, content in each other's company. And really, we're all we've got.

"Better buckle in, Rain dear," Connie says. "This shuttle can get a little bumpy."

The shuttle lurches forward, halts, then takes off at such an incredible speed it almost feels as if we're going in reverse.

Ang clicks his belt around his waist. I do the same. For now, I want to enjoy the ride for as long as it lasts. Because anything and everything can always change.

"Happy birthday, Rain," Ang remembers, then drifts off to dreamland as the underground world whizzes past.

I close my eyes and join him.

Afterword

Dear Reader,

Thank you so much for reading *Countdown To Oblivion*, the first book in my *Allies and Aliens* series. If you could take a moment to rate or review this novel, it would mean the blessed world to me.

To stay up to date on everything I'm poking my nose in, I'd love for you to join my newsletter! Beam yourself on over to shakabry.com for all kinds of literary junk. Act now and you'll receive *Our Last Halloween* a FREE short story from the *Allies and Aliens* universe!

Thanks again for reading. There is so much more to come!

Fiction is stranger than truth,
    Shaka Bry

About the Author

Shaka Bry (a.k.a. Bryon Cahill) is a conventional story's worst nightmare. In the not-so-distant past, he was an award-winning writer and editor of literary publications for teens. His stories, influenced by phantasmagorical classics such as Lewis Carroll's *Alice's Adventures in Wonderland*, do often steer off-course, alighting on the wings of the fantastical. In other words, his books don't always fit the norm.

When not writing by proverbial candlelight in the wee strange hours of morning, he is a devoted father of three and loving husband of one. He summers, winters, springs, and falls with his family along the sunny beaches of the Jersey Shore.

Other Works by Shaka Bry

Daydream Believer

Mermaids and Merliens
    Mercadia Calling
    Mercadia Falling
    Rise of The Mermaid Queen
    Mercadia Forever

www.ingramcontent.com/pod-product-compliance
Lightning Source LLC
LaVergne TN
LVHW012014060526
838201LV00061B/4300